'You are a penniless woman alone in a foreign land and in need of a protector, and I have decided that a wife could be useful to me.'

Bridget cleared her throat. 'I thank you for your offer, Captain, but does it not bother you that we scarcely know each other?'

He raised those devilishly dark eyebrows of his and drawled, 'Most couples who make convenient matches are barely acquainted.

'So, will you agree to be my wife?' asked Harry, after a pause, his heart thudding as he waited for her answer...

June Francis's interest in old wives' tales and folk customs led her into a writing career. History has always fascinated her, and her first five novels were set in Medieval times. She has also written fourteen sagas based in Liverpool and Chester. Married with three grown-up sons, she lives on Merseyside. On a clear day she can see the sea and the distant Welsh hills from her house. She enjoys swimming, fell-walking, music, lunching with friends and smoochy dancing with her husband. More information about June can be found at her website: www.junefrancis.co.uk

Previous novels by this author:

ROWAN'S REVENGE
TAMED BY THE BARBARIAN
REBEL LADY, CONVENIENT WIFE
HIS RUNAWAY MAIDEN

PIRATE'S DAUGHTER, REBEL WIFE
features characters you will have met in
HIS RUNAWAY MAIDEN

PIRATE'S DAUGHTER, REBEL WIFE

June Francis

First published in Great Britain 2011
Harlequin Mills & Boon Limited,
Eton House, 18-24 Paradise Road, Richmond, Surrey TW9 1SR

© June Francis 2010

ISBN: 978 0 263 22280 7

Harlequin Mills & Boon policy is to use papers that are natural, renewable and recyclable products and made from wood grown in sustainable forests. The logging and manufacturing process conform to the legal environmental regulations of the country of origin.

Printed and bound in Great Britain
by CPI Antony Rowe, Chippenham, Wiltshire

PIRATE'S DAUGHTER, REBEL WIFE

This book is dedicated to those readers of
HIS RUNAWAY MAIDEN who e-mailed
me wanting to know Harry's story.

Also to my dear husband, John,
who enjoys my historical romances,
in memory of a lovely holiday on the
island of Madeira for a special birthday.

Prologue

1504

If she did not act now then she would never be free. Bridget McDonald stood on the slanting deck, her hands gripping the side of the ship. A few moments ago she had caught sight of a tall, dark figure on the cliff, but now he had disappeared as the rain swept in.

Was the landfall ahead Madeira, the island she had been searching for? The master of the slave-trader ship and his remaining crew were frantically busy trying to save the vessel from being blown towards the rocks. This could be her only chance of escape. If they succeeded in saving the ship, then she feared its master would immediately come after her again. He had been eyeing her in a manner that terrified Bridget. Since disease had killed his woman a week ago, she had lost the one person who had provided her with some kind of protection from his lustful nature. She was convinced that if the storm had not blown up, he would have raped her by now. If he managed to save his vessel, she feared that this could still happen.

A wave suddenly drenched Bridget, leaving her gasping for breath, and she clung tightly to the side of the ship, trying to summon up the courage to go over the side. She thought how she might not be in this position if the man she had known as Captain Black Harry had not separated her from her father, Callum, by refusing to allow her on either of his ships, destined for the New World, almost two years ago.

She shuddered, recalling the desperate straits she was in, and knew she had no choice but to trust her fate to the waves. She might yet find her father—and if she perished in the water, at least she would not die as a slave-trader's whore but as a free woman. She took a deep breath and dropped into the sea.

Chapter One

Harry swore loudly, cursing the rain that almost blinded him as he slithered down the cliff path, gaining momentum as earth collapsed with the sheer volume of the rain, sending him hurtling towards the beach. He landed on the black sand on his hands and knees to the accompaniment of falling rocks. He drew in his breath with a hiss, his face drawn with pain, and pushed himself upright. He flicked back dripping dark hair and wiped his sodden face and beard on the sleeve of his doublet.

Had he really seen someone poised to jump into the churning sea from that ship? As suddenly as it had started the driving rain had stopped; he wasted no more time, but strode along the beach, scanning the waves for signs of that lonely figure. He was on the verge of turning back when he spotted something down by the shore. He put on a spurt and, as he drew closer, found a body sprawled face down on the sand.

He knelt down and, to his astonishment, discovered that it was a woman; and, more surprisingly, one who was able to swim—that was a rarity in his experience. She had girded the green skirts of her gown by tucking the ends into her belt at the back—no doubt so they wouldn't hamper the movement of her legs in the water. He eased her into a sitting position, but the upper part of her body flopped forwards against his forearm. She made a choking sound and he thumped her on the back, attempting to free the water from her lungs. The tension inside him subsided as she began to cough, seawater and mucus staining the sleeve of his already soaked doublet. Eventually her coughing ceased, but the action must have drained any resources she had left after such a swim because she lay limp in his arms.

A single, long braid of sodden, dark red hair dangled against his thigh as he manoeuvred her gently round so that he could see her face more clearly. His heart seemed to lurch sideways. He had the oddest feeling that he had seen her likeness before. But where? Her skin was pallid, but it did not detract from her beauty. She had the daintiest of noses, full sensuous lips and a heart-shaped countenance.

At that moment a raindrop splashed on to her face and then another and another. He thought that the rain would rouse her, but although her cheek twitched, her eyelids remained closed. God's Blood! What was he to do with her? She would be doubly soaked to the skin if he tried to carry her all the way to Machico. It seemed he had no choice but to take her to the house of his Portuguese friend, Jorge de Lobos, where Harry was staying.

His face tightened with concentration as he lifted her higher. Holding her close to his chest, he slowly rose to his feet. For a moment he swayed, but then recovered his balance, gritting his teeth against the pain in his thigh. He decided to keep to the beach as long as possible and prayed that there would be no landslides on his chosen path.

Despite the weight of her sodden garments he was able to make reasonable speed, conscious, all the time, of the woman's ashen face and shallow breathing. He took extra care on the shale when he climbed on to the main path, fearing a disastrous fall. It was a relief when he reached the house and was able to put her down on a wooden settle in the entrance hall.

He eased his shoulders and shouted for Joe. When there was no response he made for the kitchen but that, too, was deserted. By the Trinity, where was the youth? Harry returned to the hall and stared down at the woman in the green gown. He found himself remembering the tales of mermaids that an erstwhile pirate called Callum McDonald had told him when he was a boy.

Harry, too, had been plucked from the sea, although he had only been a child. He had been out of his wits when he had woken on the pirate ship, unable to remember his own name or his age as a result of a blow to the head. He had been told by the pirates that his parents had died in a boating accident that had almost taken his life and it was a miracle he had survived. He scowled at the memory, scrubbing at the beard that concealed a hideous scar on his cheek.

He wondered what to do with this unexpected guest. Normally Harry did not have women in the house, but he knew there was naught for it but to keep her here for now. He drew in his breath with a hiss. She needed to be rid of her wet garments, so Joe must ride to Machico and fetch the widow, old Juanita, to undress her. But first Harry had to find him. He left the house and searched the gardens and the stables, but there was still no sign of the youth.

Exasperated, Harry returned to the house. Immediately, he noticed that the woman had moved because she was now curled up in a ball against the arm of the settle. He shook her shoulder and her eyelids opened, revealing red-rimmed eyes the colour of cobnuts. She squinted at him as if her eyes were sore and she was trying to focus. She muttered indistinctly and shrank back against the back of the settle, lifting her arm as if to shield herself from a blow, but then it flopped weakly across her breast and her eyelids closed.

Harry's heart lurched in that peculiar fashion again and he ran a hand over his still-dripping black hair and beard. He took a deep breath and, without more ado, scooped her up into his arms and headed for the stairs, leaving a trail of water pooling on the floor. He took the marble steps slowly because the soles of his shoes were slippery and was relieved to reach the first floor without mishap. He carried her into the guest bedchamber and collapsed with her in his lap on top of the chest at the foot of the bed.

A loose damp tendril of auburn hair tickled his chin and he frowned as he gazed into the lovely face pillowed against his arm. 'Mistress, you must rouse yourself,' he said in Portuguese.

She moaned but, irritatingly, her eyes remained closed.

Harry lightly slapped her on both cheeks. 'Wake up!' he commanded.

This time she winced and her eyelids fluttered open and she appeared to stare up at him, only then to turn her face away. He could feel her shivering. 'Mistress, will you wake up?' he urged, tugging on her plait. She lifted a fist and for a moment he thought she would hit him, but then her arm dropped to her side. He smiled grimly. At least he seemed to be getting through to her. Again he lightly slapped her cheek.

'If you—you do—do that again, my father w-will m-make you regret it one day,' she stammered in the same language he had spoken.

Harry raised his eyebrows at her fractured accent and wondered where she had learnt Potuguese, as it obviously wasn't her native tongue. 'You must get out of your wet garments or you will catch a fever,' he rasped. 'There's a bed here. Get yourself beneath the covers and I'll see that food and drink is brought to you.'

She began to struggle. He found her amazingly strong, considering the energy she must have spent swimming ashore. But she could not match his strength and he captured both her wrists and held them above her head. He could feel the rapid rise and fall of her breasts against his chest and was aware of sensations that he had not experienced for a while.

'There is no need for you to fight me,' he growled. 'I will not hurt you. Now rouse yourself, undress and get into bed.'

To his dismay, her body sagged and her head fell forwards on to his shoulder. He flinched and tried to wake her once more, but whatever he did, it failed. He knew then that there was naught for it but to undress her himself.

His hands shook as he unfastened the belt from about her waist, so freeing the skirts she had girded there. Then he loosened the ties on the bodice of her gown. Noticing the design of the garment, he fingered the fabric, certain that it had been fashioned in England. So this mermaid was likely to be no peasant Portuguese woman, but could be English. What was she doing here and where was the father she had mentioned?

After removing her gown and having exposed the perfect roundness of her breasts in the damp, cream silk shift that clung to her skin, he knew that he would have had to have been made of wood, not to be stirred by their loveliness.

'Holy Mary, mother of God,' he groaned, clutching his hair with one hand and holding her off from him with the other, 'What am I to do with you?' There was no reply. Clearing his throat, he said loudly, 'Mistress, you need to remove your shift. I will fetch one of my shirts for you to wear. We have no female apparel in this house.'

'Men are s-s-such d-devils,' she stuttered, her eyes still closed.

'Women are no angels, either,' he replied roundly, getting to his feet, leaving her sprawled out on the chest.

When she did not reply, he presumed that she had slipped into that semi-conscious state again. He dragged her upright and swung her over his shoulder. Then he carried her to the side of the bed and placed her down gently. Seizing hold of the thickly woven coverlet of red and brown, he pulled it over her to ensure she stayed warm before hastening from the bedchamber.

Harry stripped off his wet garments in his own bedchamber and rubbed himself dry. Then with the cloth wrapped around his nether regions, he went over to the window and pushed wide the shutters, staring down over the sloping garden that was fragrant with the perfume of scattered blossoms after the rain. His gaze fixed on the wide expanse of ocean, but could see no sign of a vessel. For as long as he could remember the sea had been his life and a ship his main home, but on days like this he was glad to be on land since the damage to his leg.

He turned from the window with an impatient movement and limped over to the armoire and chest. He removed all that he needed and donned undergarments, shirt, hose and doublet and pulled on boots before removing another shirt from the armoire. Then, gathering up his gloves and hat, he headed for the guest chamber.

He saw that the woman had managed to divest herself of her shift. She was lying on her side, her head close to the edge of the bed with her braid dangling so that its end touched the floor. He would have liked to have seen her hair newly washed with perfumed water, smelling sweetly of camomile or lavender, and hanging loose. He drew in his breath with a hiss. What was he thinking of, fixating on her hair? He could only be glad that her naked body was mostly covered!

He placed his shirt on the bed and was in the process of pulling up the coverlet further, when he saw the scarring on her back. For a moment he froze and then his fingers gently explored the weals in the soft skin across her shoulder blades and lower back. Anger exploded inside him. Someone had cruelly *whipped* her? Could a husband have done this? He reached for her left hand that was curled on the sheet beneath and found it ringless.

He peered closer at the scars and remembered the beatings he had suffered growing up on the pirate ship. He scowled as he drew the coverlet over her. Then, gathering up her discarded garments, he left the room. He went downstairs and this time was fortunate to find Joe preparing the evening meal.

'We have a guest,' said Harry in English, placing the clothing on the table where the youth was slicing an onion.

Joseph stared at the sodden green gown and darted a startled glance at Harry. 'A woman?'

'Of course it's a woman, Joe! That's a gown, isn't it?' Harry sank on to a chair. 'And such a woman, Joe. You wouldn't believe how beautiful she is. The odd thing is that I feel I have seen her before.'

'God's Blood! A woman under *your* roof!' Joe's voice rose to a squeak as he reached for the sodden gown and sniffed a handful of material. 'This smells of the sea. Where did you find her?'

'She swam ashore from a ship that was in trouble.' Harry stared at Joe through his fingers. 'Unusual a woman being able to swim, hey, Joe? I saw her drop into the sea and later came upon her sprawled on the sand. She is in the guest bedchamber, so keep your eye on her. I need to go out. I want to find out what's happened to that ship.'

Joe had now found the silken shift and dropped it as if it had burnt his fingers. 'Me!' His blue eyes widened in dismay. 'What's she wearing if her clothes are here? Wh-what if—if she starts wandering around half-naked?'

'Enough of that nonsense,' snapped Harry, not wanting to dwell on the image the words conjured up. 'I've left her one of my shirts and I doubt she has the strength to get off the bed. If she wakes, she'll be in need of food and drink. Some soup, perhaps.'

Harry made his way to the stables and saddled up a horse. He rode in the direction where he had last seen the vessel, wanting a closer look at it if possible. He wondered if it had foundered on the rocks. If so, there was a possibility of there being survivors; if not, then others on the island might have seen the vessel and be planning to steal what they could, before those who owned the rights to salvage arrived on the scene.

Bridget was wakened by the sound of a door slowly opening and then stealthy footsteps approaching the bed. Her heart thudded as into her mind came an image of a man with shoulder-length black hair, angry dark eyes, a scar on his nose and a great black beard. She shivered, recalling the face of the master of the slave-trader ship who also had a great black beard. Her instincts were to sit up and defend herself but, not only did her limbs ache unbearably, her head throbbed and her throat felt raw. She was already aware that someone had taken her garments away and left a clean, soft woollen-and-linen shirt behind.

'Who's there?' she asked in a husky voice.

'I've brought you some soup and bread and a drink, mistress,' replied a cautious young English voice.

Bridget was confused. Hadn't her rescuer spoken to her in Portuguese earlier? She opened her eyes and stared at the youth holding a tray. He could not have been more different to the other man as night was from day. He had straw-coloured hair and a freckled face that was filled with curiosity.

'You're English,' she stated in that tongue.

'Aye, mistress.'

'What is your name?'

'I'm Joe,' replied the gangly youth.

'Where is the bearded man who was here earlier?'

'That would be the captain. He's gone off to see what's happened to the ship you deserted.'

She prayed that he would find no sign of the ship or that it was wrecked and its master drowned. 'The captain? Is he a mariner, then?' she asked, picking up on what the youth called the man who had rescued her.

'Aye.'

'He—he looked fearsome. Is he Portuguese?'

'No, he's English and you have naught to fear from him.' He gave her a reassuring gap-toothed smile. 'Here, mistress, I'll leave your food and drink on this little table here. You get it down you and then have another little sleep.'

Bridget clutched the open neck of the shirt and managed to ease herself into a sitting position. 'Tell me, where am I?'

He paused in the doorway without looking back. 'You're on the island of Madeira, mistress,' he replied and closed the door before she could ask him any more questions.

Bridget sank back against the pillows. Her relief was such that tears filled her eyes and threatened to overpower her. Praise the Trinity that she had at last reached her destination! Now she must hope that she had not arrived here in vain. She remembered her first meeting with the man she still thought of as Captain Black Harry. She and her father, Callum, had been on the coast of Ireland after escaping from a brigand called Patrick O'Malley and his cutthroats. For many a summer past Callum had set sail with young warriors from Scotland to support his Irish wife's family in their battles with the O'Malleys. That summer two years ago his luck had run out and Callum had lost not only his fortune, but his ship.

When Bridget had met Captain Black Harry, she was alone, having left her father trying to persuade the master of another ship to take them back to Scotland with only the promise of payment when they arrived there. She had been embarrassed due to his need to beg for help. Then she had walked slap bang into the handsomest young man she had ever seen. He had helped her to her feet and she had begged his pardon. He had inclined his head and asked in the Gaelic whether he could be of further assistance to her.

Impulsively she had explained their situation and he had escorted her back to Callum. Only then did she discover that the two men had sailed together when Black Harry was a boy. They had much to say to each other and had headed for the nearest tavern.

Bridget frowned as she reached for the cup on the table and gulped down the drink thirstily. If only she had overheard their discussion, she would have been more prepared for what happened the next day. Her eyes darkened. She would never forget what she considered Black Harry's hardhearted treatment of her.

She placed the cup on the table and reached for the food. She dunked the bread in the soup and, despite being ravenous, ate slowly because it hurt to swallow. As she gazed at her surroundings, her eyes began to feel heavy. The white walls appeared to waver and the blue shutters at the window shimmered. On another wall was a niche holding a statue of the Madonna and Child and they appeared to be smiling at her. She fumbled for the cup, picked it up and sniffed it. Had she been drugged? The lad might have assured her that she had naught to fear from the captain, but could she trust him? She had suffered sorely at the hands of men in the past and she felt a rising panic. Her last thought before she slipped into unconsciousness was of her father.

'You put *what* into her drink?' exploded Harry.

'Only a *little* poppy juice, Captain,' replied Joe hastily, backing away from him. 'It was what Juanita gave to me when I couldn't sleep for my aches and pains after I was attacked in the town. She dosed you with it, too! It's not that long since we returned from Africa with you wounded so bad, and I thought you'd not only never walk again, but smash every looking glass in sight.'

A muscle clenched in Harry's jaw. He would never forget seeing his scarred reflection in the mirror for the first time. Later, when he had rattled in the cart into town, the women who had previously fallen into his arms had shrunk away from him and walked by on the other side of the street. Deeply hurt and also suffering agony from the wound in his thigh, he had grown a beard to conceal the scar and chose to keep away from women altogether.

'What if she suspects you've drugged her?' Harry pointed out.

'Why should she? Surely she'll deem her feeling drowsy is due to exhaustion after swimming ashore? I was only trying to ease any pain she was in.'

Harry gazed at him with exasperation. 'I suppose you thought you were doing what was best, but I wanted to question her. Now I'll probably have to wait several hours before she wakes up. Don't ever do such a thing again without my permission, Joe, or you'll be out on your ear!' He paused. 'So what did you think of her?'

'Comely. Her eyes are hurting her. She could do with a potion to bathe them. More importantly, Captain, is the information that she *does* speak English and there is a lilt to her voice that convinces me that it is not her first language.'

Harry nodded.

'So what happened to the ship?' asked Joe.

'I could see no sign of any wreckage, so it appears that her master managed to avoid the rocks. Perhaps on the morrow I will have a search made for the ship.' He changed the subject. 'Now, Joe, what about supper?'

'I'll have it ready for you, Captain, in no time at all.'

'Then I will dine as soon as I make certain that the lady is still breathing. In the morning you can wash her clothes along with mine.'

Harry climbed the stairs, disposed of his outdoor clothes and went to visit his guest. He drew a chair up to the bed and looked down at her. Her cheeks were flushed and when he placed his hand on her forehead, he found it hot and dry. Damnation! She was feverish. Hopefully her condition would not worsen.

He leaned back in the chair, thinking as soon as she was awake he would ask what was her name and for information about the ship and her father. Now he would have supper and return here later. Perhaps she would be willing to speak to him then.

Bridget felt as if she was floating, drifting in that state betwixt sleep and wakefulness. She was aware of discomfort and of being hot one moment and then cold the next. She had vague memories of a man lifting her and being carried in his arms. He had a great black beard, but he was not the cruel master of the slave-trader's ship who had beaten her for her defiance of him. Even so, could she trust him? There was something that had happened before she fell asleep that worried her, but she could not remember what it was.

She heard a door open and footsteps. A chair creaked and she sensed it was not the lad, but *him*. He must be sitting by the bed and looking down at her. She could feel his wine-scented breath on her cheek and then she felt him lift her damp curls and feel her brow. She struggled to force open her eyelids, but when she managed to prise them apart, the candlelight so hurt her eyes that she swiftly closed them again. Even so that brief moment was long enough for her to catch a glimpse of him: he with the strong nose, dark brows, frowning eyes and that great black beard. She shivered.

'So you're awake,' he said roughly. 'You're feverish and that is an inconvenience.'

'Perhaps you should have left me on the shore to die,' she whispered.

'That's a foolish remark to make,' he growled, 'Why did you swim ashore if it were not because you wanted to live?'

'That is true. I was in fear of the slave trader. Do you know what happened to the ship?' she asked anxiously.

'I could see no sign of it.'

'So that beast could still be alive!' She grasped his arm with a tremblimg hand. 'You must not tell him I am here.'

'His ship could still be in difficulties further round the coast. I shall see what I can find out on the morrow. Now don't fret yourself about him. You are safe here.'

Was she? She gazed into his eyes, but could not read his

expression and could only pray that he was telling her the truth. She sank back against the pillows, exhausted.

'How did you come to be on his ship?' asked Harry.

'I was sold to him by a pirate in Africa,' she whispered. 'I deem originally the slave-trader's aim was to sell me to some Eastern potentate, but his woman was utterly against such a plan. She wanted me as her servant. She was very beautiful and he could refuse her nothing. We sailed to different islands with slaves, to Tenerife, the Cape Verde Islands. Sometimes we went ashore for several days and twice we returned to Africa for more slaves. I tried to escape, only to be beaten for my attempts. Then disease struck the ship and one by one people began to die.'

Harry felt anger and pity and knew that she'd had a very lucky escape indeed. But what she had said about disease disturbed him greatly. 'What was this disease?' he asked.

'I do not know its name, but I deem it was not the plague,' she said hastily.

He frowned. 'How do you know? Have you seen people die of the plague?'

'No, but I know someone who suffered from the small-pox and she described its symptoms to me.' Bridget's eyelids drooped wearily despite all her efforts to stay awake.

Harry was relieved to hear that she had not been in contact with that horrendous disease. Still, he hoped that she had not been infected by whatever had struck down those on the ship. 'Sleep now,' he said. 'We will speak again in the morning.'

The door closed behind him and she drifted into sleep. Now her dreams were not of the slave trader, but of her father and how the handsome Captain Black Harry had offered him a berth on his ship that was sailing westwards in search of a passage to the Indies. Her father's conversation to her had been full of plans to regain his lost fortune. His excitement had been infectious and Bridget had been just as eager as Callum to take part in such an adventure. But then Captain Black Harry had refused to have her on board his ship and so, rather than allowing her to accompany the men to the Indies, instead he had paid for her passage to Scotland to the home of her father's brother and his wife.

Now fear stalked her dreams. For her kindly aunt had died and her Uncle Ranald had taken her south to the home of his mistress, Lady Monica Appleby, once a McDonald and twice married. Both wanted to get their hands on her father's hoard and would not believe Bridget when she'd told them it had all been stolen. They had even tried to force her into marriage with the lady's imbecile son. She must escape! She had to get away from them!

Bridget shifted restlessly in the bed and began to cough. She was aware of the sound of footfalls and a door opened. She started with fright, for outside it was now dark and the candle burning beneath the statue of the Madonna and Child cast shadows on the walls. Her heart thudded inside her breast as she watched the captain approach her.

'What are you doing?' she asked hoarsely.

'You will need to sit up if you are not to spill this potion,' he said in a low voice.

She remembered the conviction that she'd had earlier about the drink she had downed and croaked, 'Potion! Are you wanting to poison me? I deem the drink I was brought earlier was drugged.'

'A little poppy juice, that is all,' he said easily. 'Joe deemed it would ease your pain. By the Trinity, why should *I* wish to poison you? I might consider some women cruel and self-ish, but the truth is that I heard you coughing. Now drink up and pray to God that in the morning you will be rid of the fever.'

Did he speak the truth? It was certainly true that her body ached all over. She struggled to sit up, but the act was beyond her. The captain perched on the side of the bed and hauled her upright, slipping an arm about her shoulders. He reached for the cup and held it to her dry lips. As she felt warm liquid trickle into her mouth, she was aware of the strength in the arm that held her and hated being in his power. So he considered women cruel and selfish, did he? Well, no more so than she thought some men arrogant and brutal. Even so she had no choice but to suffer the captain's ministrations for the moment. She swallowed thirstily until the cup was empty.

Harry lowered her against the pillows and watched as, with a faint sigh, she drifted back into sleep. He did not immediately leave the room, but remained sitting in the chair at her bedside. There was a definite lilt to her voice and it would not surprise him if her first language was the Gaelic. He found himself thinking of Callum McDonald and his daughter, Bridget. What had happened to Callum after he had disappeared sixteen months ago along with one of Harry's two ships, *Odin's Maiden*?

His eyes darkened with anger. God's Blood! He had made a mistake in trusting that wily old pirate when they had met again in Ireland. He should never have offered him a helping hand or been keen to assist the lovely but hot-tempered Bridget, who would now be a young woman of seventeen or eighteen summers.

He gazed down at the beautiful face on the pillow, trying to imagine how this woman might have looked two years ago, remembering how he had considered Bridget older than her years when he had first set eyes on her. Then he had discovered she was much younger than he'd thought, and knew he must put some distance between them in order to protect her from herself. She had been furious with him and he had likened her to an angry cat, spitting out accusations that he was well-named Black Harry because he had a black heart. How dare he separate her from her father, she had ranted. She had attempted to persuade Callum to get him to budge from his stance, but the old pirate had told her in Harry's hearing that it did not do to cross Black Harry. It was then that Harry realised that Callum also did not want to take his daughter with him on such a risky venture, but did not have the heart to tell her.

So Harry had parted from Bridget with her insults ringing in his ears. If naught else, her behaviour had proved to him that however comely she was, she still had some growing up to do. She knew what shipboard life was like from having sailed with her father after her mother had died. Surely her common sense should have told her that his decision was the right one? He certainly hoped she had come to realise that in the past two years.

He continued to gaze down at the woman in the bed. Was she Bridget McDonald? She certainly had a look of her. If she *was* Bridget, then where was her father? When Callum had vanished along with Harry's ship, he had wondered if the man's intention had been to cross the northern seas and make landfall in Scotland in order to be reunited with his daughter. Yet here she was in Madeira, having just escaped a slave-trader's vessel. Perhaps Callum had never arrived in Scotland and, along with Harry's ship and other crew, was now at the bottom of the ocean?

Harry could scarcely contain his impatience for her to wake up and to provide him with some answers to his questions!

Chapter Two

'You must ride into Machico, Joe, and bring Juanita here,' said Harry, turning away from Bridget's bedside. Two days had passed and he had hardly had a sensible word out of her. 'The fever is getting worse. She needs a draught that is stronger than the one you mixed for her.

Joe gazed down at Bridget's scarlet cheeks and twitching face. 'She does look bad and she's been muttering in her delirium.'

Harry shot a glance at him. 'I know. She mentioned a Lady Elizabeth and pirates and then the rest was just a gabbled stream of nonsense. I want you back here with the widow before midday. I need to visit the cane fields and see how the harvest is progressing.'

Joe nodded and left the bedchamber.

Harry resumed his seat next to the bedside and tried to contain his worry. He must persuade Juanita to stay here at the house; only then would he feel some freedom from anxiety about the sick woman he suspected was Bridget McDonald. He could not afford to change his plans and needed to be on hand to supervise the loading of the sugar cane into the carts that would carry the cargo to his ship.

He gazed down at the shivering, restless figure; as he did

so, she flung off the bedcovers and, muttering to someone to get away from her in Portuguese, attempted to get out of bed. Starting to his feet, he caught hold of her and could feel the heat emanating from her body. He lifted her back on to the bed and it was then that he noticed what looked like red pinpricks on her skin. His heart sank. Perhaps her fever was not the result of her soaking, but from that disease she had mentioned?

He considered the consequences if that was true and swore beneath his breath. Yet he had no choice but to accept that if whatever had caused the rash was infectious then it was too late for him to protect himself from its effects. He could only hope and pray that it was just a heat rash.

He left the bedchamber and returned shortly after with a cloth and a bowl of cold water. He soaked the cloth in water before wringing it out and wiping her face with it, bathing her eyes especially. Then he folded the cloth into a wet compress and placed it on her forehead. Carefully, he repeated this action and carried on doing so until she appeared less restless. When he touched her skin, although it still felt hot, it was not burning. Was the fever breaking? Or was she cooler due to his ministrations with the wet cloth? Perhaps it was both.

Suddenly her eyes opened and she stared up into his face. Her hand shot out and her fingers fastened on his wrist. 'What have you done to me?' she croaked. 'Where is my father and Captain Black Harry?'

He stiffened. 'What is your father's name?'

'Callum McDonald. Have you seen him here?'

'No.'

Her eyes showed dismay.

Harry's heart began to thud with heavy strokes. So his instincts had been right and she *was* Bridget McDonald, but it seemed she was expecting to find her father and him together. So was he right in thinking that Callum had never arrived in Scotland? It would do no good him asking her that question now. He prised her fingers from his wrist and said, 'You have a fever, mistress. I have sent Joe to fetch a healer.' He wrung out the cloth and placed it on her forehead once again.

'I need help to find him. I cannot waste time lying here,' she said fretfully. 'I must find my father. Perhaps someone else has seen him.'

She made to push down the bedcovers, but Harry prevented her from doing so by placing his hands over hers. 'You're in no fit state to go anywhere right now,' he said firmly. 'Be patient. I will fetch you a drink.'

'Where are my clothes?' demanded Bridget. 'I must find my father.'

He bit back the words that were crowding to be released and went downstairs. He went to the kitchen and made her a drink of wine and water and poured himself a measure of liquor. He decided he needed some fresh air and carried the drink and the flask outside. He sat on the terrace, moodily gazing out over the ocean glistening in the sunlight. He had survived hunger and thirst, battles and storms since last he had seen Bridget. He had been prepared to confront all these adversaries for himself, wanting adventure, as well as dis-covering new ways to increase his wealth, but he had refused her passage on his ship, determined that not only would she not have to face such dangers, but that her burgeoning beauty would not distract himself or the crew from the business in hand. Now she had come back into his life, bringing uncer-tainty and trouble.

Why was she searching for Callum here on Madeira? Who was this Lady Elizabeth she had spoken of in her delirium? On whose ship had she originally set sail before being captured and sold to a slaver?

He downed the drink in one gulp and refilled the cup. He stayed there for a while longer, thinking about the fragments of information he'd gleaned from Bridget so far. Then he went indoors, cut bread and spread it with honey and placed food and drink on a tray and carried it upstairs, hoping that she had recovered her composure and would be able to eat something.

As he reached the upstairs passage he heard a crash coming from the bedchamber and made haste. He was stunned by the sight that met his eyes. The small table had been knocked over and Bridget was writhing on the bed and babbling words he could not make out. He seized one of her hands and clasped it between his own. 'Hush, woman, there is no need for such a commotion,' he said gently. 'You are safe.'

She stared at him, but he sensed she was not seeing him because she was still muttering to herself. He wondered if she had fallen asleep and was having a bad dream. She was defying someone, saying that she would not marry their son. Suddenly she went limp.

Harry took her in his arms and brought her against his chest and spoke soothingly, recalling words in Swedish that the grandmother of his friend Alex, the Baron Dalsland, had used to comfort him when he'd suffered from his recurring nightmares. He was ashamed by the memory because he had been a youth on the verge of early manhood at the time. He should not have given in to such weakness after he had survived three years on board a pirate ship. He'd finally escaped by sneaking off and concealing himself from his shipmates behind a pile of barrels in the Swedish port of Visby. It was Alex who had found him and taken Harry to his grandparents' home. They had provided him with a roof over his head and fed him until his lean body filled out and grew strong. That first summer he and Alex had become like brothers and they were soon fluent in each other's language. Alex's grandfather, the old Baron, had a merchandising business and owned several ships. Harry had asked if he could work for him and the old man had put him under the tutelage of one of his finest captains. When the old Baron had died he had left Harry the *Thor's Hammer*.

Harry stroked Bridget's dark red hair, remembering how he had grieved for the old man. Suddenly he realised that the room had fallen silent. His patient had fallen asleep again. He waited several moments before placing her down on the bed and pulling up the covers over her. He decided to stay with her until she woke or Juanita arrived in case she should have any more bad dreams.

Bridget opened her eyes and her gaze fell on the man asleep in the chair by her bedside. His bearded chin was cupped in one hand and his elbow rested on a cushion on the arm of the chair. His thick dark lashes would have been the envy of many a woman, she thought, wondering how long he had been sitting there. He shifted suddenly and Bridget started nervously and, clearing her throat, asked, 'Captain, are you awake?'

He yawned, revealing excellent teeth, and then his eyes opened and met her gaze. For an instant she felt as if drawn into the depths of those dark blue orbs and her heartbeat quickened. 'I did not mean to go to sleep, but I've been keeping long hours lately,' he said drily.

'You mean because of me, Captain? I am grateful to you for your care.' Her voice was husky and Harry found it extremely attractive, almost as seductive as her physical beauty. 'I wish to leave as soon as possible. I need to find my father.

My information is that he and Captain Black Harry were on this island.'

Harry wondered from whom she had had this information. 'But you are ill. You cannot possibly leave,' he said firmly.

'I am feeling much better,' she insisted.

He wondered if he should tell her that her face was covered in spots, but at that moment there came the sound of voices below. He asked her to excuse him and left the bedchamber.

Bridget gazed after him, wondering if it was the healer who had arrived. She was aware that the shirt she was wearing smelled of her perspiration due to her fever. Despite this she knew it to be a fine shirt of excellent quality, so her rescuer was a man of some wealth. At that moment she heard the sound of footsteps coming upstairs and along the passageway towards her. She decided to pretend to have fallen asleep again, thinking she might discover more about the man who had given her shelter that way.

'I have seen this rash before,' said Juanita in Portuguese, glancing over her shoulder at Harry. 'It is a complaint suffered mainly by children and can sometimes kill, but the fever has broken and I have no doubt this woman will recover.'

'How soon will she be fit to leave?' asked Harry, taking coins from a pouch at his belt.

Juanita's eyes fixed on the money. 'Where would you have her go?'

'She is seeking her father, a Callum McDonald, and she has heard that he has been seen on this island. As far as I am aware he has never set foot on Madeira, but I could be mistaken. I ask that you would keep your ears and eyes open in Machico. I will have a search made of Funchal, just in case he could have anchored there at any time this past year.'

Juanita stared at him from under grey, bristling brows. 'You do that, Captain, but if her father is not here, what will you do with her then? She is young and no doubt beautiful when she does not have this rash, but she is also a foreigner. Surely you will not desert her?'

'I have a cargo of sugar cane to get to Lisbon. She needs a woman to keep her company. If I were to leave her here in Madeira, will you stay with her? I will pay you,' Harry offered.

Juanita shook her head and said firmly, 'No, I wish to leave Madeira. I am getting old and I would return to my family home in Portugal. I still have kin there and would spend my last days with them.'

Harry frowned. 'I understand, but would ask another favour of you. Have you heard aught of a slave-trader ship foundering anywhere off this coast or it may have anchored in Machico?'

'I have heard nothing, but I will make enquiries for you.'

He thanked her and changed the subject. 'Is there aught you can prescribe for her rash?'

The old woman fished in a capacious cloth bag and produced a phial. 'You may give her three drops of this liquid if the rash itches her unbearably and keeps her awake.'

Harry took the phial and handed a coin over to Juanita. 'When do you plan to leave for Portugal?'

'When the signs are auspicious.' She chuckled and patted his arm. 'If you have need of me again, send Joseph to fetch me.'

'I will bear in mind what you say.' Harry glanced towards the bed as a thought occurred to him, but he remained silent and went downstairs. He called Joe to keep a watch over their patient and headed for the fields, knowing that he could not afford to change his plans to leave the island once the sugar-cane harvest was gathered in.

Bridget inspected the rash on her arms and frowned, turning over in her mind the conversation she'd overheard between the captain and Juanita. Unfortunately, she had not been able to understand every word spoken, but she felt certain that he had asked Juanita to make enquiries about her father and for that she was grateful. Hopefully he would also have a search made for the slave trader and his vessel. What if the slave trader was still alive and came looking for her? After all he *had* bought her. A chill ran down her spine. What was she to do if the captain were to sail for Lisbon, leaving her behind here on Madeira at the mercy of any unscrupulous person?

There was a knock on the door. 'May I come in?' asked Joe.

Bridget sighed. 'Aye, please do.'

The lad entered the bedchamber, carrying a tray. 'D'yer know that at one time me and the captain thought you might die, but here you are looking a whole load better despite your rash. The captain reckons it could be caused by the fever making you all hot.' He beamed at her.

Bridget forced a smile, guessing why the captain had not been completely honest with Joe. She was also remembering that it was the lad who had put poppy juice in her drink the first day she was here. 'I am much better so I do not need any potions, Joe,' she said hastily.

'All right. But the captain said you're to eat this bread and cheese and then I'm to bring you a custard apple.'

'Tell me about your captain?' she asked.

Joe grinned. 'He's a hard man to please, but he's fair. His ship is anchored in Machico harbour and he's here to load and transport the bulk of Senhor Jorge's sugar-cane harvest to a buyer in Lisbon. It's the *senhor* who owns this house, but he's gone off with a fleet of warships, led by the explorer Vasco da Gama. They're going around the tip of Africa, hoping to find a swifter passage to the Indies. The captain intended going as well, but we were caught up in a battle with the natives at one of the Portuguese trading stations on the African coast.'

'What happened?' she asked, unable to conceal her curiosity.

Joe's eyes took on a faraway expression and he did not immediately answer, then he said solemnly, 'I don't think the captain would like me to give you the gruesome details, but I can tell you that there were more of them than us. There were spears and arrows flying through the air with us managing to dodge most of them. Then it was hand-to-hand fighting. Unfortunately whilst the captain was fighting three of them at once and winning, a spear came out of nowhere and he got wounded in the thigh. The captain drew out that spear and stuck it in one of the enemy. He has a stubborn streak does the captain. Even so that didn't stop him, but then something even nastier happened and we had no choice but to get him out of there.'

'It sounds as if he was lucky to survive,' said Bridget, admiring the captain's bravery.

'You can say that again,' said Joe, his face alight with enjoyment. 'It was the same when we sailed the northern seas and we did battle with pirates. We often ended up in hand-to-hand combat. The captain only ever used the cannon as a last resort. He's always aware that there might be innocent captives aboard who could suffer along with the sinners.'

'That's very perceptive of your captain,' said Bridget.

Joe grinned. 'I'm not sure what that means, but he's the best captain to work for that I know. Now I'll have to be going or he'll be wondering what I'm up to.'

Bridget would have liked to have heard more of the captain's exploits, but did not wish to keep the youth from his work. 'I would like some warm water, Joe, and if you could fetch my clothes I'd be very grateful,' she said persuasively.

'Certainly, the captain had me wash and dry them.'

She said softly, 'You are kind.'

He flushed to the roots of his hair. 'My pleasure, mistress,' he mumbled, and hurried from the bedchamber.

Bridget ate the bread and cheese and drained the cup of wine and water, marvelling that the captain and Joe had survived such adventures. She wondered why, if the captain was English, was he staying here and plying his trade between this island and Lisbon instead of returning home? If her father and Captain Black Harry were not to be found on Madeira it was possible that they might not be because more than a year had passed since his ship had been seen here—then she must try to persuade him to take her to Lisbon. It was possible that she might find news of her father in that bustling city. She wished Joe would hurry and bring her clothes.

However, it was the captain who knocked at the door before announcing his presence and coming into the bedchamber when she bid him enter. He was carrying a basin and had a drying cloth over his arm.

'Where are my clothes?' she blurted out. 'I want to get dressed and out of this bed.'

'I am glad to hear you say that, mistress, but are you certain you are well enough to do so? I am having a search made for your father, but if he cannot be found, I am at a loss what to do with you once you are recovered. I will be leaving Madeira soon.' He placed the basin on the table and the drying cloth on the bed.

'When will you be leaving?' she asked, sitting up straight. 'Joe told me that you are here for the sugar-cane harvest. If you are to find my father, surely it would be of help to you to have the name of the ship he sailed on? It is called *Thor's Hammer* and was last seen anchored in the harbour at Funchal.'

Harry shot her a glance. 'So it was only *Thor's Hammer* that your informant saw?'

'Aye!' Her brow knit, thinking it sounded as if he thought there should be another ship. 'It belongs to a mariner known as Captain Black Harry. He and my father set out almost two years ago in search of a north-west passage to the Indies in the wake of the voyage made by John Cabot. I was expecting my father to return last year, but he never did so.'

Harry frowned. 'Who told you that the ship could be found here?'

'A mariner in London.'

Harry drew up a chair and sat down. 'It does not necessary follow that your father was on that ship.'

She gripped a handful of the bedclothes convulsively. 'Are you saying that he could have been on the *Odin's Maiden* instead? That's the name of Captain Black Harry's other ship.'

He hesitated. 'It is possible. You must accept, Mistress McDonald, that ocean voyages hold great risk for mariners and explorers.'

She had paled. 'I am not a fool. But Cabot returned, so why shouldn't my father?'

'Why not, indeed?' said Harry, knowing that Cabot had not returned from his second voyage. He went over to the window and gazed out. 'But I have to be honest with you and tell you in the light of what you have told me that I do not believe your father to be on this island. I, too, have journeyed to the New World and your father went missing the same time as *Odin's Maiden*. This was fifteen, sixteen months or more ago.'

Bridget stared at the captain's broad back in bewilderment. 'What are you saying? That you knew my father? If that is so, why did you not tell me earlier?'

'You have been ill and out of your mind and I didn't immediately know your identity and that you were searching for Callum.'

'Were you on either ship?'

'Aye, I was a shipmate of your father's at one time and that is how I became acquainted with him.'

'Then you will know Captain Black Harry, too?'

Harry wondered how long it would be before it occurred to her that he and Black Harry could be one and the same. He was not looking forward to that moment and was determined to delay it as long as possible. He would wager a gold coin that she would blame *him* for Callum going missing!

He turned and faced her. 'Your father and the captain quarrelled. The captain was keen to sail further south along the coast of the New World, but your father was not.'

'Why not?' Her eyes were intent on his face.

'I assume it was because Callum had no taste for such a venture. I deem he realised that we were not going to find the passage to the Indies or make our fortunes, so he decided to return home. The captain, on the other hand, was keen to speak to the Portuguese explorers who had knowledge of the southern ocean and its winds and currents. Your father chose to disobey his orders and, I suspect, stole *Odin's Maiden* from the captain to make his own way home.'

'My father is no thief!' she said indignantly.

Harry raised his eyebrows. 'He was once a pirate, woman, so how can you say that? When did *you* leave home? It is possible that you and your father missed each other by a cat's whisker.'

Bridget was mortified that this man knew something of her father's past life and said stiffly, 'I left London last May. I know what you are thinking—why has it taken me so long to get here?' Her expression was strained.

'I know why. You have forgotten that you told me that you were sold by a pirate to the slave trader whose ship you escaped from.'

'That is true. I had forgotten,' said Bridget, putting a hand to her head. 'A slave trader who could be on this island and looking for me right now.' Her voice trembled. 'He paid good money for me and might not wish to lose out on his investment.'

Harry said, 'He could also be dead or have already left these waters. As for your father and *Odin's Maiden*, a mariner can always think of reasons why a ship should be delayed. A storm can blow a vessel miles off course and if a ship survives the storm, it can still be damaged, making repairs necessary. If the materials are not to hand, then the ship would need to limp into the nearest harbour, perhaps to remain there for weeks on end.'

'You're saying that this could have happened to *Odin's Maiden* and my father might have arrived home after I left,' said Bridget eagerly. 'Although, you cannot know for certain that my father stole the ship,' she added swiftly.

Harry said, 'Where else could they have both gone, along with a complete crew of men? No doubt he knew that you would be worried about him and wished to be reunited with you. He told me of his affection for his daughter, Bridget.'

Suddenly Bridget's eyes were shiny with tears. 'I can accept that as a possible reason why my father might have taken the ship. It is also possible that he might never have reached Scotland and be at the bottom of the ocean.' Her voice broke on a sob.

Harry said bracingly, 'You would give up hope so soon? He could have wintered at New-found-land, an island discovered by Cabot, whose waters are teeming with fish. This would have delayed his setting out for home.'

Bridget fought back another sob and wiped her eyes with the back of her hand. 'I will try to believe that is what happened, but if he was to search for me at my uncle's house in Scotland, then he would not have found me. He would need to go to London.'

'Why London?'

'Because that is where I was taken by my Uncle Ranald, my father's treacherous brother, after my aunt died. He decided to visit his mistress, Lady Appleby, in the north of England, and because her elder son lived in London and she wished to see him, they forced me to go with them.'

Harry wondered if this was the son she had mentioned earlier in her delirium. 'Why did they do this?'

'They believed I knew where my father's hoard was and would not accept that it had been stolen by an Irish brigand, Patrick O'Malley.' Her eyes darkened. 'If only we had not met Captain Black Harry in Ireland, who took my father away to the Indies without me, how different my life would have turned out.' Bridget scrubbed at her damp eyes. 'I would that you would leave me now.'

Harry was tempted to say that if she had not met him, then she might have been recaptured by Patrick O'Malley and what would have happened to her then? Instead he left her to her *toilette*.

Bridget so wished she knew if her father was alive or dead.

Callum usually drank far too much when life dealt him a blow and then he could be reckless in the extreme. She had believed her presence had helped rein in some of his excesses and that was another reason why she had wanted to accompany him on Black Harry's ship. Yet when Callum was sober, he was an excellent seaman and she had learnt much about handling a ship and commanding men by watching him.

She washed her face and hands and then dried them on the cloth. At least she knew more about her father than when she had arrived here. She must cling to the hope that he was still alive. She was also a free woman, so should rejoice in that and keep her spirits up. She still feared the slave trader appearing on the scene despite the captain telling her that she was safe with him. No doubt in the eyes of the Portuguese she belonged to that beast and the law would be on his side if he were to catch her again. The captain, being a foreigner on this island, might come off worse if he were to defend her. She had to get off this island as soon possible and look for her father elsewhere. As for Captain Black Harry, she would ask her host if he knew what had happened to him since his ship had been seen in Madeira last year.

Chapter Three

Harry swung into the saddle, determined not to blame himself for all that had befallen Bridget since they had parted in Ireland. Yet it was true that if he had not been prepared to pay her passage to Scotland in order for her to stay with her uncle and aunt, then her life would have been different. He remembered wanting to kiss Bridget's luscious mouth when they had first met. Even later when she had insulted him, he had wanted to grab a handful of that red hair of hers that was aflame as if it had caught fire from the sparks that seemed to fly from her in her rage and disappointment and kiss her soundly. How very different both their lives would have been if he had surrendered to his desire. But he still thought he had been right to not take her aboard his ship. A man needed to be totally focused to survive on such a perilous journey.

Harry frowned. He had little faith in Callum having survived the northern ocean in autumn despite his having told Bridget to keep her hopes alive. He was going to have to take responsibility for her, but if she knew he was Captain Black Harry, he sensed she might do something desperate rather than accept his help. She would very likely run away from him and end up in further trouble. He had to think up a plan that would ensure her safety, not just for the next week or two, but for the future. In the meantime he had to ensure that she did not realise he was the man she appeared to despise.

Bridget stirred, wondering what had disturbed her sleep. She could hear a bird singing and eased herself into a sitting position. She had been dreaming of Captain Black Harry and it was not anger she had felt, but a wild excitement. She supposed it was to be expected that she would dream of him now she was here on Madeira where his ship had last been seen. Where was he now? There had been a time after he and her father had set sail when she could not get him out of her mind.

This latest dream had shocked her and she could only believe that her mind was playing tricks on her. There was no way that she would ever take Black Harry as a lover after what he'd done to her.

Besides, she knew the man's real identity, which was one of the reasons she had set out in search of him and her father, as Harry himself was unaware of it. She had initially been accompanied by Lady Elizabeth Stanley, who had befriended her when she was in London, her ladyship's maid, Hannah, and Joshua Wood, a childhood friend of Black Harry, whose real name had turned out to be Harry Appleby. Shockingly, he was heir to a manor in Lancashire and a house and business in London, so no doubt he would not consider her good enough for him. How could she even imagine him making love to her in the light of all these facts? She must be mad!

Her eyes roamed the room and she noticed that the bowl and drying cloth had been removed. She must have fallen into a deep sleep, indeed, to have been unaware of the captain or Joe's entry. How long had she slept? She needed to speak to the captain. What was his name? Her wits had indeed gone begging for her not to have asked that simple question.

She heard voices outside and looked towards the window. The shutters were wide open, allowing sunlight and a flower-scented breeze into the room, along with birdsong. She wanted to be up and doing and longed to be outside in the fresh air. Suddenly she noticed her green gown and silk shift on the chest and her face lit up. She swung her legs over the side of the bed and stood up.

Her knees shook and she realised that she was still weak from her illness, but, by holding on to the bed, she managed to reach its foot and sank down on to the chest. Her fingers fastened on the skirt of her gown and she drew it towards her, along with her shift. She held them to her face and breathed in the smell of the ocean breeze and that of lavender. She wasted no more time, but dragged off the captain's shirt and hastened to pull the shift over her head. It proved more difficult putting on her gown, due to the weight of its skirts.

Once dressed, Bridget felt much better, so decided to unbraid her hair and let it hang loose. If only she had the company of another female to help wash and comb it. She had spent most of her childhood with women until her Irish mother, Mary, had died and her father had taken her with him on his ship, due to his fear of her being abducted by one of the rival Irish clans. She recalled her excitement and had looked forward to a more interesting life. She'd had to familiarise herself with his ship and become accustomed to all-male company. The crew had spoilt her and she had come to feel less awkward in the company of men, to love the sea and visiting new places. She had admired her big strong red-haired father, but never forgot the long weeks that she and her mother had spent waiting for his return from sea. Tears welled in her eyes as she thought of all that was lost to her. She could very likely be an orphan now.

There came a knock on the door. 'May I come in?'

Bridget recognised the captain's voice and her heart leapt. Swiftly she wiped her face, not wanting him to consider her a weak female. It had been a mistake, thinking of the past. It was the present and future that were important. She must persuade this man to help her further.

'Please do, Captain,' she called.

The door opened and he stood, gazing at her with an expression in his indigo eyes that brought a blush to her cheeks. 'You are dressed and looking much improved in health, Mistress McDonald. I deem that you are almost fit to leave this place,' he said.

The colour drained from her face; it appeared to her that he would be rid of her that day and she was not ready to cope alone just yet. Despite her wanting to be up and doing, this house had proved to be a safe haven. How could she possibly manage alone and penniless in a foreign land?

She cleared her throat. 'I do understand, Captain, your wanting to be rid of me because you have your business to attend to—but I must confess my limbs are still a little weak. I much appreciate your hospitality. I only wish I could reimburse you, but I have no money. Yet if you are prepared to continue to help me, then I will see that you are rewarded.'

'I ask for no reward,' he said abruptly. 'You look pale and still need to rest.'

'I am better than I was,' she murmured, tilting her chin.

There was a silence.

'You are English, Captain, and have told me that you were one of my father's shipmates. Does that mean you were once a pirate, too?'

Harry stiffened. 'Never.'

She flushed with embarrassment for she felt as if she had insulted him. She cleared her throat. 'May I ask why you decided to live here on Madeira? You never thought of sailing home with my father?'

'No, he never took me into his confidence before he disappeared. By the purest stroke of luck, I was able to perform a service to the owner of this villa whilst on the other side of the world. There was a skirmish with the natives and I saved his life. We conversed and discovered we had a common ambition, so that is why I set sail in company with him and his companions for Madeira.'

'What was this ambition of yours?' she asked.

'I wished to sail around the coast of Africa to the Indies. I hope that answer will suffice for the moment. Right now I would know more about you and how you came to be captured by pirates.'

She sighed and plucked at her skirts. 'When I set out from London in search of my father, I had three companions and we were accompanied by another ship. Unfortunately the vessels were separated by a storm and our ship was attacked by pirates. Our captain was killed and so were several members of the crew.'

He frowned. 'And your companions?'

'Certainly, owing to her station, Lady Elizabeth should have been ransomed, but I do not know what might have happened to Hannah, her maid, and Joshua Wood, who was also in her service. I was separated from them, you see. They remained on the captured ship and I was taken on to the pirates' vessel to be sold to the slavers.'

'It is possible Joshua Wood might have been forced to join the pirates.'

'I see.' Bridget sighed. 'Tell me, Captain—do you know what happened to Captain Black Harry?'

Harry's heart leapt. He had been waiting for this moment and he still did not know how to answer the question. His dark brows knit and he folded powerful arms across his broad chest. 'I had almost forgotten you knew the captain. This Joshua Wood, you admired him?'

Bridget gave him a startled look. 'He was a good man. Dependable.'

Harry felt a curl of envy. 'A handsome man?'

'I would say pleasant, rather than handsome.'

'You were fond of him?' he pressed.

She frowned, wondering why he asked such questions of Joshua. 'I liked him. As I have told you, he was a good man, not the kind to force himself on a woman like some,' she added, dropping her gaze and gripping her hands tightly together.

Harry thought of the slave trader and wished he had him there in front of him, so he could punch him in the face, but all he said was, 'I am glad to hear it. This Lady Elizabeth— what is her full name?'

Bridget pulled herself together. 'Lady Elizabeth Stanley. She is related to the King of England.'

Surprise flared in Harry's eyes. 'A rare prize, indeed, for a pirate. I deem you have no need to fear for her life. She will certainly have been ransomed. It is a pity she did not arrange for you to be ransomed, too.'

Bridget nodded. 'But the fault was not hers that I was taken away by the pirates and I know she was deeply concerned for me. In the past she was exceedingly kind to me. When I escaped from my uncle I was able to help in the rescue of her goddaughter, Rosamund, who was abducted by her stepbrother around that time. Afterwards, her ladyship offered to be of assistance to me. I became part of her household and she took my problems to heart and decided to accompany me on my search for my father and Captain Black Harry. Only on the way…' She became agitated and jumped to her feet.

'You can have no notion of what it is like to be desired by men who have you in their power! What I had to do just to survive…'

Harry reached out and was compelled to take her by the shoulders. He gazed down into her face and slowly lifted a hand and stroked her cheek. 'You are very beautiful.'

Bridget closed her eyes and allowed her face to rest against his hand. 'Beauty can be a bane,' she whispered, thinking of the time when even Black Harry had looked at her with a delighted expression on his handsome face. She opened her eyes and looked up into the captain's bearded face. 'Do you know the whereabouts of Black Harry?' she asked again with a troubled look.

Harry released her. 'He no longer exists.'

'What!' Bridget was taken aback. 'When did this happen? Did he die recently or was he lost in the New World and someone else took over his ship?'

Harry was surprised by her reaction. 'You sound like you care what happened to him. Yet earlier I received the impression that you despised him, so why should it matter to you if he is dead?'

'There are those I know in England who will be saddened to hear of his death,' she said.

Harry's eyes narrowed. 'If you talk of his family, he has none.'

'How do you know that? He had lost his memory and could not remember his family,' she said with a toss of her head, causing her glorious hair to swirl about her shoulders. 'If only he had not separated me from my father and gone to the New World.'

Harry's gaze fixed on her hair and he longed to touch it and run his fingers through it. Instead he clenched his fists.

'No doubt when last you confronted each other, you were showing all the signs of burgeoning womanhood.'

Bridget flushed. 'What are you suggesting? That he thought I would have an unsettling effect on his crew?'

He raised his eyebrows in a speaking manner. 'No doubt he was aware that a woman's needs are very different from a man's and to be the only female on a long voyage would have presented you with problems.'

She knew he was right about that, but was not going to admit it. 'I would have coped, Captain. A woman can adapt to difficult situations the same as a man.'

'I am not disputing your courage and stamina, Mistress McDonald, but a woman cannot help but practise her feminine wiles on a man in order to get him to do what she wishes.'

Bridget's jaw dropped and, for a moment, she was speechless and hurt that he could believe that of her. 'Are you daring to suggest that I am a coquette?' she demanded. 'I thought you were different from other men because you have been kind to me, but I see now that I was mistaken. I will seek help elsewhere. I have been called a witch in the past and accused of putting a spell on a man. The slave trader was typical of a certain kind of man who blames the object of their lust, without caring what damage they do to a woman. No doubt Black Harry was the same.'

Harry's jaw tightened. 'You do him an injustice when he cannot defend his reputation. I understand why you were desperate enough to jump into a raging sea, but I am not like that slave trader. Anyway, if you prefer to manage without any further help from me then I will leave you alone to consider your options.' He left the bedchamber, closing the door carefully behind him.

If there had been anything close by that she could have

picked up and thrown at him, Bridget would have done so. She wanted to scream at him. How could he not understand how much his words had hurt her? She had done everything possible to hide her feminine charms from the pirate crew but little good it had done her. When she had fought off the advances of the ones who had tried to steal a kiss from her, she had been repaid with a beating.

She dropped on to the bed, wondering how she could get off this island without the captain. She remembered Black Harry paying for her passage to Scotland, so she could leave Ireland as her father had wished her to do. She had to admit that it was strange behaviour on Black Harry's part if he really had lusted after her. She recalled how strong and indestructible he had appeared as he had stood on the quayside last time she had seen him. It seemed wrong that two such strong men as he and her father could now be dead.

A lump filled her throat and she wanted to weep. She must return to Black Harry's friend, the Baron Dalsland, in England, but what sad news she would be taking with her to the Baron and his wife, Rosamund, who was Black Harry's sister—the sister he did not know existed. Joshua, too, would be disappointed, as would Lady Elizabeth—that is if they were still alive. She wondered if they believed she, herself, was lost to them for ever.

A tear trickled down her cheek. Perhaps it would be better if she did not return to England because then she would not have to give them such disappointing and sad news. But that was a cowardly thought and she must consider some way she could get back to them.

She wondered if she were to get down on her knees and kiss the captain's feet and beg his pardon he would extend his helping hand to her again. Her proud nature baulked at the very notion of behaving in the way she had been forced to act whilst in the power of the pirate chieftain when she had rebelled against his orders. Fortunately, where he was concerned her beauty had saved her from rape, because she was worth more to him as a virgin.

A knock on the door and her heart began to race and she felt quite faint at the thought of coming face to face with her host again. He was beginning to have the most odd effect on her. Had he returned to tell her that he did indeed want her out of the house immediately?

'Who is it?' she asked in a trembling voice.

'It's Joe.'

She felt a mixture of disappointment and relief. 'Come in.'

He opened the door and peered round it cautiously. 'The captain said that you were vexed. He told me to make sure not to get too close to you with a knife.'

His words came as such an anticlimax that Bridget laughed. 'Your captain jests. I would not hurt you, Joe. I look upon you as my friend.'

'Honestly?' He pushed the door wider with his hip and came further into the bedchamber. 'I've got no female friends, but I've food here that's real appetising. It'll nourish you and make you strong.'

'I suppose you don't get a chance to become acquainted with a suitable lass being away at sea so long,' said Bridget.

'Aye. But, to be honest, I don't know what to say to lasses, unlike some of the crew. Women and drink are the first things they think of as soon as we drop anchor in port.' He reddened. 'I suppose I shouldn't be talking to you about such matters…' His voice trailed off and he looked even more embarrassed.

Bridget lowered her eyes and toyed with her fingers. 'Does the captain go with women?'

Joe placed the tray on the chest and made for the door. 'No, he steers clear of them. There was a woman he once loved, but she was in love with his closest friend.' Joe looked guilty. 'The captain would have me hide if he knew I was gossiping about him. Now you eat your fish and bread.'

Bridget gazed down at the pure white fillets swimming in a creamy herb sauce as if in a daze. 'What kind of fish is it?'

'Forget its name, but it has a real ugly head. Anyway, you're not going to have to look at that because I chopped it off.'

'Did you catch it yourself?' she asked.

Joe grinned. 'Aye. Captain's too busy to go fishing. Time's money and he reckons the winds will be blowing in the right direction soon to take us to Lisbon.'

The lad's words made Bridget feel almost as desperate as she had felt when she had dropped into the sea. 'Tell me, Joe, what is your captain's name?'

'We call him Captain Mariner.'

'Mariner?' She stared at him in surprise. 'But that is simply another name for a sailor.'

Joe nodded. 'Aye, the captain was an orphan like me, so he chose his own name.'

Bridget supposed it made perfect sense. 'And what's your surname, Joe?'

'I'm Joseph Cook because that's what I am. I'll leave you now, mistress, to enjoy your meal.'

After Joe left, Bridget forced herself to eat whilst she mulled over what he had told her. If the captain had naught to do with women, it meant that she was safe from any advances from him. She wondered about the woman he had loved and recalled the expression in his eyes when he had looked at her earlier. He was all man and no doubt could have made many a woman happy. She regretted speaking to him the way she had done now. He must have been deeply hurt when the woman had preferred his friend. Somehow she had to overcome his misgivings about her and convince him that it would serve him well to take her with him on his ship to Lisbon.

Harry stood outside Bridget's bedchamber. He had calmed down and now regretted upsetting her. He should have taken her sufferings into more consideration and considered his words before he spoke. But he had spoken honestly when he had told her that she was beautiful. He desired her and wanted her for himself, but for the moment he had to keep those feelings under control. She was penniless, far from home and her situation was unlikely to improve if Callum was at the bottom of the ocean along with Harry's ship and its crew. She might speak of friends in England, but that country was thousands of miles away. Her beauty, as she had said, was a hindrance rather than a help, and she needed protecting from other men. He could see only one way of ensuring such protection and security for the future. But if she knew him for who he really was, then she might reject his suggestion. If it were not for his beard, she might possibly have guessed who he was by now.

How long before she realised he was deceiving her? He had not actually lied to her when he'd told her that Black Harry no longer existed but she had reacted to the news as he intended, by believing that he had meant he was dead. Harry had always hated being called Black Harry and no one had called him by that name for years, so in a way he did no longer exist. Now Harry, as his alter ego, Captain Mariner, needed to apologise to Bridget McDonald if he was to lay his plan for their future before her. Taking a deep breath, he wrapped his knuckles on the panel of the door and asked for permission to enter.

'Of course, Captain Mariner, do come in,' invited Bridget.

Perhaps he should not be surprised by the sweetness of her tone, aware how desperate was her situation. He half-expected to find her lying on the bed, resting, but she was standing in front of the statue of the Madonna and Child. He cleared his throat. She turned and their eyes caught and held, and he guessed she was trying not to show how nervous she was of him.

'I hope you will forgive me for having spoken words that were hurtful to you?' said Harry quietly.

Bridget did not drop her gaze, but her insides were quivering. 'I, too, spoke out of turn earlier, Captain Mariner. I really am grateful for all you have done for me and I really do need your help. If I had any money, I would pay you to take me aboard your ship and provide me with passage to Lisbon.'

'And what would you do when you reached Lisbon?'

'I would hope that there would be an English ship whose captain would be generous enough to take me to London. I am sure my friends would willingly reimburse him for his trouble.'

Harry frowned. 'You cannot be as foolish as you sound, Mistress McDonald. I refuse to believe that you have forgotten already your earlier fears about the slave trader still searching for you. I deem what you really want is for me to take you all the way to England.'

She blushed. 'It would certainly be the perfect answer to my dilemma.'

Harry muttered, 'Sit down, Mistress McDonald.'

She hesitated and he rasped, 'I cannot sit down until you do and I've been on my feet for hours.'

Hastily she sat on the bed. 'You are busy supervising the loading of the sugar-cane harvest?'

'Aye. All is nearly ready and I will be departing soon.' He paused and was silent for so long that she thought he was going to refuse to take her. Then he took a deep breath. 'I have a proposition to put to you.'

'What kind of proposition?' she asked warily.

He frowned. 'There is no need for you to look so apprehensive, but you are an attractive woman and could cause havoc on my ship.'

'Joe told me that you—'

He glared at her. 'What did he tell you?'

She changed what she had been about to say. 'That you were an orphan just like him, so you chose your own name.'

Harry said drily, 'I don't believe that was your first choice of words, but no matter.' He paused, putting off the moment when he would put his proposition to her. 'Would you like to know how Joe came to be in my employment?'

'Aye. I know that he is fond of you and thinks you are the best captain he knows.' She smiled.

Harry scrubbed at his beard. 'I found Joe being tormented by a couple of bigger lads down by the waterfront in London, so I took him under my wing because I knew what it was to have no one of your own to fight your corner. He's been with me ever since. He's like a son to me now.'

Bridget felt a strange warmth inside her. 'Surely you're not old enough to have a son his age?'

Harry gave a twisted smile. 'A younger brother, then. I do not know my exact age, but I reckon I must have seen twenty-four summers.' He paused. 'How old are you, Mistress McDonald?'

'It will be the eighteenth anniversary of my birth in a few months.'

He nodded. 'Then it is time you were wed.'

Her mouth tightened. 'You would tease me, Captain Mariner? What kind of man would marry a dowerless woman?'

'I will marry you,' said Harry simply.

Bridget went still and was convinced that she must have misheard him. 'I beg your pardon, Captain? I didn't quite catch what you said.'

'A marriage of convenience, Mistress McDonald,' he said, meeting her gaze squarely. 'You are a penniless woman alone in a foreign land and in need of a protector, and I have decided that a wife could be useful to me.'

She was stunned by his suggestion. 'I cannot believe you would wish to marry me. I have naught to bring you.'

'You are a beautiful woman and will enhance my life. I have roamed the seas for years and it has seldom bothered me that I have no wife or house to call home when I make landfall. Now I have decided that I will buy a house in some port and you can live there. Will that not suit you? You will not have to constantly tolerate my presence for I will be away on business some of the time. You can make a home for me and Joe. Do you think you can manage to do that? If you feel it is beyond your capacities, then say so now.'

Bridget was still feeling stunned by his proposal, but his reasoning sounded sensible. She had to give it serious thought, because what would happen to her if she turned him down? He might feel he no longer needed to feel responsible for her. He had been kind and tended her when she was ill. No doubt he had saved her life and not once had he taken advantage of her dependency on him. He appeared to be an honourable man. But what did he mean exactly by a marriage of convenience?

She cleared her throat. 'I thank you for your offer, Captain, but does it not bother you that we scarcely know each other?'

He raised those devilishly dark eyebrows of his and drawled, 'Most couples who make convenient matches are barely acquainted.'

Bridget knew this to be true. Even the King of England's daughter, Margaret, had married the King of Scotland by proxy without ever having met him. 'That is certainly true. You speak of a marriage of convenience—does that mean you intend this to be a match in name only or shall it be a proper marriage?'

He hesitated. 'Perhaps we can discuss that when we are better acquainted.'

She could see the sense in that because it was possible that they both might have a change of heart in a few months' time. But even so— She frowned. 'Wouldn't a housekeeper do you just as well?'

Harry blinked at her. 'Am I to presume you would rather be my housekeeper?'

'No! For what security would that give me?' she said honestly, reaching out and touching his arm. 'Yet what if, against all the odds, you were to meet another woman and fall in love with her? You might decide that you'd rather be rid of me.'

'It is hardly likely, Mistress McDonald,' he said ruefully. 'But your point is worth considering, only maybe it will be you who will fall in love with another man. You are lovely. It isn't as if you are stuck with an ugly visage like mine. Maybe you will come to hate looking at my face.'

She hesitated. 'I confess I do not have a fondness for black beards. Perhaps if you shaved it off, I would marry you.'

Harry's hand went to his beard in a defensive gesture. 'Is that really necessary?'

'No, it's just that the slave trader had a black beard and I would rather not be reminded of him,' she said.

Harry did not want her constantly thinking of the slave trader, either, as that would not bode well for their future. On the other hand, when she saw him without his beard and recognised him, as well as getting a good look at the disfiguring scar currently hidden beneath his beard, she would have more than one reason for refusing his offer. 'What if I were to promise to shave it off after the wedding?'

She smiled. 'That is a rare promise. I cannot believe you are as ugly as you say you are. I deem you just hide behind that beard because you wish to keep the women at bay.'

He grimaced. 'I would like to hear you say that when you see me minus this beard,' he said, touching his whiskers.

'I deem you dwell too much on the importance of a person's appearance. Surely it is what one's heart is like that is more important.'

'You can say that because you are lovely,' said Harry, 'not that I disagree with you about a person's nature. I would add that, if you decide to accept my proposal, I will expect your complete loyalty to me once we are married.'

His words surprised her. 'Why should you doubt my loyalty? You are offering me a home where I will rule when you are not there. I have no dowry, so no other man of worth would take me as I am. A home of my own is something I have never had before. Just like you, my home was a ship for several years. Even when I lived on land before sailing with my father, my home was either in my Irish grandfather's keep or my uncle's castle. It is true that there will be much for me to learn about organising a household, but I have seen how it is done and I have certain housewifery skills, such as sewing and cooking.'

'Then you will agree to be my wife?' asked Harry, his heart thudding as he waited for her answer.

Chapter Four

Bridget said hesitantly, 'You are offering me so much. I only wish I had part of my father's hoard to give you, then I would feel more worthy of you. I would that neither of us will regret my agreeing to be your wife.'

'I have no need of a dowry,' said Harry, relieved. He took her hand and lifted it to his lips and kissed it. 'Obviously there will be no time for banns to be read, but I will visit the priest in Machico today and, for a few pieces of silver, I am sure he will obtain a special licence so we can wed before we leave Madeira. I pray that you will feel well enough to make the journey in the next few days.'

'If that is your wish.' Bridget could feel her skin tingling where his lips had touched it. 'How will we travel there?'

'On horseback or you could ride alongside me when I drive the cart into Machico. After the ceremony we will go aboard my ship. I will need to oversee the loading of the cargo and, God willing, we will set sail the following morning on the outgoing tide.'

'You have it all planned,' said Bridget, attempting to conceal her sudden apprehension. Could he have planned this from the moment he had discovered her identity? But why should he have done? He had, after all, given sensible reasons why he wished to marry her.

'Naturally, I gave my proposal some thought before broaching the matter,' said Harry. 'Of course, plans can easily be overturned by forgetfulness or misfortune,' he said idly. 'If you can think of aught I might have forgotten, then I will be glad if you will inform me of it. I will leave you now and speak to you on my return.'

Bridget watched him go. She found it difficult to think of anything other at the moment than this man who had saved her life. She had a fair notion of what life was like being married to a mariner. Lonely, if one did not have a family or friends living close by. She felt a tightness in her chest and a moment's panic. Had she made the right decision? He had made no mention of wanting children. Yet she knew from listening to married women talking that most men wanted a son. Her mother had wanted a son, but it had never happened.

There were footsteps outside in the passage that she recognised and her heart began to thud. 'Is that you, Captain?' she called.

He entered the bedchamber and smiled down at her. 'I have been thinking you might like to sit outside on the terrace. I am certain the fresh air and sunshine will do you good.'

Instantly his thoughtfulness banished her ponderings. 'I would like that,' she said sincerely. 'But I have no shoes.' She lifted her skirts to reveal her bare feet. 'I lost them in the sea.'

He frowned and stroked his beard. 'I should have thought of that earlier. No doubt you could also do with more clothes for the journey. I shall see what I can do about such matters when I go into Machico.'

She thanked him.

'I think it is best if I carry you downstairs as this will be the first time you will leave your bedchamber since your arrival,' he said.

Before she could protest and say that she was quite capable of walking, he scooped her up into his arms and carried her from the room. 'But, Captain, my condition is much improved,' she assured him.

'Aye, but you have been close to death and need to conserve your strength for the journey.' Harry was not going to deprive himself of the pleasure of holding her close to him.

On those words, Bridget decided to remain silent, conscious of the strength in his arms and the beating of his heart. It gave her an odd feeling to be cradled in his arms that was not unpleasant.

He set her down in a chair on the terrace where she could gaze down over the garden to the glistening ocean below. 'How calm the water looks today,' she said.

'Aye, it is hard to believe that it can turn into a raging monster with little warning,' said Harry. 'If you will excuse me. I will be back soon.'

'Of course,' said Bridget hastily, watching him until he was out of sight.

Then she turned and looked again over the garden, determined to make the most of these moments of tranquillity. Soon she would have to strengthen her will to face going aboard ship again. What the captain had said about the sea being a raging monster had struck home. But she would not mention her fear of getting caught up in another storm to him.

'Taste this and give me your opinion,' said Harry, handing a goblet to Bridget.

Grateful that he was treating her as he would a normal guest, she took a cautious sip and then a mouthful of the wine. 'It is sweet and fruity with an unusual flavour. If you could bottle it, I'm sure you could make your fortune.'

He smiled. 'I see you have a business head. The unusual flavour is spirit fermented from the processed liquid sugar for the estate's own use. Perhaps one day enough will be produced to make it worth my client's efforts to turn the liquor into a profitable business. At the moment Jorge does not possess enough agricultural land to do so.'

'Jorge is the man who owns this house?'

Harry nodded. 'You have not had the opportunity to discover that Madeira is a heavily forested mountainous island. A lot of trees have to be felled to clear the land for the plough and many of the fields are on a slope. The sugar-cane harvest makes him a decent profit as it is and he also grows vines.'

'So you ship Madeira wine, as well?'

Harry nodded. 'It is a popular wine.'

'Do you have a buyer?'

'I doubt I'll have difficulty finding one in England.' Harry poured a little more of the drink into her goblet. 'I had, until recently, thought of making my home here, but now we are to be married no doubt you will wish to live near your friends in England. I have heard that Lady Elizabeth has a fine mansion near the Strand in London.'

'That is true.' Bridget gazed at his bearded face and tried to imagine his profile clean shaven, but it was not easy and she gave up.

'I have also heard she is an eccentric and prone to do exactly what she likes if she takes a fancy to someone, having no husband to rein in her wayward behaviour.'

Bridget smiled. 'She is also extremely wealthy because he died without issue and she inherited his fortune. She is so droll and says exactly what she thinks, even if it is insulting.

Yet her heart is warm and once she heard my story, she was determined to help me to find my father.'

'Kind of her, indeed,' said Harry drily. 'I presume it was she who provided the ship you sailed on.'

Bridget shook her head. 'No, her goddaughter had recently married the Baron Dalsland and it was he who placed two of his ships at our disposal.'

'What!' exclaimed Harry, sitting bolt upright.

She looked at him, startled. 'Of course, you will recognise the name. The Baron was a close friend of Captain Black Harry. After we discovered that *Thor's Hammer* had been seen in Funchal harbour, the Baron was determined to have him found.' She drew in a trembling breath. 'As you can imagine I was desperate to leave England as soon as possible, fearing the ship would be gone if I delayed, but the Baron insisted that we wait until the weather improved.'

'Wise of him,' rasped Harry. 'You are fortunate in your friends.' He longed to ask about this woman whom the Baron had married, but knew it would be more sensible not to show too much interest, if he was to keep his identity secret a little longer. Yet he was extremely curious to know why Alex had not married Ingrid Wrangel, the woman with whom they had both been in love.

'I sincerely hope that Lady Elizabeth is back in London where she belongs,' said Bridget.

'Would you like to live in London?' asked Harry.

'Surely where we live will depend on your trading interests, Captain?'

He did not dispute it because he had seen Joe approaching with food.

Bridget watched as the youth set a basket of bread on the table, as well as dishes of meat, soft white cheese and fruit. She had regained her appetite and her mouth watered. Joe left for a few moments and returned with plates and knives and a jug of wine. She reached for bread and meat and, for a while, neither she nor the captain spoke, but gave all their attention to consuming the meal set before them. It was a while since she had tasted food so good as that she had consumed in this house.

'Perhaps you would prefer to live in Scotland?' suggested Harry, picking up the conversation where they had left off.

'Not particularly. My memories of life with my kinsfolk are not particularly happy ones. I was happier with my mother's family in Ireland, but I would not like to return there. There are too many memories of her in that place where she died and it would make me sad.' She sighed heavily. 'If only my father had not gone to the New World and she was still alive.'

'You can't rewrite the past, Bridget,' said Harry gently. 'You just have to do your best to redeem it.' He pushed back his chair and stood up. 'I will speak to you again in the morning. I have arrangements to make now. Don't overtax your strength,' he called over his shoulder as he walked away.

As Bridget watched him vanish around the side of the house, she thought how right he was that one could not rewrite the past. She must set her mind on the future. If only she knew what had happened to her father; how she wished that his fortune had not been seized by Patrick O'Malley. She still felt unworthy of the man she was to marry, coming as she was to him dowerless.

It was peaceful sitting there. Joe came out a couple of times and asked if there was aught else she wanted. When she told him that she had finished, he cleared the table. She remained there, watching the sun vanish beyond the horizon and the sky streak with apricot, gold and silver, wondering when the captain would return and if the priest would accept his silver in exchange for a special marriage licence. She felt a stir of apprehension mingling with a tingle of excitement, anticipating the days ahead.

'Christian, I have a task for one of the men,' called Harry from the quayside.

'What is it, Captain?' asked the tall, muscular, blond-haired Swede, leaning over the side of the ship.

'I want the name *Thor's Hammer* painted over with the words *St Bridget.*'

The man screwed up his ice-blue eyes. 'Has the sun got to you, Captain?'

Harry smiled. 'You might believe that even more so when I tell you that I am getting married and my bride's name is Bridget.'

The sailor's mouth fell open. 'You jest!'

'No. She is Callum McDonald's daughter and has come in search of her father. He never arrived home, which means that he and the crew and my ship are most likely at the bottom of the ocean.'

The Swede scowled. 'That is no reason for you to marry her.'

'Isn't it?' Harry frowned.

'No! It is not your fault. I was master of the *Odin's Maiden* and he tricked me into going ashore. If he had not done so, then he would not be missing. You must not forget it was Callum who stole your ship,' said Christian fiercely. 'He showed you no loyalty. *I* would never have behaved towards you in such a way.'

'I know,' said Harry, clapping a hand on his shoulder. 'But she is not to blame for that.'

Christian placed his hand over Harry's resting on his shoulder. 'Neither are you. He knew the risks. He had spoken to the settlers on New-found-land on the outward voyage and even then was hell-bent on returning the way we came. I wonder how he managed to persuade the men to crew the ship and disobey your orders?'

Harry shrugged. 'Perhaps they, too, thought I was mad to want to continue down the coast and preferred to return home, albeit empty-handed. Be that as it may, I still feel some responsibility for Bridget,' said Harry, removing his hand. 'Especially as she is all alone.'

Christian froze. 'Why is she on her own?'

Harry leaned against the side of the ship and his eyes darkened. 'The ship she was on was attacked by pirates and she was sold into slavery.'

'How did she escape?'

'She swam ashore from the slave-trader's ship and I found her on the beach in a state of exhaustion. She needs a protector.'

'That is still no reason for you to marry her,' the Swede insisted.

Harry's mouth set in a firm line. 'I have not made this decision lightly and I do not wish to discuss it further. I've persuaded the priest to perform the ceremony on the morrow, so there will be no delay.'

'Why such haste? Have you considered that she might have been raped by her captor?'

Harry did not answer.

'You have! Yet you would still marry a defiled woman?'

'You've said enough,' said Harry, a warning note in his voice. 'I will not have you questioning my actions and you will speak respectfully of my future wife.' He felt odd enunciating those last two words. 'You can expect the cargo on the morrow.' He did not linger to see the effect of his words on the Swede, but left the ship.

* * *

The following morning Bridget awoke early and instantly remembered that this was to be her wedding day. There was a peculiar feeling in her stomach, but she told herself that it was natural she would feel nervous. She was relieved to see that the rash was fading. Hopefully by afternoon it would be scarcely noticeable. She could only pray that neither the captain nor Joe had caught the disease and wondered if her future husband had given any thought to her infecting his crew. Perhaps he believed she was no longer a threat to anyone.

Not waiting for either of them to knock on her door to rouse her, she dressed swiftly and went downstairs in search of the kitchen. There she found the captain in conversation with an old woman dressed in black. They stopped talking the moment she entered the room and Bridget guessed that they had been discussing her.

'It is good to see you up and about so early, Bridget,' said the captain. 'I want to introduce you to the widow Juanita who came to see you whilst you were ill, but you were sleeping. She will be travelling with us as she wishes to return to her family in Lisbon. I thought you would enjoy the company of another woman.'

Bridget marvelled at his consideration. 'I appreciate your forethought, Captain.'

She turned to Juanita and greeted her in Portuguese, stumbling over some of the words.

A smile flooded the older woman's face and she responded graciously, saying that she was happy to travel with the lady who was to be the captain's wife.

'I was of a mind that if you felt well enough that you might like to go with Juanita into Machico this morning and choose some cloth to make a couple of gowns for yourself,' said Harry, taking Bridget's arm and drawing her aside. 'There will be no need for you to return here. Juanita will take you to the chapel and I will meet you there.'

'As much as I would like to do that,' said Bridget in a halting voice, 'you are forgetting that I have no shoes.'

'Of course!' He looked annoyed. 'Then you'll have to stay here and wait for my return. You will have to trust Juanita to choose what is best.'

'I can easily suggest the fabrics and the colours I would prefer,' said Bridget. 'Sewing will help pass the time during the voyage.

'What about shoes?' asked Harry. 'Let us see the size of your feet.'

She lifted her skirts a few inches and he gazed down at her slender ankles and small feet and then at Juanita's; the latter's were much bigger. 'I deem what is needed is a template,' he added thoughtfully.

Within a short space of time Bridget found herself standing on a drying cloth whilst the captain drew round her foot with a stick of charcoal. She found the whole operation physically disturbing. Her toes twitched and she wobbled; to keep her balance she had to place her hand on his shoulder. Every time his muscles bunched, she remembered how he had carried her downstairs as if she weighed no more than thistledown. Gazing down at his dark hair, she was tempted to press a hand to its springiness.

'Now the other foot,' he said gruffly, gripping her right ankle.

To distract herself Bridget asked him the name of his ship. He hesitated before saying, *'St Bridget.'*

She was amazed. 'What a coincidence.'

'Not at all. I decided to rename her once you agreed to marry me. I've always had a fondness for the saint. She knew what she wanted and wouldn't allow anyone to get in her way.'

'You make her sound selfish,' said Bridget, hoping that he did not think she was the same. 'But, of course, you must know that what she wanted most of all was to serve God. She even asked Him to take away her beauty so no man would want to marry her.'

'You're right. I do know the story,' said Harry drily, unable to resist tickling her toes.

She jerked her ankle out of his grasp, wondering whether he had tickled her deliberately. If so, what had caused him to behave so frivolously? It was unlikely behaviour for the man she was beginning to get to know. 'If you have a pair of spring scissors, I could cut out the shapes,' she offered.

'No, leave them as they are,' said Harry, knowing that he should not have given in to temptation to tickle her, 'that way the shoemaker only has to place a pair of ready-made shoes on the cloth to see if they fit.'

Juanita was handed the cloth and a chinking purse changed hands. Bridget told her what she wanted and the widow left the house.

Bridget wished she was going with her, wanting some task to perform. 'Perhaps I could make breakfast,' she suggested. 'I am sure you and Joe have much to do.'

'There is no need,' said Harry. 'Joe will be back shortly with fresh bread from the bakery and there is the remains of a chicken to eat. Why don't you sit outside and enjoy the garden whilst you can? Joe will need to go into Machico to oversee the food supplies being loaded on to the ship. Perhaps you could go with him instead of me. You would not have to walk far.'

Bridget nodded, disappointed that he was fobbing her off on to Joe. It was not that she would not enjoy travelling with

Joe because she liked the lad. But she would have enjoyed the journey more with her future husband. They could have become better acquainted and there was also the fact that he was an interesting man and could have told her more about the island and his travels.

'Is there nothing I can do whilst I am waiting here?' she asked, a little forlornly.

Harry hesitated. 'I have a tear in a shirt that you can repair.'

Her face brightened. 'I will mend it for you.'

He smiled and had left the kitchen before she could remind him that she would need needle and thread, so she hurried after him, only to have to rest against the banister due to a sudden dizziness.

He found her there a few moments later. 'What is wrong?' he asked sharply, fastening his shirt as he came down the stairs. She thought she caught a glint of a silver chain at his throat and wondered if he wore a medal of St Christopher, the patron saint of travellers.

'I was rushing to tell you I had need of needle and thread and came over dizzy,' she said, loosening her grip on the banister.

'You came rushing upstairs just to tell me that, woman,' he chided. 'It is obvious that you still have not recovered from your illness. You could have slipped and broken a leg. There is a sewing box in the kitchen. Now take my arm and let us take the stairs slowly.'

She slipped her hand through his arm. 'I did not want to be a bother to you, although I suppose it is a little late for me to say that now. I've already caused you so much extra time and trouble.'

'I'll not deny it—but it was my decision to take you in and look after you,' he said. 'Do you know, when I first saw you

I was reminded of a mermaid. You must swim like a fish to have accomplished that distance from the ship to the shore and survived. I, too, enjoy swimming, although I have no memory of how I learnt.'

She felt flattered by the admiration in his voice. 'My father taught me as soon as he took me on his ship. He told me how he remembered being thrown into the water as a boy and was terrified he would drown. Somehow he managed to doggy paddle to the shore and after that he determined to become a good swimmer. Besides, he discovered that he enjoyed it.' She swallowed a lump in her throat. 'I cannot believe he is dead,' she said huskily.

'Then do not believe it,' said Harry, gazing down at her from fathomless dark blue eyes.

For a moment she felt quite breathless and as if he was drawing the soul from her body. Then she forced herself to look away. 'I will do as you say. I would not like you to regret your decision to marry me, but if my father is still alive, would you allow him to live with us?'

'He might not wish it. Let us wait and see,' said Harry diplomatically.

They had reached the bottom of the stairs and Joe was waiting there for them. Harry raised her hand to his lips and kissed it before saying, 'Go outside and I will join you shortly. I must have a word with Joe.'

Once outside Bridget did not sit down, but walked slowly past the terrace and into the garden. The sun already felt warm on her face and was drawing out the scent from the yellow blossom of a mimosa tree. There were a multitude of flowers, many she had never seen before. She breathed in their fragrance as she wandered down to the foot of the garden where there was a low wall. She noticed that there was a sheer drop on the other side to the beach, although it was not very high.

She perched on the wall with her bare feet nestling in the grass and gazed over the ocean. She thought how pleasant it would be to swim with the captain in the warm waters of this island. She thought about what he had said about mermaids and tried to imagine them both with tails, half-naked, plunging through the surf and able to breathe underwater. Of them coming together and kissing. She blushed at her foolishness and considered how swiftly her own life had altered since she had met him. She was filled with a sense of unreality. Soon she would wed and become the possession of a man she was only just starting to get to know.

Suddenly she heard her name being called. 'I'm here,' she shouted, getting to her feet and beginning the climb up the sloping garden.

The captain appeared a few yards above here. 'What were you thinking of, wandering away without saying where you were going?' he chided.

She bristled at the tone of his voice. 'Where could I go? I have no shoes, cloak, hat or money and I am unlikely to do anything as foolish as to jump from the wall on to the shore.'

'You could fall and it is not unknown for pirates to land on this coast.' He took her arm. 'Come! I have much to do this day and have no time to waste. I have decided that instead of delaying to break your fast here, you can eat on the journey.'

'What about your shirt?' she protested. 'Was I not to mend it?'

'You can do that on the ship.'

'If that is your command,' said Bridget.

The severity of his expression relaxed. 'You do not like my

giving you orders,' he said softly, touching her cheek with a gentle hand.

'You are to be my husband, so I will have to become accustomed to it,' she said, a spirited sparkle in her eyes.

Harry reached up and plucked a blossom from a tree and placed it behind her ear. 'I am glad that you understand that,' he teased. 'Some flowers in your hair and you will look like a bride.' He took more blossoms and handed them to her and then he kissed her lightly. 'I deem I will give myself the pleasure of taking you to the ship. No doubt there will be much of interest for you to watch down at the quayside whilst I am busy.'

Bridget clutched the flowers to her bosom. Never had she expected such *courtly* behaviour from this bearded rescuer of hers, so different to what she expected. Not only did he give her flowers, but he seemed to know what she enjoyed already. She had always found anchoring in a new port fascinating. She went with him, still wishing wistfully that her father could be there to give her away and that she had a dowry to give to her captain.

Chapter Five

Joe was obviously pleased to be going with them to Machico. He was smiling and humming a tune beneath his breath. She was aware of his eyes on her as the captain helped her up on to the wide seat of the cart before climbing up beside her. She placed the blossoms in her lap.

'You might find the journey a little bumpy,' Harry said.

'I'm sure I'll survive. I will hold on tightly.' Her hand sought the metal guardrail at the edge of the seat.

'Good.' He nodded to Joe. 'Now don't drive too fast.'

'Aye, aye, Captain,' responded the youth, touching his cap with the end of his whip. He clicked his tongue against his teeth, flicked the reins and the horse began to move.

The captain placed his arm around the back of the seat, his hand resting lightly on Bridget's shoulder. She was very aware of his closeness as the cart bumped and jerked along the path. He told her a little more about the island and it did not seem long at all to Bridget before they were crossing a bridge over a river, the banks of which were covered in lush vegetation. Then Machico came into view.

The town was backed by steep hills and the captain pointed out to her the Chapel of the Miracles and told her that was where the marriage ceremony would take place. He said that it had been erected over the resting place of a pair of lovers, one of them an English adventurer, Robert Machim. 'Apparently he set sail from Bristol in the fourteenth century with the lady of his heart, Anne d'Arset, to escape the wrath of her father,' he added.

Bridget was surprised that he should know of such a romantic tale. 'I thought Madeira was not discovered until early in the last century by the Portuguese.'

'The lovers' destination was Brittany, but a storm blew them off course and they ended up here.'

'I can understand how that could easily happen,' said Bridget seriously, hoping that they would encounter no such storms on the journey to England. 'Is there another church? The chapel does not look very big.'

'A larger church is being built and there is another chapel to the west of the town,' informed the captain.

She noticed a construction on a headland. 'And what is that building?'

'A fort. The people have to be prepared for attacks from the sea even here.'

'Is nowhere safe from pirates?' She sighed. 'Where is your ship anchored?'

'You'll soon see. Then I will introduce you to Master Larsson.'

'Who is he?'

'My second-in-command. He is expecting you.'

Bridget wondered what Master Larsson had been told about her. Had he approved of his captain's decision to marry and take her aboard his ship?

As soon as she set eyes on the tall Swede with a shock of flaxen hair, she knew that he had not. He might welcome her aboard the ship in his strongly accented English, but he had such cold eyes when he looked at her. His disapproval was even more obvious when he went with her and the captain into his cabin. He removed a cloak hanging on the back of a chair and left without a word.

'I deem Master Larsson does not like me,' said Bridget, looking troubled.

Harry thought how perceptive she was in some ways. Yet she had not recognised *him* beneath the simple disguise of a beard! 'You must not concern yourself about what he thinks. It is nothing personal. He just does not approve of women aboard ship.'

Just like Captain Black Harry, thought Bridget, feeling an odd ache at her heart. She gazed about her at the latticed window and large table with charts and instruments of navigation on its surface. There were a couple of chairs screwed to the floor, as well as lockers beneath a wide bunk bed that would take two people if necessary. Only now did it occur to her that most likely she and the captain would have to share this cabin. His crew would expect it. Her heart began to beat heavily and she knew that she should try to pluck up the courage to say something about their sleeping arrangements.

But before she could speak he said, 'I'll leave you now, Bridget, I have matters to see to,' and he was gone.

Bridget stood motionless for a moment, wondering what to do next, then realised she was still clutching her flowers. If she did not put them in some water, they would soon wilt. She found a bucket of water in the cabin, as well as a pot, and dealt with her blossoms. She decided not to linger here, but went up on deck and padded across to the side of the ship. She took several deep breaths in an attempt to calm herself. Already she knew what it felt like to be held in the captain's arms and to feel the gentle touch of his lips on hers. But what would it feel like if he were not to behave so gently? She chewed on her lip. She had seen cattle in the fields mating so knew what coupling entailed. She only stopped chewing her lip when she tasted blood.

She was not yet prepared to welcome the captain into her body. He had begun to court her, but she still barely knew him. How would he react once he had his ring on her finger? She was filled with trepidation as she rested her arms on the polished wood and gazed down at the quayside.

'Senhorita McDonald!'

Bridget's eyes searched for the owner of the voice and she caught sight of Juanita. The widow was not alone, but accompanied by a man carrying several rolls of cloth. Bridget forced a smile and waved to them. Once they were on board, she suggested that they take the cloth to the cabin. The man dumped it on the bed and left the two women alone.

'I did not expect to see you so soon,' said Bridget.

'No doubt it would have taken me longer if we had discussed at further length what you wanted,' said Juanita, glancing about the cabin. 'This is a great adventure, no?'

'Aye, I suppose it is.' Bridget darted a look at the bed.

Juanita's eyes followed hers. 'There is no need for you to fear him. He might look fierce, but he is a good man.'

'Of course, but—' Bridget hugged herself and paced the floor.

'You do not quite trust him because you do not know him very well. But the captain needs love, so you must give it to him.'

Bridget hesitated. 'Why do you say that? Is it that you have heard that he loved a woman and lost her? He has told me that he wants me only to keep house for him.'

Juanita laughed. 'He would marry you to be his housekeeper? I do not believe it. I remember what the captain was like when he first returned with Senhor Jorge. They caused a great stir amongst the young ladies in Machico.' Juanita set aside the paraphernalia on the table and spread out the cloth. 'Is this not fine?'

Bridget scarcely glanced at the cloth. 'You mean he went with women? I don't believe it!'

'Why? He was very handsome then, so handsome.' She sighed gustily. 'Not handsome, anymore, because of the scar on his cheek and some of the women look at him askance, so he grows a beard, but still I deem he is an attractive man, so big and so strong. Also he is not poor.'

Bridget thought about the captain's reluctance to shave off his beard. Obviously, he really did fear she would be repulsed by *his ugly visage* if she saw the scar before they were wed. Perhaps she should have insisted that he shave his beard off before their marriage. Yet what right had she to do so when he had offered her so much for so little in exchange?

'You like the colour?' asked Juanita, changing the subject.

Bridget saw that the roll of material was of blue wool. 'Aye, it is what I told you to get.'

'The wool is from Flanders. The seller must have paid a pretty penny for it and the captain even more. He wants you to dress like a lady, so he can be proud of you. This blue, it is the colour of the Madonna's robe. She smiles on you and will bring you good fortune. You will have his child.'

'Who are you that you can foretell such things?' said Bridget, startled. 'Is it that you consider yourself a seer?'

Juanita's eyes widened. 'He is lusty and you are beautiful, so why should you not make fine children?'

Bridget chose to ignore her words. Why should she believe her? Juanita picked up the material and swirled it around Bridget's shoulders. 'Many men have worshipped the Madonna. Children will forge your union and make it

strong.' She paused and murmured, 'This is of great importance because I sense there is a woman waiting for him in
England.'

Bridget stared at her in disbelief as she felt the material
slither from about her neck. Was it possible this woman
the captain loved might not have married his friend and
still awaited his return? But Juanita could not know this
and was surely saying these things to make herself sound
important.

'You are talking nonsense. Please, say no more,' said
Bridget.

Juanita shrugged. 'You will see. And now what about your
shoes? I hope you will like them. I purchased two pairs as the
captain ordered. A pair of soft leather slippers and another
of strong leather with tough soles.' She displayed them. 'Try
on your slippers, my pretty. You do not want to go to your
wedding in your bare feet.'

Bridget reached for the slippers.

'You have pretty feet,' said Juanita. 'Sit down and I will
help you on with them.'

Bridget hesitated, then sat on the bed. She remembered
how the captain had tickled her toes and a pleasant heat
pooled in the pit of her stomach. Why was she feeling like
this just at the memory of his touch? Then she recalled the
strength of his arms and a tremor shot through her.

'A perfect fit,' said Juanita, 'and so pretty.'

Bridget held out a foot and could not but agree with the
old woman. What had she been thinking of buying red shoes
with tiny flowers painted on them? Yet it seemed a long time
since Bridget had worn anything so delightful. She removed
the slippers, aware of Juanita watching her. 'You are right.
They are pretty. You have made a good choice.'

'Now the other shoes,' said the old woman, smiling. 'You will need them if you are to walk on difficult terrain.'

'What are you forecasting now?' asked Bridget.

'I forecast nothing. There will always be times in one's life when the way is rough. You will see.'

Bridget had had enough of her comments and asked her politely to leave as she wanted to rest. Juanita fixed Bridget with her dark eyes and gave a throaty chuckle before shuffling from the cabin.

Bridget sank on to the bed and stared at the shoes. She picked them up and went over to one of the lockers; finding it empty, she placed them inside. She picked up the slippers and put them on. Then she went over to the table to collect the rolls of cloth, scissors, chalk, needles and thread. She was in the process of placing them with the shoes when she heard the captain's voice. Her heart seemed to lurch sideways and she knew that she did not want him to find her in his cabin, acting as if she had already taken possession of it. She opened the door and went on deck.

Harry was instantly aware of Bridget and thought she looked pale and apprehensive. Briefly, he considered leaving the complete supervision of the loading of the sugar cane to Christian Larsson and making his way over to her side to ask if all was well. He was aware that he had given her little time to become accustomed to the idea of becoming his wife. For an instant their eyes met and she darted him a nervous smile.

God's Blood! Surely she was not frightened of him? The thought angered him. Had he not proved in the last few days she was safe with him and that he had her well-being at heart? If he were to die, all that he possessed would come to her as his wife. He was not a fabulously rich man, but he could provide her with a comfortable lifestyle. He realised that now was not the right time to tell her that. There would be time enough for that after the wedding.

The loading of the sugar cane was finally completed and the cargo of wine stored. Joe returned with a loaded cart and several of the crew helped him to stow everything away, although the coops of live chickens were wedged on deck in a manner that meant they would not be flung about once the ship sailed.

During this time Bridget was aware of the curious glances of the men. Whatever their thoughts of their captain's behaviour, none of them was speaking them aloud. She returned to the cabin and wove the flowers into a garland as best she could and adorned her hair with it. When she emerged into the sunlight again she was aware of the eyes of the captain and the crew upon her. Even when it came time for them to leave the ship and go to the chapel, not one of the crew seemed to think that congratulations to their captain and his future bride were in order. She felt uneasy, wondering if Master Larsson was causing trouble for them both behind the captain's back. No doubt the Swede had also known Black Harry and her father. Was her father the reason why Master Larsson looked so disapprovingly at her? Had he known Callum had once sailed a pirate ship?

She clenched and unclenched her hands, telling herself that she was marrying Captain Mariner, not his second-in-command or the crew. She would behave with decorum and they would realise that, although she was her father's daughter, she knew how to behave. She felt a deep sadness thinking of her father, trying to convince herself that he was alive. Yet her mood was dark and it took an effort to pin a smile on her face.

Juanita and Joe were to accompany them to the chapel. As the captain drew her arm through his, Bridget asked, 'How long will it take us to reach Lisbon?'

'If all goes well, within a sennight,' he answered. 'Hopefully, we should be in England within the month. Is there aught else you wish to ask me?'

She hesitated, remembering that wide bunk in the cabin, but her courage failed her.

'Do the shoes fit well?' he asked, gazing down at her bent head.

She lifted her skirts to show him the soft red slippers.

'Not sensible, but suitable for a wedding,' he said with a chuckle.

The sound caused her to jerk up her head and stare at him. 'Why do you laugh?'

'Because I am pleased to be marrying you. I would that you had a bridal gown to wear, but at least you have pretty shoes for your pretty feet.' He added in a whisper, 'You have naught to fear from me, Bridget.'

Her nod was almost imperceptible, but he took it for agreement and, without more ado, led her through the bustling streets of Machico to the chapel.

Bridget had wondered if at the last minute something would go wrong. Perhaps the priest would not marry them after all or the captain might have forgotten the ring. Possibly she would panic and be unable to say her vows. How she wished her father was beside her! Would he have approved of her marrying Captain Mariner? As it was, she felt as if it were someone else speaking when it came to her playing her part. As for Captain Henry Mariner, his voice was rough but clear when he spoke the words that would bind her to him.

They emerged from the chapel into the evening sunshine.

Bridget was conscious of the heavy gold ring on her finger. It spoke to her of his ownership and, for an instant, she was reminded of the manacled African slaves on the trader's ship. Then she told herself that to compare her situation with those slaves was nonsense. The captain had shown her kindness. Of her own free will she had agreed to marry him. At least now she could believe that she legally belonged to him and the slave trader had no remaining claim on her.

They made haste in returning to the ship, where a special meal was prepared for them, accompanied by a fine Madeira wine. It made Bridget pleasantly sleepy, if still a little apprehensive because since Juanita had spoken of the captain being lusty and of her having his child, she did not know how best to behave. Would she have the courage to tell the captain she was not ready to have him in her bed if he should decide that he wanted to consummate their marriage? He was stronger than she and could overpower her if he chose.

She lingered on deck, watching the activity on the quayside. The crew had been given permission to go ashore for a couple of hours, but now they were returning to rest before making ready to sail on the morning tide. She was aware of her husband's eyes on her. What was he thinking? He rose suddenly and, without a word to her, went and spoke to Joe before making his way to his cabin. His actions startled her. She had it in mind that he would expect her to retire before him, so she could prepare for bed and snuggle beneath the covers before he made an appearance. But perhaps he had only gone to fetch something and would make a reappearance, so she stayed out in the fresh air, waiting to see if that was what would happen.

She saw Joe carrying a steaming pot into the cabin and wondered what was taking place in there for he did not immediately reappear. She watched Juanita wrap herself in a cloak and curl up on a pallet beneath an awning on the deck. She was conscious that some of the crew kept glancing her way. She began to feel restless, wondering why Joe was in the cabin so long. Suddenly he reappeared, carrying the pot. He waved to her and then vanished beneath the awning.

The sun had set and the stars were beginning to prick on in the darkening sky. She knew that she could delay no longer and made her way to the cabin. Hopefully her husband would not be angry because she had stayed on deck so long. Her heart beat heavily as she entered the cabin and closed the door behind her. A lantern hung from a hook in the ceiling, but the light it cast was not strong and she could only make out the shadowy outline of the bed and her husband's strong shoulders and profile. She started when he addressed her.

'I thought your curiosity might have brought you here the sooner. You asked me to shave off my beard and Joe has done so for me,' he said in a strained voice.

'So that is why he was in here so long.' Her hand searched for a chair because her legs felt suddenly weak. 'I confess that I had forgotten that I had asked that of you.'

He made a noise in his throat as if clearing it. 'So I could have kept my beard?'

'No. I am glad you have shaved it off and I am curious to see how you look, although, in this light—'

'I can do naught about the light, but if you come closer you might have some notion of how I look without a beard. If you were blind you could read my features with your fingers, although, if you explore my face in such a fashion you will soon discover just how ugly I am.'

'I cannot believe that you are as ugly as you believe yourself to be!' exclaimed Bridget, crossing the cabin towards the bed.

It was darker there, so she could barely see his features.

Was that what he'd intended? Taking a deep breath, she sat on the edge of the bed and placed her hands either side of his face. Instantly she could feel the twisted outline and jagged skin of the scar that covered most of his cheek. She could feel him trembling and, despite having been warned of its ugliness, was shocked by the extent of the damage to his cheek.

'What caused this?' she asked.

'A jab with a burning torch during a skirmish in Africa,' he said hoarsely.

'It must have hurt.'

Unexpectedly he chuckled deep in his throat. 'An understatement, my dear Bridget. It burned like hell's fire.' He placed his arms at either side of her waist and drew her closer to him.

'Joe made no mention of a burn although he did tell me of the wound to your thigh,' she said, feeling slightly breathless, still cradling his face between her hands and very aware that he was holding her so that their bodies were pressed against each other. She was relieved that he was still wearing his shirt.

'I wager he made me out to be some kind of idiotic hero.' He brushed his lips against the inside of her wrist and she felt her nerves tingle.

'A hero, certainly,' said Bridget, easing a throat that was suddenly tight with emotion. She felt such sympathy for him that she wanted to bring him some comfort.

'He's prejudiced in my favour.'

'I cannot blame him. You did after all rescue him from being bullied and have taken care of him ever since.' She removed her hands and rested them on his forearms and gazed into his shadowy face. 'In a way, you have done a similar thing for me. You might not have done battle with the slave trader who held me prisoner, but you have rescued me from my fear of him.'

'It was pure chance that I was standing on the cliff and saw you drop into the sea.'

'You do not consider fate meant us to meet?' She found it easier to say these things to him in the dark.

'Fate, chance? What is the difference?'

'I thought you would know that,' she said.

'You are saying I was meant to see you and to find you? I deem you are more of a romantic than I would have thought, Bridget. I wonder if you will feel the same in the morning when you see me in the light.' Leaning forwards, he pressed his lips against hers. 'Now undress and go to sleep. It's been a long day for both of us and no doubt you are still recovering from your illness.'

'My health is much improved now.'

She wondered what would have happened if her lips had yielded to his. Now he had turned away from her and was lying down. She had no choice but to share his bed. No doubt when he purchased a house for them, they would have separate bedchambers. She was relieved that he had no intention of forcing himself upon her this night, but was also aware of a vague disappointment that he obviously found her easily resistible. She would like to rid him of the memory of that woman who had preferred his friend.

She dragged the garland of blossoms from her hair and removed her gown and slippers. Then, still wearing her shift, she climbed into bed and turned her back on him and tried to settle to sleep. But sleep would not come because she was too aware of his presence, although he made no move towards her and his breathing was steady and even. Obviously he was already asleep and her sharing his bed did not bother him a jot. She closed her eyes and instantly was conscious of a wave slapping against the hull as the ship rocked at anchor. She willed sleep to come, but it did not, and she lay there gazing into the darkness, thinking of Juanita's words to her.

Harry lay awake, listening to the sound of Bridget's gentle breathing and conscious of the swell of her bottom against the small of his back. He longed to turn towards her and take her in his arms and ravish her mouth with kisses and make love to her. Yet he had married her under false pretences and should never have done so. Once she saw him for who he was, then she would not want to consummate their union, and he desperately wanted her.

Why had he agreed to her request to shave off his beard, so revealing his ugly self to her censure? There was no doubt in his mind that when she saw his face by the light of day, she would feel revulsion as well as fury. Surely she would recognise that side of his profile that was undamaged. She might run away from him as soon as the opportunity arose. He could not allow that and would perhaps have to lock her in this cabin for her own protection. He would not like doing so, but what else could he do to prevent her from fleeing into danger?

Suddenly she turned over and his pulses raced. Cautiously he rolled over so that he was facing her. He caught the gleam of her eyes in the darkness. 'Can't you sleep?' he whispered.

'No.'

She wondered what he would say if she told him what Juanita had said about them having a child. She was tempted to ask him whether the old woman had a reputation as a seer. She remembered how lonely a mariner's wife's life could be when her husband was away at sea, so that when he suddenly drew her close to him she did not resist. He nuzzled her ear and then the side of her face before covering her mouth with his and kissing her gently; when she did not pull away, he kissed her more deeply. Skilfully, he slipped the strap of her shift from her shoulder and then caressed the side of her neck with his lips, easing the garment down until her breasts were bared. Then his fingers gently stroked her nipples.

The breath caught in Bridget's throat because the sensation caused by his caresses was extremely pleasing, but really she should ask him to stop. But then his mouth covered hers again and instinctively hers opened beneath his. He ran his tongue along the inside of her lower lip and all the time his fingers were creating havoc with her senses. Then he lowered his head and took her nipple into his mouth and instantly she felt a warm, pleasant heat pool between her legs as he suckled her. She began to tremble and he lifted his head and kissed her mouth again, but this time his tongue dallied with hers and she felt as if her whole body was a mass of differing sensations. His hands were sliding down her hips, taking her shift with them. She thought that she really must tell him to stop as his gentle fingers began to explore her most private place, only instead the word that she uttered was, 'Please!' for never had she experienced such physical delight, which grew and grew until she was gasping and a voice in her head was saying *don't stop*!

Bliss suddenly flooded her being, so then when he entered her she was unable to resist him. Instead she clung to him as he pushed further and further into her and another wave of ecstasy took her with him as he climaxed.

Chapter Six

When she woke the following morning, the first thing Bridget set eyes on was the silver amulet nestling in the dark hairs on her husband's chest as he lay on his side a few inches away from her. The amulet was fashioned in a cross from a miniature *Thor's Hammer* and she had seen one like it before.

Her heart began to thud in an unpleasant manner as she lifted her head and gazed at his handsome profile, unable to see the scarred side of his face. Only now did she recognise him for who he was and it gave her such a shock that she shot up in bed and banged her head against the wooden wall of the ship, which was dipping up and down in an alarming manner. She yelped in pain. Her husband opened an eye, but said not a word. She was so angry that she lifted a fist and punched him in the chest. 'Captain Black Harry, you *cur*!' she exclaimed, as the full extent of her position and his actions hit her.

He flinched and his eyes darkened. 'Why do you insist on calling me Black Harry?'

'Because that is your name and you have a black heart,' she cried.

'It is *not* my name,' he growled. 'It is the one Callum gave me when I was a boy on the pirate ship and I hated it. I was always given the filthiest tasks to do so was always dirty.'

'You deem by telling me that that you will rouse my sympathy?' Her voice rose several octaves. 'You have deceived me! You told me you were dead and I thought I would never see you again and now I will have to put up with your company until you die again,' she added on a sob, raising her fist once more.

He seized her wrist. 'I know my being alive must come as a shock to you, but surely you cannot wish I was dead again?'

'You were never dead in the first place!' she cried. 'You lied to me! Have you no conscience? If I'd known it was you I was marrying, I would never have taken holy vows and let you near me,' she added, struggling to free herself.

'That is why I never told you. I knew you'd probably do something foolish, such as running away, if I'd been honest with you.'

'You never gave me the option. If you would let go of my wrist, then I will do that right now.'

'Too late, Bridget. We're at sea and there's nowhere for you to run to, so why don't you be sensible? Accept that we are man and wife and be glad that you won't have to worry about where your next crust is coming from and will have a roof over your head.'

'You think that makes your deception acceptable?' she asked incredulously. 'I might as well have stayed on the slave-trader's ship instead of swimming straight into your arms, for I am as much your captive as I was his after last night.'

'Don't talk such nonsense!' he thundered, outraged by her comment. 'I did not force you to consummate our union. I wooed you.'

'You *seduced* me!' she hissed angrily.

'I know you are angry, but how can you possibly compare my actions in any way to that despicable slave trader?'

'You *bought* me,' she accused.

'I *married* you!' he protested.

'I thought you were Captain Henry Mariner, a different man altogether,' she said.

'No, Bridget, he is me,' said Harry softly, 'so get that into your head and perhaps then you will begin to realise that I am not the black-hearted villain you insist on my being.'

'Maybe I would have realised it sooner if you had been honest with me. Instead, you spoke falsely because you had no faith in my judgement. You looked upon my outer appearance and saw a woman you desired, but you believed that inside I was still the girl you refused to have on your ship two years ago.'

He hesitated. 'There is some truth in what you say, but that is because you made it obvious this past week when you spoke about Black Harry that you still held a grudge against him for separating you from your father. I knew then that you would cut off your nose to spite your face if I told you the truth. And you've proved that to me a few moments ago by calling me a cur as soon as you recognised me without my beard. I was right to do what I thought was best for you.'

For a moment his sheer arrogance took her breath away. 'You were not my father that you should make my decisions for me!' she said in a seething voice, wrenching her wrist out of his grasp. 'I am getting dressed and going out on deck. I need some fresh air.' She reached for her gown, only to overbalance and fall off the bed. She went careering across the floor and ended up beneath the table and lay there, winded.

Harry was out of the bed in a flash and hauled her out by her feet. The indignity of her position brought tears to her eyes. She struggled as he lifted her up and staggered with her across the cabin. He dumped her on the bed and kept his arms around her. It was only then that she realised he was wearing only his shirt.

She gasped and tried to hide her eyes, but she could not get her hands free. 'Let me go!' she cried. 'I do not want a repeat of last night.'

His eyes glinted. 'But you found pleasure in it. Still, you're a fool if you deem I would take you in the mood you are in at the moment. Now keep your voice down. We don't want the whole ship knowing we are quarrelling.' He released her and moved away from her.

'I want our marriage annulled,' she said in a shaky voice, rubbing a grazed elbow.

He shook his head. 'Out of the question after last night. Besides, you promised to remain with me for fairer or fouler.'

'And *you* are the fouler.' She tossed the words at him.

She was aware of the weight of the silence that followed as his hand flew to his cheek. She remembered how the skin had felt beneath her fingers last night and suddenly she was scared and waited for the blow to fall. Only he did not touch her, but instead turned his back on her. She struggled with anger, pain, shame and pity, and part of her wanted to reach out to him and beg his pardon. But the thought that she was his wife and he had such power over her held her back. Why could he not have told her the truth?

A few moments later she heard the cabin door open and close. What was she to do? Escape was impossible. Now frustration was her uppermost emotion. She had been in this position of wanting to escape so many times before that she shook with the strength of the anger that accompanied her frustration. For a moment she considered behaving like the girl he still thought her to be. She would dress, leave the cabin, cross over to the side of the ship and throw herself into the sea. That would show him just how much he had hurt her. It would say to him that she would rather die than have to live with him. Only she did not want to die—rather she would live and find some way to pay him back for his arrogance and deceit!

She should have insisted that he shave off his beard before instead of after the wedding. Only she had been so grateful to him for all that he was offering her: a home, his name.

His name! She paced the floor. She suddenly recalled that even though he didn't yet know it, her new husband was Harry Appleby, heir to Appleby Manor, a business and a house in London. Was their marriage even legal? He had married her under the name of Captain Henry Mariner, so perhaps it wasn't. Her spirits lifted and she thought that she would go out on deck and tell him that they weren't legally married. When he asked why, then she would tell him it was because he wasn't who he said he was when they had exchanged their vows. She hated him for his deception, when she had been so honest with him. Despised him for his lack of faith in the woman she was now.

She must get dressed. Carefully she made her *toilette* before donning her gown. Then she put on stockings and her sturdy shoes before taking several deep breaths and going outside.

Almost immediately she was aware of Master Larsson, who raked her with one of his frosty glances, and several of the seamen looked her way. Her husband, though, appeared intent on ignoring her, seemingly absorbed in commanding his ship. He held himself upright and from the angle she viewed him now his profile was as handsome as when she had first set eyes on him in Ireland and been charmed by him.

Then he turned his head and she saw that horrific damage

to his face. Seeing it in the bright light of day, she sternly suppressed feelings of compassion, determined to remain angry with him. Then his cold gaze touched her face and she knew he was utterly furious with her. Her own grievances rose once more and threatened to choke her and she looked at him with disdain. For a further moment she did consider going through with her plan, only it struck her afresh that their marriage had been consummated and what would that make her if she spoke out and said their marriage was not a true one? His *mistress*? The thought was unpalatable to her.

She was relieved when Joe hailed her and she turned away and carefully made her way across the deck, clinging to a rope that had been slung between two masts. The youth's smile melted some of the ice in her heart and she exchanged a few words with him. She ate her breakfast under the awning and forced herself to converse desultorily with Juanita about the fabrics she had brought her. But all the time she was aware that her husband was only yards away and no doubt listening to every word she spoke.

Harry was deeply hurt, not only because Bridget had spoken her mind about how she felt about his appearance, but also for comparing his behaviour to that of the slave trader. His aim in wanting to possess her was completely different. Bridget was also mistaken about his opinion of her. He had admired the woman he had rescued for her courage, as well as her beauty. He had also not simply married her because he had wanted her for himself, but had done so out of concern for her protection and to make amends for the ills that had befallen her since she had taken her farewell of her father.

It had taken an enormous amount of will-power to keep his gaze averted from his wife's comely figure when she came out on deck, but eventually he had been unable to resist glancing her way and what had been her response? She had looked at him as if he was beneath her. No doubt now she knew him for that sorry boy on the pirate ship whom her father had befriended, she considered him unworthy of her. A boy with no name, only the one that he had given himself. What right had she to consider herself better than himself? She was only a woman. A lovely woman to be sure, but a woman, nevertheless. Her grandfather might have been a Scottish lord, but her father was a pirate and had stolen one of Harry's ships. A ship that Harry had paid for to be built in Sweden when he'd decided to go into business for himself.

He had worked hard to get where he was; although he had often longed to know his family name and background, he had learned to live with the fact that he might never know the truth about himself and to be proud of his achievements. He had been mad to marry Bridget, but it was done now and he was determined that she would learn to accept his rule. After all, she had all to gain and little to lose.

He watched his wife rise from her seat under the awning and go towards the cabin. He thought she might have stayed out longer on the deck, but obviously she would rather not linger where she could see him. He turned away and went to speak to Master Larsson.

Bridget entered the cabin, wondering if her husband would follow her, but thankfully he did not. She took out the blue cloth he'd purchased for her new dress and stared at it for several moments before tossing it aside as her anger rose again. She wanted nothing from him. If only her father had kept his hoard in a sensible place instead of having it all with him on his ship! She wondered where her husband kept his money. There was a chest in the cabin that was locked, so perhaps it was hidden in there.

She went over to the window and stared out over the sea and thought the surface looked a little choppy. She longed for the journey to be over and wished she could wake up on the morrow and be in London. But that was impossible. The voyage would take at least a month and the thought of sharing a cabin for all that time with her new husband filled her with dismay. How was she going to pass the time if she did not occupy herself with sewing? Also she did not fancy wearing the same gown and shift all the way to England. She turned back to the table, picked up the material again and, seizing the shears, took the plunge and cut the cloth.

Bridget ate the midday meal in her husband's company on his orders, but during that time he exchanged no words with her, so she was also silent, thinking that if she began to talk she might say more than she intended. The rest of the day passed agonisingly slowly and she wondered what would happen when they were alone together that night. Would he attempt to force his will on her and make her submit to him?

She need not have worried because he spent only a few brief moments in the cabin that evening before telling her that he would be spending that night on deck, as the weather was on the change and it might be a rough night. She felt a curl of fear in her stomach. No doubt he wanted to make certain the cargo was doubly secure and to keep his eye on things. He said that he would send Juanita to be with her. She thanked him in a cool voice.

Shortly after there was a knock on the door and the sound

of Juanita's voice requesting permission to enter. Bridget told her to come in.

'I wish I had stayed in Madeira now,' said Juanita as the wind took the door from her hand and slammed it shut. She was wearing a black cloak and carried a bag containing her possessions. 'Perhaps it was God's will that I stayed there and I have disobeyed him.' The old woman clung to any object she could get a grip on as she crossed the cabin towards the bed.

'You believe that just because the sea is rough? Perhaps you'd best start praying,' said Bridget seriously.

'That is my intention,' said Juanita. 'Is it acceptable to you that I share your bed?'

Bridget did not see how she had any choice in the matter. She could hardly expect the old woman to sit up all night if the weather was to get worse. 'Of course.'

Juanita thanked her and Bridget organised their sleeping arrangements and suggested they say their prayers once they were in bed. The old woman agreed. Once that was done, to Bridget's surprise Juanita offered her a drink of poppy juice from a flask. She refused as gently as she could, preferring to have her wits about her if a storm were to blow up as her husband predicted. After all she had no reason to doubt his seamanship. So whilst the old woman snored, Bridget lay, listening to the wind and waves and thinking of Harry out in the elements along with the rest of crew.

She remembered being confined to a cabin with Lady Elizabeth and her maid, Hannah, during the storm that had raged last year. Her ladyship had remained calm and tried to soothe their fears by talking of her travels as a young woman after she'd been widowed. It had been a very different case altogether when Bridget had been confined to a cabin with the slave-trader's woman during a ferocious storm. That had raged for days and she recalled the woman's terror and conviction that she was going to die.

Bridget sighed and rolled on to her side and gripped the wooden rail at the edge of the bed. She remembered the storm that had blown the vessel to Madeira and that dark figure on the cliff. How would she have felt if she had known it was Black Harry? Would it have given her hope? It seemed that it *was* fate that had led him to that point that day—would she have survived if he had not seen her and she'd remained on the beach exhausted and soaked to the skin? She did owe him her life, but how she wished he could have been honest with her. She might just have accepted his offer of marriage for that reason alone. But instead he had deceived her. Still, however angry she was with him, she realised that she was going to have to tell him soon that he was Harry Appleby, heir to all that had been his father's, and that in England, his sister waited for his return. He deserved to know his true identity. Perhaps he would decide that their marriage was still legal because Mariner had been the name he was known by? Eventually she dozed off with that thought in her head.

She was wakened shortly after dawn by Harry entering the cabin. Juanita was still asleep by her side. Bridget sat up cautiously as the ship was rolling terrifyingly. All was grey outside of the window with clouds racing across the sky. Her husband staggered towards the bed and she noticed that his hat and cloak were sodden. 'You are soaking wet and will catch a chill,' she shouted.

He shrugged and held out some hard biscuits and fruit to her. 'You don't have to pretend that you care about me,' he yelled. 'You will have to make do with these for now. You must both stay here in the cabin until the storm abates.' He went back outside.

Bridget determinedly quashed her fear and tried to concentrate on anything but the storm, but the noise made it difficult. She decided there was no point in waking Juanita and ate a piece of fruit and then nibbled at a hard biscuit. She prayed silently for the safety of the men on deck and for the ship, that the storm would die down and that they would not be blown off course. She wondered when she would get the opportunity to tell her husband the news of his true identity. Obviously not until the storm had passed—it wasn't exactly a subject she could explain in one short sentence. As it grew lighter in the cabin, she decided to get on with the task of sewing her simple gown in an attempt to take her mind off what might be happening on deck.

Juanita woke a couple of hours later, refused food and downed another dose of poppy juice and lay drowsing on the bed. As she sewed, Bridget could hear her muttering in her own tongue, but could not make out what she was saying. Bridget thought that if Juanita had any supernatural powers that it would make sense for her to use them now.

She thought of her father with tears in her eyes. She tried hard not to imagine him caught up in a furious storm that could have sunk the ship that carried him. She knew it did her no good to think so negatively. Now Harry filled her mind. Had he been able to forgive her father for stealing his ship? After all, a ship was a valuable commodity and it meant that Harry could not transport as many cargoes as he might have done. She wondered if Callum had been drunk when he had stolen *Odin's Maiden*. Whichever way she looked at it, Harry had every right to be furious with the McDonalds. Still, that was no excuse for his deception over their marriage!

* * *

Joe staggered into the cabin several hours later, bringing them more cold food. He looked harassed and sad.

'Are you all right?' asked Bridget, concern in her voice.

'One of the men has been washed overboard. He was swept away before we could do anything to save him,' he shouted. 'The captain's real upset about it, I can tell.'

Her fear soared and it took all her will-power to bring it back under control. She wanted to scream out for the storm to stop and to weep for the man who had lost his life. She wondered if he had a wife and family back home, wherever home had been for him. 'Have you experienced such a storm before, Joe?' she cried.

'Aye, and the captain got us through it then and he'll do so again,' he said stoutly, 'so don't you worry.'

She was touched by Joe's faith in his master and experienced a sudden yearning for those last couple of days at the villa on Madeira when she had not known who Harry really was.

Joe left the cabin and Bridget forced herself to eat another piece of fruit and a biscuit. Fortunately she had never been seasick in her life. Then she prayed again, asking Almighty God and all the saints that no more men's lives would be lost.

It was evening when Harry called in to say that he thought the storm would blow itself out through the night. Bridget thought he looked exhausted and said, 'You need some sleep.'

He looked at her as if he could not credit that she could be concerned for him. 'I shall sleep when I deem it is safe for me to do so,' he snapped. 'In the meantime you will stay where you are.'

'Can't I go on deck for just a few moments?' she asked.

He shook his head. 'It is safer for you here. The deck is slippery and you would be putting yourself and others at risk. Do what I say in this, Bridget, I will not have you disobeying my orders,' he said harshly, and slammed the door behind him.

She knew what he meant by risk, but considered there had been no need for him to add that part about *disobeying his orders*. She was a mariner's daughter and had more sense than he gave her credit for, she thought indignantly.

Bridget spent most of that night listening not only to Juanita snoring but in praying and trying to make out if the sound of the wind was lessening. At least the rain had stopped. It occurred to her that Callum must have really trusted Harry to have agreed to sail across the great ocean under his command. Yet no man was infallible. What if Harry should collapse for lack of sleep and be washed overboard? It did not bear thinking about, especially as Master Larsson would then take over command of the ship. She quashed that thought and managed to doze off as the storm finally began to die down.

She woke to find that dawn was not far off and that Juanita was finally up and dressed and sitting at the table. Bridget put on her own gown and shoes and went out on deck. The sky was a washed-out silver grey tinged with streamers of pale peach clouds. There was all sorts of debris littered across the deck and the sails were reefed as she would expect. She found her husband slumped over the side of the ship and she thought at first he was gazing out over the sea. Only when she brought her face down to his level and he did not move did she realise that his eyes were closed.

'Harry, wake up,' she said, shaking him by the shoulder and discovering that his cloak was still sodden.

'What is it?' he muttered, struggling to lift his eyelids.

'You need to get some sleep,' said Bridget, surrendering to her better self and slipping her arm beneath his cloak and attempting to hoist him upright.

He yawned and then stared into her face. 'What are you doing here?' he asked.

She noticed that his black hair hung lankly about his cheeks and that he had a couple of days' stubble. She avoided looking directly at his scar in case it annoyed him. 'I came to see where you were and it is good that I did, for you might have toppled into the sea.'

'Would you have cared?' he asked quietly.

'That is a foolish thing to say,' she retorted angrily.

'Why? If I was dead then you would not have to live with me and look at this foul visage every day,' he commented drily, having noticed her deliberate attempt not to look at his damaged cheek.

'I suppose I deserve that, but do you have to throw my words back in my face?'

'Maybe, maybe not.' His expression was strained. 'I will not argue with you now. You are right in saying that I must get some sleep.'

'I will have Juanita leave the cabin so you can undress and get into bed.'

He nodded wearily and, removing her arm from about his waist, straightened up and limped across the deck to his cabin. She followed him, realising that the wound in his leg must be causing him pain. Pain was not something that she wished on him. She was aware that several of the crew sat, slumped on barrels, whilst others were unfastening the sails. A couple were staring at Harry whilst Master Larsson was looking at her with an unreadable expression. Suddenly it occurred to her to wonder if he considered it unlucky to have women aboard ship. Her father had told her that there were such mariners who superstitiously believed in such things.

When they entered the cabin it was to find that Juanita was still sitting at the table, but now she was gazing down at a chart.

'What are you doing?' asked Harry.

She glanced up. 'I am trying to make sense of this. Look here, is this Lisbon?' Juanita placed a finger on the chart. 'I pray that we have not been blown too far off course.'

Harry limped over to her. 'Now the skies are clear once more we shall soon find out,' he said.

Juanita stared into his face. 'You are in pain.'

'I will survive,' he said.

'Of course, but you must rest now. You are a clever man and I think your seamanship saved my life and for that I am grateful. I have a little poppy juice still and will leave it for you.'

Harry nodded and watched her place the flask on the table before leaving them alone. He glanced at Bridget. 'You do not have to stay.'

'Why not? I am prepared to help you,' she said stiffly.

'I can manage without your help.'

She was hurt at having her olive branch thrown back in her face. 'If that is your wish, then I will leave you alone.'

'Tell Joe to come here.' His tone remained brusque.

She paused with her hand on the handle of the door. 'Do you not think it will appear odd Joe coming to your aid whilst I am here to wait on you? After all, I *am* your wife.'

'A rebellious wife, at that. I don't care how it appears to the crew. I prefer Joe to do what is necessary for my comfort.' He sat down heavily in the chair. 'Now, please go!'

Bridget felt hot with embarrassment and anger as she left the cabin, determined that if her husband was ever to have need of her help, then he was going to have to beg for it!

Chapter Seven

Harry swore vigorously as Joe helped him off with his hose and then he collapsed on to the bed, perspiration beading his forehead and naked chest.

'You all right, Captain?' asked the lad anxiously.

He did not answer, but lay there, panting.

Joe peered at the red and swollen scar that formed part of Harry's thigh where a chunk of infection had been cauterised, leaving a hole in the muscle. He shook his head. 'You've been on that leg too long,' he said.

'I know, but I had no choice,' he gasped.

'You're going to have to rest it.'

Harry did not answer, but muttered, 'Pass me the poppy juice and the bottle of spirit I brought from the villa.'

Joe did as ordered and also brought a pewter tankard. He mixed the spirit with the juice and was about to add water when Harry said, 'No, give me it as it is.'

'But it'll knock you out, Captain!'

'That is exactly what I want it to do,' growled Harry.

Joe looked uneasy.

Harry said, 'That's an order, Joe!'

'But what of the mistress? She's not going to be pleased

when she's seen so little of you these past two days and nights.'

'She said I needed to sleep and that's exactly what I'm going to get and I don't want any pain keeping me awake,' said Harry, propping himself up on an elbow. 'Now hand me the drink and then fetch me a clean shirt.'

Joe followed orders, watching Harry down the drink before helping him on with his shirt. 'The mistress would enjoy doing this,' said the lad.

'Shut up, Joe!' Harry growled. 'You can leave me now and get cooking some hot food for the crew.'

'I suppose you'll do without until you wake up.'

'Aye,' said Harry, lying down and pulling the bedcovers over him. He thought of Bridget and how it had felt making love to her. He would like to experience the pleasure all over again. Yet he still felt stricken by what she'd said to him about being the *fouler* option. He remembered the expression on her face when she had seen his scar for the first time and his hand wandered to his cheek. His fingernails rasped the two days' growth of beard there. Then he finally felt the pain in his thigh begin to ebb and slipped into oblivion.

Bridget quietly opened the door and entered the cabin. This was the seventh time that she had done so since her husband had told her that he had no need of her. Each time she gazed down at his slumbering face, her eyes were drawn to the scar on his cheek. She had come partly due to a conviction that the crew expected it of her and partly because she felt compelled to keep her eye on him despite the hurt and anger he had caused her. The more she was able to peer closely at the savage scar, the more she was becoming accustomed to it. She would have wished it away if she could, but only because it had such an adverse effect on him. He might deny caring what others thought about him, but she did not believe him. The scar made him vulnerable to people's opinion of him. Otherwise, why had he grown a beard? Without this scar she might have recognised him.

She ventured to hold a hand over the scar, blocking it out so that it was easy to see how he had looked without it two years ago. She lightly touched it with her palm, only to start back as his eyes suddenly opened. A sailor's curse tripped off her tongue and she crossed herself. He did not speak, only staring up at her before his eyelids closed again.

She wasted no time leaving his side and sitting at the table. Was he pretending to be asleep or was he awake? Perhaps she should go outside. But she still felt she needed to be here. Joe had told her that the captain's leg was causing him a great deal of pain because he had been on it for most of the storm, so she had to make allowances for his temper. She would remain quietly here and wait and see what he did next. Soon it would be nightfall and the cabin would darken. If he woke, would he leave the cabin and spend the night on deck? If he remained asleep in here, then she could wrap her cloak around her and rest in this chair. Although she would rather he woke. She did not like him being asleep so long with Master Larsson in charge. She preferred Harry on deck, commanding his ship, not his rather dubious second-in-command.

'What are you doing over there?'

Bridget almost jumped out of her skin. 'You're awake!'

'Obviously I'm awake if I'm speaking to you.' He sat up and wiped his face with his hands.

She did not like it when he made sarcastic comments. 'You'll be hungry. No doubt that is another of my unnecessary remarks,' she said.

'Aye. You can go and tell Joe to bring me some food.'

She rose to her feet and without another word left the cabin.

What had she been doing earlier bending over him? wondered Harry, flinging back the bedcovers. He yawned and ran an unsteady hand over his untidy hair before getting out of bed and searching for his belt that had a pouch attached to it. Having found it, he removed a key from the pouch before limping over to the chest and unlocking it. Way down at the bottom of it beneath his clothes were business papers and a bag of coin, but the bulk of his money was with the bankers.

He took out clean hose and, gritting his teeth, sat on a chair. He managed to pull them on, but had to rest before removing a fresh doublet from the chest. Then he fetched his comb and tidied his hair. He was putting on his shoes when the door opened. He glanced up and saw Bridget enter, balancing a tray on her hip. 'Where's Joe?' he asked.

'Preparing the crew's supper. Surely you do not object to my bringing your food?' He did not answer, so she closed the door and carried the tray in both hands and placed it on the table. 'You've dressed—does that mean you plan on going out on deck?' she asked.

'For a while, but I will be back here later.'

She nodded, but did not ask if that meant he would be sharing the bed with her. She felt unexpectedly weak at the knees, remembering the bliss she had found in his arms when they had consummated their marriage. She asked to be excused and left the cabin. She took deep breaths of fresh air, trying to ban the memory of that night as she walked around the deck and thinking that she still had to find the right moment to tell him that he was Harry Appleby.

* * *

The sun had set by the time he came out on deck and she wondered what he had been doing all this time. She noticed that he was still limping as he went over to Joe and spoke to him. Then he went to different members of the crew and talked to them until it grew dark and the stars twinkled on in the night sky and the moon rose. She gazed up at it in wonder, scarcely able to believe that the last two days of storm had taken place.

'It is time you retired to the cabin, Bridget,' said Harry.

She lowered her eyes and stared at him. 'Do you have any idea if we are far off course?'

'If we are, then it is only by a small margin. If I read the sky aright, then I would not be surprised if we arrived at Lisbon earlier than I estimated.'

'That is good news,' she said, relieved.

'Aye, I am sure you want to reach England as soon as possible to see your friends.' He turned away and left her standing there.

Impulsively she called, 'Harry, wait a moment. There is something I wish to tell you.'

He turned, but before he could make a move towards her, Master Larsson loomed up out of the darkness and spoke to Harry. He stood, listening, and then obviously answered him. Then the Swede talked a little more and Harry nodded and said something else.

Bridget, realising that they were going to be a while, returned to the cabin where she found the lantern was already lit and, to her surprise, that the bed was divided into two parts by a bolster set in the middle. She felt an odd ache in the region of her heart. What was she to make of her husband's actions? Was he saying that she need not worry that there would be a repeat of their wedding night as he would respect her wishes? Or was he saying that he no longer desired her so and could not even bear that their bodies might brush against each other?

Her mouth quivered with emotion and then hardened as she fiercely controlled herself. Whatever his reasoning, it suited her too, she told herself. She prepared for bed, said her prayers, thanking her Lord, his Holy Mother and the Saints for making the storm pass. She also prayed for the sailor who had been lost and his family if he had any. Then she wrapped herself in a couple of blankets and lay down on one side of the bolster and tried to sleep. At least she would not be bothered this night by Juanita's snores and mutterings. Then she thought of the old woman sleeping under the awning and hoped she was not too uncomfortable.

It had been some time before Bridget had fallen asleep, but eventually she had done so. When she woke it was morning and there was no sign of Harry, but his side of the bed appeared to have been slept in. The fact that he was already up and about caused her to wonder if he was deliberately trying to avoid her. She could play his game if he wished, but surely they wouldn't be able to keep it up aboard ship for long. If they were living in a house, of course, it would be different. More room to stay out of each other's way.

She wondered why that thought made her feel sad—how could she make a proper home for them if they had no time for each other? *House, home!* She decided that now was the time to tell him that he was Harry Appleby, a man of property. He needed to know the truth, regardless of how she felt about him. She made her *toilette* and dressed before leaving the cabin.

To her annoyance she found that Master Larsson was also up and about and once again in conversation with Harry. It struck her that her husband probably spent more time talk-ing to his second-in-command than he did to her! They both glanced her way and their looks were enough to convince her that Harry had been talking about her to the Swede. The next moment he curtailed his conversation and approached her.

'You are up early, Bridget,' he said.

'You were up even earlier despite losing two nights' sleep,' she countered. 'Tell me, where does Master Larsson sleep?'

'Why should you be interested? Do you consider him hand-some?' he said, frowning.

'No! He has cold eyes, and as I have said before, I deem he does not approve of me. I am just curious; he always seems to be hovering and wanting your attention. When did you meet him and where?'

'In Sweden whilst I was working for Alex, the Baron Dalsland, whom you have met. I remember you mentioned that Alex supplied the ships for you to search for your father and myself. Hopefully I will find my friend in London, al-though, it is possible that he might have returned to his home in Sweden. I have to confess that I was surprised when you said he had married someone other than a Danish woman called Ingrid Wrangel. I believed they were in love and would definitely marry.'

'Mistress Wrangel proved to be an adulteress, a thief and a double-agent spy at the very least,' said Bridget vehemently. 'He would never have married her!'

Harry stared at her with a fixed expression, stunned by the news. 'I don't believe it! You must be mistaken. She, Alex and I worked together for years, collecting information. She would *never* have betrayed him. She loved him.'

Bridget instantly realised that Ingrid must be the woman *he* loved too. Her tone gentled. 'I didn't realised that you knew her so well but I am sorry, Harry, there is definitely no mistake. Yet if you choose not to believe me, that is your prerogative.' She turned and walked away.

'Bridget, come back here!' ordered Harry.

She turned and looked at him, but made no move towards him.

'Now, this instant!' he roared.

She was instantly aware that those on deck had gone quiet and were watching them. She glanced in Master Larsson's direction and saw that he was smirking. She felt degraded and was furious with Harry for making her feel like this, but she knew that she could not ignore her husband's command because it would undermine his authority with his men, so she obeyed him. She kept her eyes down in what looked to be a submissive manner, but really it was so he would not see the hurt and anger in her eyes.

'What is it you want from me?' she asked in a low voice.

'I want to know why you say these things about Mistress Wrangel,' he demanded.

'I say them because they are true,' she said.

'That is not the answer I am seeking. What proof can you provide that would convince me that you are telling the truth? Master Larsson has also known Mistress Wrangel for several years and he would vouch for her character.'

His mention of Master Larsson was enough to increase her anger and hurt. She lifted her head and stared at him. 'Can you not just take *my* word that I know what I am talking about?'

'I knew Ingrid a lot longer than I have known you, Bridget,' Harry pointed out.

'So you are saying that my word is not good enough for you! May I suggest that you did not know her as well as you thought,' she hissed, her anger simmering just below the surface of her voice. 'Perhaps when you reach England, you will discover who are your true friends and who are not. Now may I go? I have some sewing to do.'

Harry's eyes narrowed. 'When I reach London I will find out what this is all about and why you feel the need to slander Ingrid.'

'You do that, Black Harry,' she said insolently. 'Now may I go?'

He dismissed her with a wave of the hand and it took her all her will-power not to slap his face. She returned to the cabin with angry tears in her eyes. There she paced the floor with her arms folded across her breasts, hugging herself and thinking, why, why had it had to be the Danish woman whom Harry had loved?

Eventually she calmed down and told herself that once they reached London, she would be vindicated and then he would realise his error. Yet perhaps he might still feel some love for the beautiful Danish woman with her silver-blonde hair and magnolia skin. The thought caused a further lowering of her spirits and Bridget forced herself to do something to take her mind off such thoughts.

She took up her sewing and made the final touches to the gown. Having done that, she decided to cut out a shift from the plain cream material Juanita had brought her. She moved the charts and instruments of navigation on the captain's table to one side and as she did so she caught sight of the wedding ring on her hand and felt a sharp stab of pain in her breast. How dare Harry speak to her the way he had done? He had deceived her and she must never forget that he had tricked her into this marriage. Sooner or later she knew she would have to tell him the truth about his true identity because she could imagine what such tidings would mean to him. But in light of his accusations towards her, he probably wouldn't believe her! So perhaps she should not bother to try telling him, but instead wait until they reached London and then he would know the kind of company his precious Ingrid Wrangel had kept and he would find out for himself who he really was.

Bridget's stomach rumbled and she realised that she had not had breakfast. She decided to go and see Joe about food. As she left the cabin she passed Harry and Master Larsson on the way in, but chose to ignore them. She guessed that they needed to consult the charts and apply Harry's instruments of navigation.

Whilst speaking to Joe, it suddenly occurred to Bridget to ask him if he had ever met Ingrid Wrangel.

'Aye,' he said, a grim expression on his face.

Bridget had never seen Joe look like that. 'You did not like her?'

'She treated me as if I was dirt beneath her feet, but never in the captain's company. With him her words were always honey sweet and she chose to ignore me then. That suited me because I didn't want to upset the captain by complaining about her. Yet she's no better than I am because she was an orphan like us for all she gave herself airs. She was placed with the nuns as a child and brought up by them.'

'A nun's habit is one of her favourite disguises,' murmured Bridget, glad that in Joe she had someone who knew Ingrid Wrangel for what she was. 'She is a dangerous woman.'

'Aye, I was glad when the captain made the decision to leave London and her behind, only it also meant severing his ties with the Baron,' he added with a touch of regret in his voice.

'You liked the Baron,' said Bridget.

He nodded. 'I'm hoping he and the captain will heal the

breach between them caused by that Danish witch and be friends again.'

Bridget assured him that she felt certain that was a strong possibility. Then she changed the subject and, taking a plate of food from Joe, went and joined Juanita. She was sitting on a barrel, darning hose. 'How are you today, Juanita?' she asked.

'I am happy because the captain tells me that soon we will reach Lisbon,' she replied. 'But the captain, he is not looking happy. You have displeased him.'

Bridget darted a glance in her husband's direction—he had obviously not spent much time in the cabin. 'We have displeased each other.'

'But he cares about your welfare, otherwise he would not have married you. The crew, they often watch you. I have seen them doing so. Of course, most of them knew your father and there are those who sympathise with the dilemma you were in and understand why the captain married you.'

Bridget sighed. 'I do not need their pity.'

'It is better than hate. Maybe your father asked the captain to take care of you in the event of an evil fate overtaking him.'

'If that were true, I don't know why the captain has never mentioned it to me,' said Bridget, thinking that he could have easily done so. After all, as Captain Mariner he had told her that he had sailed with her father in the past.

'A man does not tell a woman everything he knows,' murmured Juanita. 'Soon we will reach Lisbon and I will leave you. You must take care of yourself for the child's sake.'

Bridget blushed and was startled into saying, 'I do not know if there will be a child yet. It is far too soon to tell.'

'It will bind you together.'

'I don't see how that can be. The captain will choose to

continue his travels despite having a wife and child, no doubt. We will be parted for months on end and that will hardly serve to strengthen our relationship.'

Juanita patted her hand. 'The wound in his thigh still gives him much trouble. I see change in the air for both of you.'

Bridget thought it did not take a seer to forecast change when one was leaving one country for another and a couple were newly married. Although, if Harry's wound was bothering him, then it was possible he might choose to give up the sea once he learnt of his inheritance.

She thought about that and realised that she would prefer that he chose to stay on land. She might be angry with him about his deception and his defence of Ingrid, but she would rather have him where she could keep an eye on him. It bothered her that he was in pain, and his disability could mean that he was not as fleet-footed as he once was and result in his having an accident aboard ship that could lead to his death.

The thought caused a shiver down her spine. She glanced in her husband's direction and caught him looking at her with a louring expression. Her mouth tightened and she turned her head away and continued her conversation with Juanita.

Harry was in a foul mood. Why couldn't his wife hold his gaze longer than a few seconds? Was it that she could not bear to look at his scar or was it because they had disagreed so strongly over Ingrid? Well, the latter would be sorted out. But if it were the former, then he would have to grow a beard again to conceal his scar despite her aversion to big black beards. At least back at the villa on Madeira, she had never looked at him with such distaste in her eyes. Despite their disagreements he still desperately wanted her, but whilst she so disapproved of him there was no way he could make love to her. He would never force an unwilling wife.

He shifted uncomfortably from one foot to the other, knowing the only way to ease his pain was to lie down and rest for a day or so, but he could not do so because it would make him appear a weakling in front of his crew. The pain was such that he could not bear his leg being touched and that was another reason why he had placed the bolster in the middle of the bed—in case, by chance, Bridget should kick him in her sleep. He would have taken more poppy juice for the pain, but there was none left.

Bridget gazed at Harry through half-closed eyelids and watched him blow out the candle in the lantern. What was he doing? He had not undressed and she wondered if he was going to sleep out on deck again, but now she could see his shadowy figure approaching the bed. To her astonishment he stretched out fully clothed on his side of the bed on top of the bedcovers. She did not know what to make of his behaviour. What was preventing him from getting beneath the bedclothes as he had done so last night?

She wanted to ask him, but feared if she did so he might snap her nose off, so she lay on her side, gazing at him through the darkness, willing him to say something. Since he had entered the cabin, they had not exchanged a word. Perhaps he was lying there, thinking of Ingrid, she thought with a mixture of irritation and sadness. Ingrid, who had not known Harry's true identity until after he had sailed away without telling her or the Baron where he was going. It was only Bridget who had known his destination, but she had managed to keep that from Ingrid and her lover, Edward Fustian, Harry's evil stepbrother, until she was able to inform the Baron and Harry's sister, Rosamund.

Bridget felt a strong conflict of emotions that was holding her back from telling Harry the truth about himself. Perhaps she needed to rethink the decision she had made about letting him discover for himself the truth when he reached London? Whichever way she looked at it, she realised that he would no doubt be even angrier than he was with her right now if she kept the truth from him. She must not forget his feelings for Ingrid in all this. Thinking his deep, even breathing meant he had fallen asleep already and she had once more missed her chance to tell him, she sighed and turned away from her husband and eventually fell asleep herself.

Bridget was mistaken in thinking that it was Ingrid who occupied Harry's thoughts. His body was afire with desire for his wife despite his aching thigh. He wanted to feel her naked skin against his own, to caress and kiss every inch of it and to bring her to that point of ecstasy again. Hearing her sigh, he wondered what was on her mind. No doubt she was regretting marrying him, but they had to make the best of the bargain they had made. He forced himself to concentrate his mind on what lay ahead: the task of unloading the sugar cane and speaking to the buyer when he reached Lisbon. It had an excellent harbour situated on the right bank of the Tagus River and it was from here that Vasco da Gama had originally set sail on his voyage of discovery to the Indies. Situated on the furthest western point of Europe, the port was ideally placed for trade with northern Europe, London, Scotland and Africa. Now with a new passage to India underway and the discovery of the lands across the great ocean there was no doubt in his mind that the port would increase in power and wealth.

He looked forward to arriving there and no doubt Bridget could not wait to escape him for a while, he thought grimly, remembering how she had struggled to obey him earlier that day. Perhaps he should have insisted on her telling him what she knew about Ingrid that he did not. Instead he had given no thought to how Ingrid might have changed since he had left. What could have led her to betray the Baron? Bridget had spoken of Ingrid being an adulteress. Was it possible that she had fallen in love with someone else and this man had persuaded her to act against her better nature? He needed to know the truth, but could he trust Bridget to be honest with him when she was so obviously cold towards him?

Eventually Harry had dozed off, only to wake again whilst it was still dark. His thigh was no longer aching and he was filled with a sudden restlessness. As Bridget seemed sound asleep, he decided to get up and see how the men on watch were faring.

The air was fresh and filled with the scent of the sea, but mingling with it he caught the smell of vegetation. One of the men on watch glanced his way. 'I deem we should make Lisbon this day,' he said.

'Good!' Harry eased himself down on to a barrel and gazed up at the sky. Suddenly he was filled with a sense of wonder and peace, remembering Bridget being on deck after the storm had blown itself out. She, too, had looked up at the stars and no doubt marvelled at the Almighty's creation. 'I'll be staying on deck if one of you wants to get his head down,' he said.

The men exchanged glances and one nodded. The other thanked the captain and went to catch up on some sleep. The remaining mariner and Harry talked idly until the sun rose and the rest of the crew began to stir.

When Bridget came out on deck she instantly went over to where her husband stood at the wheel. 'You're up early,' he said, without looking at her.

'You were up even earlier. It is a fine morning. How much longer before we reach Lisbon?' she asked, thinking sadly that he obviously had not wanted to remain alone with her in the cabin any longer than necessary.

'Hopefully later this day.' He pointed to what looked like a cloud on the horizon. 'There is the coast of Portugal.'

Bridget's spirits soared and she put aside those things that rankled and said, 'I cannot wait to set foot on land again. Will you allow me to do so, Harry? I need to purchase such items that are essential to a woman's *toilette*. I had thought of going with Juanita. I have been to the city before, but I cannot say that I know it well.' She gazed up at the several days' stubble on his face and, when he did not answer, added impulsively, 'Harry, I pray that you do not intend growing a beard again.'

Harry stared down at her, wondering if her words meant that she preferred the sight of his scar to being reminded of the slave trader. If that were true, then perhaps he had mis-understood her use of the word *fouler* and she'd not meant his appearance, but only how he'd deceived her.

She touched his bristly jaw with the back of her hand and pulled a face. 'Please shave?'

He gazed down at her with a light in his eyes that she had not seen there for several days, but he did not say aye or nay, only took some coins from the pouch at his belt and handed them to her. 'Buy what you need, but promise me that you will be back here before dark.'

Her eyes lit up. 'I promise.'

A couple of hours later Bridget saw Joe carrying a pan of steaming water into the cabin, which Harry had entered a short while ago. Her breath caught in her throat and it oc-curred to her that perhaps after all she had some influence over her husband. She decided that tonight she would definitely tell him the truth about himself and what she knew about Ingrid's perfidy, which included the attempted abduction of Harry's own sister.

Harry watched Master Larsson supervising the loading of the cargo of sugar cane into wagons. Joe and one of the crew had already gone ashore to purchase fresh supplies and another two were handling the filling of the water containers. Harry had already spoken with the harbour master and his buyer and looked forward to taking aboard a cargo of sherry. He had no buyer for it, but he had no doubt he would find a market for it in London.

Suddenly Bridget and Juanita appeared at his side. 'It is time I left, Captain,' said the latter. 'I am looking forward to introducing your wife to my family and I will show her the best places to buy all that she needs.'

'Make the most of your time here because the journey to England will take us longer than it took us to reach here, Bridget,' he said.

She surprised him by standing on tiptoe and kissing his scarred cheek before hurrying down the gangplank after Juanita. She did not look back.

As he gazed after them, Harry thought of how he would have liked to show his wife his favourite places in Lisbon and buy her some pretty trinket. Yet despite that kiss it seemed obvious to him that she did not want his company, but preferred that of another woman.

He was about to turn away when he noticed a stranger standing in the doorway of a tavern, looking up at his ship. He was powerfully built and had a rugged, weatherbeaten face. As Harry watched, the man crossed the quayside, apparently to take a closer look at his ship. He walked alongside its length and stopped where the ship's name was inscribed. He stood there so long that Harry's curiosity was about to get the better of him when the man stepped back and returned to the inn and went inside.

Harry left the ship and stood where the man had done and saw that the paint was peeling, revealing the words *Thor's Hammer* in faint letters. Now why should that man be so interested in the name of his ship? He crossed the quayside and went inside the tavern. He spotted his quarry talking to another man, so he made his way towards them. He knew the moment the bearded man saw him because he started to his feet. 'Who are you?' demanded Harry in Portuguese, seizing him by the front of his doublet. 'Why are you interested in my ship? Are you that filthy slave trader who bought my wife?'

Chapter Eight

The man's companion spoke rapidly to Harry. 'He does not speak Portuguese, Captain. He is English and is seeking a woman called Bridget McDonald and a man known as Captain Black Harry.'

At this revelation, Harry released the man and stared at him with interest. 'What do you want with them?'

'Yer've seen the lass?' rumbled the man, smoothing the fabric of his leather jerkin with an unsteady hand.

'You tell me who you are and what you want of them first,' demanded Harry.

'Name's Joshua Wood. Does that mean aught to yer?' he asked, peering at Harry intently.

Names tumbled through Harry's mind. He remembered what Bridget had told him about her companions with whom she had left London and realised this man could be the man she had spoken about.

'Maybe,' he answered.

'Can we get out of here?' asked Joshua Wood, a quiver of excitement threading his voice. 'The light's that bad in this place that I can't quite make out—'

Harry led the way outside and was instantly the object of Joshua's scrutiny once more. He was starting to get annoyed because the man had the audacity to bring his own face so close to Harry's that their noses almost touched.

'What is it that you're looking for?' growled Harry. 'Back off, man.'

Joshua ignored his words and reaching out, touched the bridge of Harry's nose before withdrawing his hand. 'I gave yer that scar, Master Harry, but not that really bad one on yer cheek,' he shouted. 'God's Blood! I thought that I'd never see this day, but here yer are alive, and if not as handsome as yer were as a boy, it—it *is* you!' He choked on the words and wiped the back of his hand across eyes that were suddenly damp.

Harry stared at him in disbelief. He felt light-headed and extremely odd. Such a meeting was something that he had occasionally dreamed about, but never believed would happen. 'You knew me as a boy?' he asked quickly.

'Aye! We used to play together, regular-like. That scar on yer nose, I caught yer a whack with one of them wooden swords me father made us. He was yer father's woodcutter. Fancy yer not being able to remember that! It didn't half bleed and yer were out to spill my blood afterwards.' Joshua chuckled and then sobered up immediately. 'But there, the Baron Dalsland did tell us that yer couldn't remember those days because yer'd been clean knocked out. It's one of his ships that brought me here.'

'Bridget told me about you and her ladyship being captured by pirates and how the Baron had supplied the ships to search for me and Callum McDonald,' said Harry, feeling totally dazed.

Joshua gave him a searching look. 'Is she all right? We feared for her virtue and her life.'

Harry nodded. 'You must excuse me, Master Wood, but I feel a need to rest against this wall. You cannot imagine how peculiar it is to meet someone who remembers that part of one's life that one cannot remember.'

'Certainly, Master Harry,' said Joshua, surveying him anxiously. 'But I'm sure once we have a good ol' chinwag, the memories will come flooding back.'

'You really believe so, Master Wood,' said Harry, leaning against the wall of the tavern, unable to take his eyes from the other man's face. 'I presume the Baron could not come seeking me, himself, because he is now married?'

'Aye, Master Harry. I see yer know about his marrying your sister and I presume yer on yer way back to England to be reunited with them.'

Harry was utterly dumbstruck by the news that he even *had* a sister, but tried to appear as if it came as no surprise to him. Why had Bridget not told him all this? He cleared his throat. 'Aye. As you can imagine it came as welcome news to me. Of course, there were gaps in what she knows and I would be interested to hear everything you can tell me about my sister. For as long as I can remember I've had these nightmares involving a dark-haired girl mouthing words to me from the top chamber of a tower and of a woman falling down some stairs.' He stopped, unable to carry on because it suddenly occurred to him that the girl was very likely his sister. He was overcome by emotion and turned his face away, ashamed to be seen in such a vulnerable state.

'There now, Master Harry,' said Joshua gruffly, patting his shoulder. 'That girl would be Mistress Rosamund.'

Rosamund! He could not understand why Bridget had not told him that his friend Alex had married his sister. She must have realised how much he would have welcomed such news! He managed to gain control of himself. 'You must forgive me, Master Wood,' he said, his voice unsteady. 'I have not mentioned my dreams to Bridget.'

'Name's Josh,' he said, smiling. 'From when we were almost in the cradle I was always Josh to yer. Mistress Rosamund used to trail after us, wanting to join in our games. She grieved badly when you went missing, as did your father.'

Harry wiped his face on his sleeve and took a deep breath. 'My father—' His voice cracked.

'Sir James Appleby of Appleby Manor in Lancashire. Sadly he is dead now.'

Harry rocked on his heels. The name repeated itself over and over in his head very slowly. *Appleby, Appleby, Appleby! Why had Bridget not told him this, either?* But Joshua was continuing. 'At least, yer don't have to avenge his murder. Those responsible have already paid the price, so all yer have to do is come home and claim yer inheritance. Yer shouldn't have any difficulty proving who yer are despite that nasty scar on yer cheek. I'd like to hear the tale of how yer got that. Yer always did want to go adventuring, Master Harry. I suppose now yer'll be thinking of settling down at Appleby Manor. I'll vouch for yer, and so will the Baron, who's more important, and so will Mistress Rosamund.'

Why had Bridget kept all this from him? Why? Why? Harry presumed as there was no mention of his mother that she was also dead. His mouth felt dry. 'As I said, I saw in my dreams a woman being pushed downstairs. There was another woman there and she—'

Joshua gazed at him in fascination. 'I do believe that was no dream, but could be a memory. The first woman was likely to be your mother, God rest her soul, and the second would be Mistress Fustian, who was supposedly taking care of her whilst yer father was away. Mistress Fustian became Sir James's second wife. She was kin to Bridget's father's cousin and it was she who had you abducted so you wouldn't

rightfully inherit and told your father you'd drowned. I hope
I'm telling yer things yer already know?' he asked.

'It is interesting to hear it from your point of view,' said
Harry hastily. It was obvious then that some of the McDonalds
were involved in his abduction, but had Callum known of it?
'I was told by the pirate captain when I awoke aboard his ship
with no memory of who I was that my parents had drowned
at sea in a boating accident.'

'Well, he would speak falsely to you, wouldn't he?'

Harry agreed. 'Why was my father murdered?'

Joshua looked at him oddly. 'I suppose Bridget might not
have known about that because it was before she came on the
scene. It was because he spotted you in London, but didn't
have a chance to speak to you. Besides, he thought he could
be mistaken and so he made the mistake of mentioning it to
Edward Fustian, your stepbrother. He also mentioned it to
the Baron, but unfortunately you'd sailed away by then.'

Harry's head felt as if it was going to burst with all this
startling information. 'I never liked Fustian. In fact, I knew
he was a dishonest, unsavoury character as soon as I met him
in London. If I had realised then he was my stepbrother...'
His voice trailed off.

Joshua gave a grim smile. 'You don't have to worry about
him. As I said, he's dead and so is his mother and Bridget's
uncle.'

Harry was suddenly beginning to feel suspicious of
Bridget's motives in keeping all this from him. He remembered her mentioning her uncle forcing her to go to London
and that it was there that she had met Lady Elizabeth.

'No doubt Bridget will be wondering about Lady Elizabeth,'
said Joshua, as if he had read Harry's mind.

'We thought a ransom would have been paid for her.'

'Aye, we were convinced that Bridget was lost to us and

a captive in a harem. But God's Blood, Master Harry,' burst out Joshua, 'as your sister said, if it weren't for Bridget then we'd never have set sail in search of yer and her father in the first place, so we had to find her. It was she who told us yer'd both gone off to the New World after yer disappeared from London. She was desperate to find you both. So can I see her?' asked Joshua.

Harry was also desperate to see her, but not for the same reason as Joshua! 'Regretfully you have just missed her. She has gone to purchase a few essentials for the journey home.'

Joshua looked disappointed. 'Is her father with her?'

Harry shook his head. 'He decided not to travel with me to Madeira, but to journey across the northern ocean, so it is possible that he did not survive the crossing.'

'That would be sad tidings, indeed, for Bridget,' said Joshua, frowning.

Harry decided it was time to inform Joshua of his marriage. 'Aye, it was and because of that I asked her to marry me.'

Joshua stared at him in astonishment and then a smile broke over his face. 'God's Blood, that is good news.'

'I am glad you think so,' he said lightly. 'I know the thought of waking up every morning to see this face of mine on the pillow next to them might put some women off marriage to me, but Bridget was happy to accept me as I am.'

'I wasn't going to say aught about yer face, Master Harry, but that yer always did have a kind heart. Yer never thought anyone beneath yer. Not that I'm saying aught against Mistress Bridget.'

Harry smiled falsely. 'No doubt she complained of my having a black heart because I parted her from her father, but we have had to deal with our differences. Besides, if I had not found her when I did, God only knows what might have happened to her.'

'It was fate,' said Joshua solemnly.

'Exactly, Master Wood,' said Harry smoothly. 'I am more grateful than words can say for your coming in search of us but I am afraid I must go now. We have not long anchored here in Lisbon and I have business I must tend to, and as I have no notion of the hour Bridget will return, I suggest you come to my ship in the morning when we would both be delighted to see you and to talk some more.'

'Certainly, Master Harry,' said Joshua hastily. 'I didn't mean to keep you from your business.'

'I would much rather continue talking to you, Master Wood,' said Harry sincerely, 'but you understand that I must see to matters here in Lisbon.'

The two men shook hands and parted.

How could Bridget have kept so much from him? wondered a seething Harry. Was she far more vengeful and devious than he ever thought she could be? His thoughts so occupied his mind that as he went aboard his ship, he failed to notice Master Larsson trying to attract his attention. It was not until he planted himself in front of Harry and spoke directly to him that he became aware of his presence.

'Who was that man you were talking to?' asked Christian in a sharp voice. 'You seemed to have a lot to say to each other.'

Harry started. 'You're not going to believe this, Christian, but that man, Joshua Wood, knew me when I was a boy. We used to play together. His father worked for my father and he came here on one of the Baron's ships in search of me and Bridget. He was one of her companions on the pirate ship and he told me that my name is Harry Appleby and that I'm heir to a manor and business in England!'

'No wonder you look so pleased,' said Christian, his eyes lighting up. 'You will be able to buy another ship.'

Harry was taken aback. 'I have only just received this news; I've had little chance to make plans.'

'But you will consider buying another ship?' urged Christian. 'I have served as your second-in-command since Callum stole the *Odin's Maiden* and I would like to be master of a vessel again.'

'I understand your feelings, but I cannot make such an important decision so soon,' said Harry. 'When we arrive in England will be time enough for me to do so. In the meantime I have much to do and must speak to my wife.'

Christian's expression altered. 'It is always her that possesses your thoughts now. Do you not consider it peculiar that she did not tell you about this? Surely if this man was one of her companions and knew of your new status, then she would have done so, too? Perhaps it is the reason why she married you?'

Harry had begun to wonder about this, himself, but he did not like hearing it from Christian. 'I would rather you did not make such accusations against my wife,' he said coolly.

'Why not? Face up to the truth, Captain. Once she realised that Callum was at the bottom of the ocean, she knew herself to be in dire straits and so played on your sympathy. Knowing you were a man of substance, she'd reason that, if you knew the truth, you'd want a different kind of wife than her. For God's sake, Harry, she's the daughter of a thieving pirate!'

'That's as may be, but there's no way she could guarantee that I would ask her to marry me,' snapped Harry.

'You think not?'

'Aye! She loathed my very name.'

'All the more reason for tricking you into marriage. Even

I can see that she is a beautiful woman. You've been taken for a fool by a devious woman,' he said scornfully.

Harry's anger spiralled out of control and he saw red and punched Christian squarely on the jaw. He went flailing backwards on to the deck. 'You go too far!' thundered Harry. 'You forget your position.'

Christian picked himself up from the deck and stared at Harry from furious eyes. 'She's bewitched you. You are not the man you were, but have grown soft.'

Harry said icily, 'Our friendship is at an end. I will pay you what is owed to you and you will leave this ship.' He walked away from Christian, raging inwardly. How dare Bridget put him in such a position that he looked a fool! What was going on in her mind that she should keep such momentous news from him?

Bridget was later than she had intended and it was dusk by the time she returned to the ship. Juanita had been as good as her word and taken her to visit her kinsfolk and they had insisted on her sharing their meal. Afterwards she had enjoyed herself wandering around the city with Juanita and a couple of her nieces. She had been able to purchase several scarcely used items of clothing as well as bindings for her monthly courses that were due soon. She prayed Harry would not be vexed with her for being late.

There was no sign of her husband on deck, so she presumed that he was still ashore and was relieved. She went immediately to the cabin, thinking to stow away most of her purchases, only to find Harry waiting there for her in the gloom as he had not lit the lantern.

'So you've returned at last,' he said.

Bridget thought that his tone of voice did not bode well for her. Faced with a powerful man who was angry caused flashbacks to the slave ship she'd been on. Her stomach began to quiver and she found herself babbling. 'I beg pardon for being late, only Juanita's sister insisted I share a meal with her family and then I had items to purchase as I mentioned to you. I hope you like the garments I bought with your money.' She placed them on the table.

'What price do I have to pay for the truth from you, Bridget?'

The question took her by surprise as did his suddenly springing to his feet. She backed away from him and felt the rim of the table dig into her waist. 'I—I don't know what you're talking about?'

'Are you certain of that? Think, Bridget! What information might you have that I would be eager to possess? Such glad tidings that I would have given you the moon if I'd heard it from your lips.' He seized her by the throat and punished those lips with a fierce kiss.

Bridget's heart seemed to take a nose dive into the pit of her stomach and she felt sick. She did not struggle, but remained motionless in his grasp. He lifted his head and his glittering eyes seemed to be able to see into her mind. 'Well, what have you to say for yourself?' he demanded in a silky voice. 'And I want the truth this time.'

'Who told you?' she whispered.

'Someone who knows Harry *Appleby*. Don't pretend and tell me that you've never heard that name before.'

She had trouble swallowing. 'I deem it would be a waste of my time, seeing as you already seem to be aware that I have,' she croaked.

'I need to know why you kept my identity a secret from me.'

'I am having difficulty speaking with your hand around my throat.' Her heart was pounding in her chest.

He loosened his grip and pushed her into a chair and moved to the other side of the table. 'Well?' he demanded.

She sighed. 'I did not realise before we married that you were Black Harry, so how could I tell Captain Mariner that he was Harry Appleby?'

'So you say but I don't know if I can believe you any longer. I gave you enough clues to my identity and marvelled even then that you did not pick them up.'

'I was ill! I wasn't expecting Black Harry to take care of me,' she protested.

'That could be a falsehood. Master Wood said that I've always had a kind heart. Surely when you were in his company he must have talked about me and you realised that I was a better person than you had thought?'

'Joshua is here!' she exclaimed with delight and started to her feet.

'Sit down,' roared Harry.

She jumped out of her skin and immediately sat down, frightened once more of this angry man. 'How did he recognise you?'

'You mean with this damned scar on my face?' He fingered it. 'Suffice to say he did so by the smaller scar on the bridge of my nose. Why didn't you, Bridget?'

'Y-you had a thick beard w-when I first set eyes on you again. Perhaps if I hadn't asked you to shave today then Joshua m-might not have recognised you.'

Harry nodded. 'I will allow you that, but I deem he saw more in my face than that small scar. My hair, my eyes. You barely hesitated before accepting a proposal of marriage from a man you believed to be a complete stranger.'

She was indignant. 'I would have refused, but you persuaded me that I had no choice but to accept your offer. Besides, you'd told me that you knew my father.'

'So you were prepared to trust me because I was acquainted with Callum, an erstwhile pirate and a thief?'

Her eyes flashed with annoyance. 'I was obviously a fool to do so, but I did trust Captain Mariner, especially when he told me that he was ugly beneath his beard when I asked him to shave it off.'

'You could have asked me to shave off my beard because you wanted to make certain that I was Harry Appleby because you had already recognised me,' he said, looming over her.

She shrank back in the chair. 'No!'

'Aye,' he contradicted her. 'You set out in search of me with your companions, knowing that Black Harry was Harry Appleby. No doubt you couldn't believe your good fortune when you woke up and saw me bending over you. When you recognised me and discovered your father was most likely at the bottom of the ocean, you decided that marrying me would be a good idea. After all, you are a beautiful woman and although you said that beauty is a bane, you decided to use it to your advantage. You probably just didn't expect me to ask you to marry me so soon.'

'I don't know how you can say I used my beauty when I was covered in a rash and suffering from a fever half of the time!' she retorted indignantly. 'Anyway, you didn't shave off your beard before we were married, so how could I have been certain it was you? You waited until our wedding night and afterwards I only saw you in poor light, such as now.'

His eyes flickered over her face and she could feel his breath on her cheek as he brought his head close to hers. 'But the next morning you immediately recognised me, Bridget, despite my *foul* scar. You could have told me the truth then. What have you to say to that?'

Bridget felt a familiar anger stir inside her and stared at

him stonily. 'When I woke up the day after we were married and realised you were Black Harry all I could think of was that you had deceived me. For days I had believed you to be Captain Mariner, an admirable man who had saved my life. Suddenly you were no longer that person, but Black Harry, who had parted me from my father,' she said heatedly.

'Even if that was true you'd have known then that I was Harry Appleby, a man of property. You must have been very pleased with yourself later when your anger abated and you realised exactly to whom you were married,' he said bitterly. 'Perhaps you thought that Harry with the ugly face should be grateful to someone as beautiful as you for marrying him?'

She was aghast. 'It did not even occur to me. The truth is that I was staggered when I realised who I had married and that I would be tied to you for life. I even suggested we get an annulment!' she exclaimed.

'Yes, only afterwards, when there could be no annulment. *You* had all to gain whilst *I*—'

Her anger erupted and she sprang to her feet. 'If you re-member, I pointed that out when you made your proposal! I said that it was unfair that you were giving so much and I came to you dowerless.'

'Very clever of you. You roused my compassion,' he retorted.

'I have had enough of listening to this,' said Bridget.

She made a rush for the door, but before she could wrench it open, he had seized hold of her and dragged her away. He lifted her and flung her on the bed. 'You will stay here.'

'I will not!'

She struggled to sit up, but he pushed her down and put his arms either side of her. 'You *will* obey me.'

'If Joshua Wood is here, then I will leave you and return

to England with him,' she said. 'You can forget that you were ever married to me. After all, you married me in the name of Captain Henry Mariner, so perhaps our marriage is not legal anyway.'

'Don't be a fool! It was my legal name for years and is on many a document. You will remain with me whether you like it or not. I will need an heir now I am the owner of a manor and after our wedding night you could be carrying my son. When Joshua Wood comes aboard tomorrow I expect you to behave as if all is well between us. I have no wish for him to realise that you kept my true identity from me.'

She was in agreement with him that she did not want Joshua to know how she had behaved. 'What of your crew—will they not wonder why you didn't inform them of your good fortune?'

'Leave the crew to me. They owe me loyalty and would not dare to question my actions openly,' he said, thinking only Christian Larsson would do that. 'Do you understand, Bridget?'

'Aye, you want me to act as if I am delighted to be married to you.'

He nodded.

'I will try. But if you had told me from the beginning that you were Black Harry, we would not be in this position now.'

'You are putting the blame on me again, I see,' he said vexedly.

'But it is true,' she protested. 'I would have told you that you were Harry Appleby if you had done so.'

Harry wanted to believe her and it was true that he had deliberately set out to deceive her. 'Let us say that is a real possibility, but it still leaves me with the question—why did you delay once you realised the truth? I can only believe it was out of spite.'

'No! The reasons I have given you are the true ones—and, of course, I didn't see you for days after our marriage because of the storm. Then when I did, all we seemed to do was argue and I never got the opportunity to tell you.'

He frowned down at her despite being unable to make out her features. 'I can see that we could continue to argue about this all night.' He rose from the bed. 'I must go. I have a task to perform and must go ashore.'

'When will you return?' she asked.

'I do not know. I have much to celebrate even if you are still my wife,' he said harshly, opening the door and closing it after him.

Chapter Nine

Bridget lay there in the darkness, thinking over what had just taken place. She accepted that whilst Harry's actions in deceiving her were reprehensible her own behaviour did not bear scrutiny, either. She could have told him earlier about his being Harry Appleby and it was true that she had intended doing so on more than one occasion. If only she had told him before going ashore instead of deciding to leave it until this evening, his opinion of her would be so different right now.

How different? While she had delayed telling him, she would have told him sooner if he had not sprung to Ingrid Wrangel's defence in the way that he had. Why could he not believe her about the perfidy of that woman? After all, Bridget had told him that the Baron had married someone else other than Ingrid. Surely that should have given Harry cause to wonder why his friend should have changed his mind about marrying the Danish woman?

Bridget sighed. No doubt she would have more questions to answer later. What if he returned drunk? Her stomach quivered, remembering how uncontrollable her father used to be when in his cups. She could only hope that her husband had more self-control but those words *I have much to celebrate* echoed in her head. She decided to go up on deck and see if anything was happening outside.

Bridget gazed down at the quayside. Some buildings were in darkness, but lights could be seen coming from several taverns and the sound of voices and laughter was being carried on the air. There was the smell of meat and fish being grilled over charcoal and that of fried onions.

'You all right, *Mistress Appleby*?'

Bridget started at the sound of Joe's voice as he sidled up to her. His elbow nudged hers and she turned her head and looked at him by the light of the lanterns on mast, stern and prow. 'So the news is already out,' she said.

'Aye, the captain told me,' replied Joe, grinning at her. 'He explained why he'd kept it a secret until it had to come out once Master Joshua Wood came looking for you both.'

'He did?

'Aye, he didn't want the crew feeling unsettled, wondering whether he'd be giving up the sea. He knows I'm no good at keeping secrets so I was kept in the dark, too.'

So her husband had thought up an excuse to give to the crew, thought Bridget. 'What do you think about it, Joe?'

'Whatever the captain decides is all right by me. He'll not be sending me away if he decides to settle down. He told me that there is a home for me wherever he goes. I'd be content to give up the sea as it's not easy cooking on a ship. I'd really enjoy cooking in a proper kitchen.'

Bridget could understand why Joe felt that way. But would her husband be able to settle down when the sea had been his life for so long or would he hate staying in one place? He'd had little time yet to think much about it and decide where he wanted to make his home.

'You hungry, missus?' asked Joe, rousing her from her thoughts.

Bridget did not have much of an appetite, but decided that at least having a meal would help pass the time. 'Aye, Joe,' she said with a smile.

'Like to eat it up here on deck?'

She nodded.

In no time at all Joe was serving up a platter of grilled fish in a sorrel sauce with fresh crusty bread. He poured her a glass of wine and bid her, *'Bon appétit!'*

As she sipped her wine, she noticed Master Larsson on the quayside. He was staring directly at her with such an unpleasant expression on his face that she felt a chill run down her spine. He called out to her, but she could not make out the words. She stood up and moved closer to the side of the ship and only then did she noticed that his face appeared to be swollen. Then suddenly she saw Harry come into view and expected him to greet his second-in-command. To her surprise, they ignored each other and Master Larsson strode off in the opposite direction.

She watched as Harry came aboard ship, thinking that she had not expected him back so soon. He spoke to Joe before approaching her. 'What are you thinking of sitting here all alone in full view of men passing by, Bridget?' he said sternly. 'What did Master Larsson say to you?'

'I did not catch his words.'

Her husband seemed relieved about that and sat down on a cask the other side of the makeshift table. He tapped his fingers on it and his expression was now so forbidding that she half-expected him to order her to the cabin. She would have liked to have known his thoughts, but no doubt he would consider the question an intrusion.

She had finished her supper by the time Joe placed a plate of food in front of Harry before pouring wine for him and replenishing Bridget's goblet. Harry took a mouthful of fish and sauce, said something complimentary to Joe and then dismissed him.

It was a clear night and in other circumstances she might have found it romantic. But there was naught loving about the way her husband felt towards her and her feelings towards him were not loving, either. They were very mixed and confused. In this light she could not make out his scar and she recalled the first time she had set eyes on him. She remembered his smile and how it had warmed her heart and, unexpectedly, she longed to see him smile at her in such a way again.

'What are you thinking?' asked Harry, glancing up from his plate and gazing at her.

'The first time I saw you,' she answered, taken off guard.

He raised his eyebrows and reached for his wine. 'You trusted me enough then to speak the truth.'

'You listened to me and I believed that you would help me and my father.'

'And I did…' Harry paused. 'Tell me honestly, Bridget, did Callum know of my abduction when I was a child? The fact that it was he who named me Harry when I awoke on the pirate ship causes me to wonder if that is a possibility.'

She supposed in the circumstances that the question should not have come as a surprise. 'I was only a child at the time. If he had mentioned it to my mother, I was unaware of it.' She hesitated. 'Besides, if my father had known who you really were, I cannot see him keeping quiet about it for long.'

'At least you are now being honest and I deem you are right. Callum would not have been able to resist revealing such knowledge when we met up again if he knew me to be a man of substance. He'd have told me and expected a reward for handing me such welcome news.'

'So we can agree that my father was not party to your abduction,' she said, 'And I did not know your true identity until the beginning of last year when I was in London and made the acquaintance of the Baron and your sister, Rosamund.'

Harry's expression darkened. 'How could you keep the news that I had a sister from me?'

'Harry, I honestly tried to tell you on a couple of occasions. During the storm I was going to tell you, thinking you should be aware of who you were in case aught happened to you and you went to the grave not knowing the truth.'

'When was this?'

'When you brought me and Juanita some food, but we could hardly hear the other speak, so I decided it was not a good time.'

'You could have told me afterwards.'

'You mean after the storm when you slept for a whole day.'

'I cannot deny that we saw little of each other during that time, but there has been time since.'

'Not much time,' she pointed out. 'And if you remember, we had that disagreement over Ingrid Wrangel. That was another time I approached you to tell you the truth about yourself and got distracted, which I am very sorry for.'

He was silent. As if from a distance she could hear the sounds of laughter and people talking. A dog barked and there came the gentle slapping of waves against the hull of the ship causing it to rock gently.

'Are you saying you would have told me then if we had not argued?' he demanded. 'I remember you making accusations against Ingrid that I found difficult to accept.'

'I thought of telling you before you doubted my word about that woman,' she replied coolly.

'You only *thought* of telling me, but you did not!'

'Afterwards there never seemed the right moment and you would glare at me so.'

'And you viewed me with disdain!'

'I was angry and hurt because I had believed Captain Mariner a man worthy of my respect and he had turned into the man I—I—'

'Despised,' finished Harry, wanting done with this conversation.

'I do not despise you, but I needed time to adjust, Harry,' said Bridget quietly. 'When I met you in Ireland, we spent but a short time in each other's company before you spoke to my father and then our ways parted acrimoniously.'

'I know what you are going to say—then we met again and I rushed you into marriage under false pretences after only a week. I still deem you should have told me I was Harry Appleby sooner.'

'I would have told you this evening if Joshua had not turned up. I had made up my mind to do so,' she confessed.

'You expect me to believe that?' said Harry. 'I deem you still do not understand how momentous this news is to me. I am no longer that little frightened boy your father named Black Harry or the person I named Captain Henry Mariner because I hated being called Black Harry with its connotations of filth and being subjected to beatings by a pirate captain whose obnoxious trade I hated. It was one of the reasons I felt compelled to fight against piracy in the northern seas along with the Baron and members of the Hanseatic League. Now I have a sister, Rosamund, who is married to the Baron, who was like a brother to me, and you kept that from me too!' He almost choked on the words.

She felt exceptionally guilty and would have asked him to forgive her, only the words stuck in her throat because she could not forget he had deceived her too and believed her guilty of an equally awful deception, that of marrying him for his position and money. 'What are you going to do with me?'

'You're my wife—what do you expect me to do to you? Beat you?' he said bitterly.

'Some would say you have a right to do so. Master Larsson, for instance.'

'I do not hit women,' he said in a low voice that had pent-up anger running through. 'Just go to the cabin and stay there.'

Bridget was glad to escape from his anger and retire to bed. The bolster was still in place, but would he be joining her there? Perhaps he would go ashore again and escape into some woman's arms. In the mood he was in, it was highly unlikely he would want her.

It seemed that she was correct in that assumption because he came to the cabin shortly after she did, but behaved as if she did not exist.

The following morning they both rose early and after breakfast they returned to the cabin. Now she was trying to ignore Harry's presence as he perused one of his charts whilst she inspected the clothes she had purchased.

One of the gowns was dark red and made from what she was certain was silk. She had bought it from a used-garment stall and the hem and sleeves would need shortening. She had also bought a robe of a russet colour that she liked very much. When she was younger, Bridget had not bothered her head about fine clothes and had even worn a youth's breeches and shirt when she had needed to disguise herself after escaping from her uncle and his mistress. But Lady Elizabeth's love of fashion in clothing and jewellery had stirred Bridget's own interest.

There came a knock at the door. 'Who is it?' asked Harry.

'Master Joshua Wood is here to see you, Captain,' called Joe.

Harry gave Bridget a warning look before opening the door. She glanced over and saw Joshua's sturdy figure in the doorway. Instantly she expressed delight at seeing him and invited him to sit down. For a few moments they talked about Lady Elizabeth and then Bridget asked him whether the Baron and Rosamund's expected baby had arrived safely.

Joshua grinned. 'She and the Baron have a fine boy. They have named him Douglas Alexander Harry James and he has the Baroness's eyes and the Baron's flaxen hair and fine nose. Hopefully yer'll see for yerself once yer back in England. They were leaving for Appleby Manor when I left London.'

'This is good news, is it not, Harry?' said Bridget.

Harry nodded agreement and she realised he was in the grip of a strong emotion. Suddenly it occurred to her that he had not known Rosamund was having a child, either. Did this mean as soon as Joshua left that she would receive the sharp edge of Harry's tongue once again?

She watched him as he went and poured wine and handed around the goblets. 'Let us drink a toast to my nephew,' he said.

So they drank to the health of Douglas Alexander Harry James. After doing so Joshua suggested a toast to Master Harry and Bridget and wished them a long and happy life together. 'To my wife,' said Harry, raising his goblet.

'To my husband,' she murmured, following suit, thinking

how difficult it was to behave as if all was light and happiness between them.

Yet they must have played the part well because Joshua said, 'It does my heart good to see you both so happy.' Then he turned to Harry. 'So, Master Harry, what do you say to my coming back to work for you at Appleby Manor?'

'You would leave her ladyship's employment?' asked Harry, surprised.

'It is what she will expect once she hears the news that you have been found,' said Joshua, turning the goblet between his hands. 'I only went to work for her because your stepmother dismissed me. Lady Elizabeth was staying at Lathom House, the home of her cousin, the Earl of Derby, and she hired me. She was a friend of your mother and remembered me as a boy. Only my heart is in the north at Appleby, Master Harry,' he said earnestly, 'and I long to be back there.'

In the face of such eagerness, Harry could only say, 'Then I will be happy to welcome you back.'

A grin split Joshua's face. 'It won't quite be like old times, but I'm certain you'll be happy there once you find your feet again. You had a great fondness for the place and used to know every inch of your father's land.'

Harry was looking forward to seeing his old home and wondered if once he set foot on his land whether the memories would come flooding back. Often he had visited places and thought that they reminded him of somewhere. Perhaps it had been Appleby? Then he thought of Bridget and wondered if they would ever be able to turn it into a happy home the way they felt about each other at the moment.

Joshua asked could he make the journey back to London on Harry's ship and he agreed, certain that he would learn much from Joshua about his boyhood on the voyage home. Then they talked of London and his father's house and business, and Harry wished he could remember Sir James and grieved afresh for his dead parents. Joshua asked about his travels and Harry suggested they go up on deck because he did not wish to reveal some of the gory details in front of Bridget.

She did not realise that was his reasoning behind the suggestion that the two men go on deck. It was obvious he did not want to be in her company and much preferred that of Joshua. She wondered what Master Larsson would make of their friendship.

When Harry returned he found Bridget turning up the hem of the gown she had bought. She did not look up at him, but carried on with what she was doing. 'You played your part well,' he said. 'Just make certain that you keep it up in Joshua's company.'

Bridget gave him a speaking glance.

Harry frowned. 'It should not be too difficult. I must tell you that we will not be sailing alone to England, but will have the company of the ship that brought Joshua here and that Master Larsson has transferred to that vessel.'

Bridget was astonished. 'Why?'

'I do not need to explain that to you,' said Harry. 'I have a new second-in-command now, Master Hans Nilsson from that same ship.'

Bridget wondered what had happened between her husband and Master Larsson. Perhaps he had not been as pleased as his captain that Harry had come into an inheritance. Could it be that Master Larsson was jealous? Maybe he had decided that Harry was likely to give up his seafaring life and had made a move to another ship now. Whatever his reasons, Bridget was glad to be finally rid of Master Larsson's cold disapproving presence.

When his wife remained silent, Harry continued, 'The

master of the other ship expects to find the Baron or his representative in London and will be looking for fresh orders. It is possible that ship will be ordered to Sweden.'

'Are you saying that Master Larsson is likely to sail with her and that I will never have to see him again?'

Harry nodded. 'I need to go back on deck, but I will see you later. If you decide to leave the cabin, then wrap a scarf around your neck. I regret that there is some slight bruising where I seized you roughly last evening.' He did not wait for her reaction, but went out. Bridget put a hand to her throat and gazed at the door as it closed behind him, thinking that was most likely the nearest she would ever get to an apology from him. She would be glad when they set sail. The sooner they arrived in England, the better she would feel.

They left Lisbon the following morning and in the days that followed little seemed to change between Bridget and Harry. In company they pretended that all was well between them and that they were looking forward to seeing their friends and making their first home together once they arrived at Appleby Manor. They spent scarcely any time alone as Joshua often joined them or Harry was busy discussing the business of the ship with Hans Nilsson. He seemed a good man with a ready smile for Bridget, but when she told her husband so she was surprised that he did not seem pleased with her comment. During the night when Harry was not on deck, the bolster remained in place in their bed.

After a week, Bridget wondered how long they would go on like this. When would they start feeling the need to forgive each other? She stood at the side of the ship, gazing over the sea. Above the slap of the waves and the sound of sawing of wood by the ship's carpenter, Andrew, she could hear the conversation between Harry and Joshua.

'Nothing beats good English oak,' Joshua was saying as he thumped a foot on the wooden deck.

Harry said, 'I would not deny it, but this ship was built in Sweden.'

Joshua chuckled. 'My mistake. Yer have some fine trees on Appleby Manor, Master Harry, not just of oak but chestnut, hornbeam, willow and beech. There's also plenty of hazel that provide a fine crop of nuts in the autumn.'

'You fill me with even more longing to be there,' said Harry. 'Let us talk livestock. I seem to remember you saying that I have no sheep.'

'Aye, that is true.'

'Why not? Their wool would make a good cash crop.'

Joshua grinned. 'You're thinking like a merchant, Master Harry. Trees also bring in the money.'

'I would not argue.' He smiled and took Joshua's arm. 'Come, let us leave Andrew to his repairs.'

As the two men moved away, Bridget sighed and wondered what their life at Appleby would really be like. Despite Harry's enthusiasm for his childhood home, surely he would not find it easy after being accustomed to the feel of the deck rolling beneath his feet as his ship forged through the waves and his eyes being accustomed to the far horizons of the seas. It would be a very different kind of life to that which he had known for so long.

She knew the same could be said for herself. It would be arduous taking the organisation of Harry's household into her inexperienced hands and the thought excited and scared her at the same. No doubt he would be watching her every move, so she must not fail. Yet if she were to have his child she felt he would forgive her much and she, too, could forgive him for what he had done to her, for the child would belong to them both. She prayed daily that she was already pregnant from that one coupling on their wedding night. She tried to think about the pleasure he had given her because it filled her with longing. At least her monthly courses were overdue so it was possible that she was indeed already with child.

Suddenly she noticed the Baron's vessel was near enough for her to see some of the mariners going about their work. She became aware that she was being watched and, with a sense of shock, realised that it was Master Larsson who was gazing at her. Once more, there was that in his expression that filled her with unease. Then he shifted his gaze to where Harry was talking to Joshua. Was it possible that the Swede might have it in mind to cause trouble for her and Harry in the future despite Harry saying that he would most likely go home to Sweden?

That evening Harry came into the cabin as Bridget was performing her *toilette* before retiring to bed. She was wearing the russet robe and he stopped short when he saw her and his eyes fixed on the upper curve of her breasts. Her hair hung loose down her back and she was polishing it with a cloth.

'You look—' He drew in his breath.

She ran her hands over the robe in a very feminine way and blushed. He was conscious of an instant arousal and carefully sat on a chair to remove his boots.

'You might think I am making a fuss over naught, Harry,' said Bridget after a moment's hesitation, 'but I noticed Master Larsson watching us from the Baron's ship this morning and I deem he will cause us trouble if he can.'

'I don't see how that is possible.'

'Neither do I, but my instincts tell me that he will try to do so. Did you fear you might have had a mutiny on your hands if he had stayed on this ship? I know he did not approve of your marrying me and perhaps several of the men felt the same.'

Harry shook his head. 'I cannot believe my crew would mutiny, especially now Christian has gone, but some might be dissatisfied. We did not leave the New World richer men. The rewards were greater when we were battling with pirates in the northern seas and defeating them.' He paused. 'I am glad that you have mentioned this, though. I will promise them a bonus when we reach London and I come into my inheritance, and that should ensure their loyalty.'

Bridget considered that a worthy idea and told him so. He flushed. 'I am glad I am redeeming myself in your eyes.'

He padded across the floor to where she was sitting on the bed and sat beside her. Her pulses began to race as he slipped his hand inside her robe and caressed her breast and kissed her. The kiss took her unawares and weakened the emotional and physical barrier she had put up against him, but she was uncertain what he expected of her. The kiss deepened and despite her inner struggle to resist him, her lips yielded to his and she did not protest when he eased her down on the bed and unfastened the girdle that held her robe together. His hands roamed over the silk of her night rail and the breath shuddered in her lungs as he bent his head and kissed her breasts through the material. When he finally took possession of her, such was the urgency she felt to respond to him that she could not rein it in. His passionate reaction took her unawares, but it only increased her desire for fulfilment at his hands. Such exquisite pleasure was hers that she clung on to him, kissing his chest, shoulders and his lips as he finally found release in her arms.

Afterwards she felt a deep disappointment when he immediately turned his back on her and fell asleep.

The following morning she woke and instantly knew that something had changed because she felt different. Perhaps at last she and Harry could talk about their feelings. She rolled over only to find that he was sitting up on the side of the bed, getting dressed.

She did not know what made her say, 'Do you miss the excitement of doing battle with pirates and savages?' It was not what she had intended saying at all!

Harry shrugged. 'I came near to losing my life several times and more recently in Africa.'

'I have not forgotten Joe telling me you fought like a lion, battling with several men at once single-handed. He made you out to be a real hero.'

'Joe exaggerates.'

'But I am aware that scar on your face is not your only wound.'

'No.' He hesitated. 'Give me your hand.'

Bridget hesitated and then placed her hand into his. He took hold of it and guided it inside his hose to his bare thigh. 'Can you feel the scar?'

She felt her heart thudding as her fingers found the dent in the muscle of his thigh. 'It must have been a terrible wound.'

'I thought I would lose the leg.'

'But you fought back and survived.' She was about to withdraw her hand, but he stayed it with his own and she was suddenly aware of his manhood hovering so close that she could have touched it. She began to tremble, unsure what he expected of her. Did he want her to take hold of it? The next moment he sighed and lifted her hand and placed it back on her lap.

Bridget was aware of that confusion of emotions she felt towards him. She had believed after last night he would want to couple with her again this morning. Instead he was finishing getting dressed and a few moments later he left the cabin. What was she to think of his actions? Was he regretting giving in to his desire for her last night? Did she wish he had not done so? She could not say that she did, but perhaps if he were to want her again she would not show herself so willing. After all, she didn't want to be rejected again come morning as had just happened to her.

She dressed and went out on deck. Her husband was talking to Hans Nilsson, so she went over to where the carpenter, Andrew, and Joshua were talking. Now Master Larsson had left the ship Bridget felt more at ease with the crew and asked Andrew whether he had a wife and family.

'Aye, I had three lads and a lass when I left home,' he said. 'I'm hoping that they and the wife are still there to welcome me. They live with my father-in-law so she had help with the lads. I will be glad to see them as I have been a long time at sea and pray that they have not forgotten me.'

Bridget glanced at Joshua. 'I know that you did not have a sweetheart in London, Josh, but was there a woman you had a fondness for back at Appleby?'

'Not a woman and not at Appleby, but a young lass who lived in a nearby town. I made her acquaintance when Master Harry and I were boys, but her father wouldn't tolerate me back then; no doubt she'll be betrothed by now.'

Bridget considered that a pity because she believed Joshua deserved some happiness and a woman to take care of him. He had been such a loyal friend to Rosamund and Harry that he deserved some reward.

'Master Larsson, now, he never bothered with the women,' said Andrew. 'It was always work with him, and he and the captain sailed together for many years. I was surprised when he left and went to the other ship.'

Joshua glanced at him. 'Are we talking about the mariner who is on the Baron's ship now? If so, I can tell you that he was boasting a swollen jaw when he came aboard.'

'You think he'd been in a fight?' asked Bridget.

Joshua nodded.

Bridget was musing over what Joshua had told her later that day in the cabin. Harry had finished consulting his charts and instruments with his new second-in-command and was now sharpening a quill to fill in his log.

'Joshua was saying that Master Larsson had a swollen jaw when he went aboard the Baron's ship. It looked as if he had been in a fight. Do you know aught about it, Harry?'

'Damnation!' he exclaimed savagely.

Bridget looked at him and went over to the table. 'You've cut yourself!'

'Your question startled me,' he said, scowling at her.

Worried at the sight of the blood, she took hold of his hand and sucked his bloodied finger.

He stared at her in amazement. 'What are you doing?'

'Oh, my goodness, what *am* I doing?' Bridget dropped his hand. 'I beg your pardon. I don't know what came over me.'

'Obviously.' A faint smile played round his lips and he lifted his cut finger and put it to his own mouth.

'I only did what my mother used to do when I cut myself,' babbled Bridget. 'She told me that Jesus used spittle for healing. I doubt I've done you any harm. I will bind it for you.' She hurried over to one of the lockers and took out scissors, salve and binding, and returned to him. She looked at the bloodied digit. 'I think I should clean it first.'

He watched her cross the cabin and scoop water into a small bowl from the pail hanging from a nail. She moved with a natural grace that pleased him. His anger and hurt had abated somewhat in the past week, but it still rankled with him that she could have kept so much from him. There were times still when he wondered if she had done so because she wanted to hurt him for deceiving her over his identity before marrying her.

Bridget took hold of his hand and wiped away the blood. Suddenly her limbs felt as if they were turning to water and she was intensely aware of the smell of his herbal soap, over-lying that male scent that was particular to him. She felt dizzy and as she tried to take off the top of the jar of salve it slipped from her fingers.

Chapter Ten

'Bridget!' Harry's tone was sharp. 'Are you all right?'

She leaned against the table. 'I feel faint. It must be the sight of the blood.'

'You certainly look pale.' He stood up and took hold of her arms and sat her in the chair he had vacated. He felt anxious as he gazed down at her as she rested her head against the back of the chair with her eyes closed. 'You stay there. I'll get you a drink,' he said.

Bridget had no intention of moving, but was thinking that she could not remember the sight of blood ever having this effect on her in the past.

Harry poured her some wine and brought it to her. He held it to her lips and she sipped it slowly. After a few moments she gradually began to feel better. 'I can bind up your finger now,' she said.

'You'll stay where you are,' said Harry, frowning. 'I don't want you falling down and banging your head. I'll deal with my finger. Perhaps you should rest.'

Before Bridget could say aye or nay, he had swung her into his arms and carried her over to the bed. He sat her down and knelt in front of her and removed her shoes. 'You really should not have to do these things for me,' she said, surrendering to a compulsion to touch his wind-tangled hair and smooth it down.

'I do not mind acting as lady's maid to my wife,' said Harry, glancing up at her. The breath caught in his throat because she looked so lovely, sitting there. Her expression altered and tears filled her eyes. 'What is wrong?' he asked, concern in his voice. 'Do you still feel unwell?'

Bridget did not answer him, but her tears fell thick and fast. He was dismayed and sat on the bed and lifted her on to his knee. He stroked her hair and kissed her cheek. 'Is it that you are thinking of Callum?'

She turned her head and gazed at him through a sheen of tears. 'Are you certain my father didn't ask you to take care of me if aught happened to him?'

Harry glowered at her. 'Do you really think Callum would trust you to a man you believed had a black heart?'

'No, but perhaps he didn't believe you had a black heart,' she wailed.

'Perhaps not. Anyway, Callum believed himself indestructible. He used to talk about how he survived so many adventures.'

'If that is true and he survived crossing the great ocean to the west, then perhaps I should have refused your offer of marriage and had more faith in him.'

Harry's expression altered. 'It is too late to go back now. You are my wife, but no doubt you would have it differently?'

She hesitated and then reached up and clasped her hands behind his neck and drew herself up against him. Her lips touched his as lightly as a butterfly's wing. 'I would not say that. I am thinking, Harry, that perhaps I felt faint not because of the blood but because I am with child.'

Harry's heart began to thud. 'You really think so?'

Her eyes searched his face. 'But if I am, Harry, that will make you happy, will it not?'

'It will.' He cupped her face between his hands and returned her kiss, feeling a stirring in his loins. He so wanted to make love to her, but how could he when she had nearly fainted away? 'We must take care for we do not want to risk hurting the child.' She nodded, and he drew away from her, wondering if he detected regret in her lovely eyes.

A week passed and still the 'curse' did not come and then one morning Bridget rose and felt so nauseous that she vomited into the chamber pot.

Harry gazed at her with concern. 'I cannot believe you're seasick, not after all the time you've spent at sea.'

'No, Harry, I am not suffering from *mal de mer*,' she said, feeling wretched. 'I deem it is the sickness a woman suffers when she is with child.'

'So you are certain that you are with child?'

She nodded. 'My monthly courses are overdue so I deem it is as we hoped.'

'Is there aught I can fetch you? What about breakfast?'

She lifted her wan features. 'Food is the last thing I want right now.'

'Poor Bridget,' he said sympathetically, kissing her forehead. 'I will take care of you. You stay in bed until you are feeling better.'

Bridget did exactly that and prayed that the sickness would soon pass and that the journey home would not be disrupted by storms and be achieved in a winning time.

The next few days only served to convince Bridget even more that her diagnosis of her condition was indeed the correct one. Every morning Harry would rise, look into her pallid face and fetch a bowl. It seemed that for now all that had gone wrong between them was forgotten because they were having a child. Unfortunately, Bridget did not get her wish for a swift journey to England and even more annoying was that the sickness did not confine itself to mornings only; she felt sickly in the evenings, too.

Another storm blew up and their ship was separated from that of the Baron. They were delayed in a French port for several days. By then the crew were aware of her condition. She had always eaten breakfast, so naturally Joe had been the first to notice her affliction and mentioned it to Harry. He told him the happy news.

Joe was delighted and said to them both, 'We'll be a proper family with a baby in the house.'

To have his own family was what Harry had always wanted and he was solicitous of his young wife for the rest of the voyage. Bridget appreciated his care, although there was part of her that would rather he did not feel he had to hold the bowl for her while she was being sick. No woman looked their best at such times, but she kept her thoughts to herself, not wanting to appear ungrateful.

One day Bridget was sitting on deck eating the midday meal with Harry and Joshua, when the latter surprised her by saying, 'No doubt you will be wondering what happened to the Danish woman, Ingrid Wrangel, in your absence, Bridget?'

She was instantly aware that Harry's attention had been caught and it was he who said, 'Aye, we would like to have the latest news of her.'

Joshua glanced at him. 'I was forgetting that you were acquainted with her too, Master Harry. No doubt Mistress Bridget has told yer about her double dealings and how she managed to escape punishment for her crimes. Just before I

left London the Baron told me that there were rumours that
a nun of the Bridgettine Order has been seen in the vicinity
of yer house in London, as well as down by the headquarters
of the Hanseatic League near the Thames.'

'He deems it could be Ingrid?' asked Harry, feeling deeply
uneasy at Joshua's mention of Ingrid's crimes. 'I know she
was placed as a child with that order in Sweden and was
reared by the nuns. I remember taking her by boat to one
of their houses near Richmond, but why should she now be
dressed as a nun?'

'It is one of her favourite disguises,' said Bridget. 'She
used it to gain entry into Richmond Palace. Not only was she
involved in a plot with Edward Fustian, her lover, to abduct
your sister and to destroy the Peace Pact between England
and Scotland, but with her other lover, Lord Bude, she stole
a jewel box from Lady Elizabeth's mansion. I had hoped to
never set eyes on her again,' said Bridget, aware of her husband's stunned expression.

'Yer not alone on that score,' said Joshua, nodding his head
vigorously. 'The Baroness feels the same.'

Bridget glanced at her husband again and decided to
change the subject, feeling little satisfaction in having her
word backed up by Joshua when Harry looked so upset.

Later when Harry and Bridget were alone in the cabin,
he sat down at the table across from her and said one word,
'Ingrid.'

Bridget glanced at him. 'You want to talk about Ingrid
now?'

Harry frowned. 'Aye, from what Joshua said it seems I have
not been fair to you. I thought a short while ago that I should
ask what you knew about her, but events overtook me.'

Bridget raised her eyebrows, remembering how hurt and

angry she had felt when he had doubted her word. 'What do you want to know?'

'Why Ingrid should want to abduct my sister?'

'Two reasons. The Baron had enlisted Rosamund as one of his spies and along with Lady Elizabeth the three of them and Joshua foiled the plot I mentioned. Part of it was to murder the Queen of Scotland.'

'The Baron should not have involved my sister in such dangerous work,' Harry said harshly.

'I would not argue with you, but shall we leave the Baron out of this for now? I can see that you still want to believe that Ingrid is the woman you left behind in London.'

He frowned. 'You're mistaken. How can I dispute what you say when Joshua agrees with you? What else can you tell me?'

'She was in league with your stepmother and my uncle, as well. I can't remember if I told you that they wanted me to marry William Fustian, Edward's younger brother. They had some crazy notion that by doing so they would get their hands on my father's hoard. They could not accept that it had been stolen.' She smiled faintly. 'I will add that Ingrid did me one favour when she killed William.'

Harry swore beneath his breath. 'Why did she kill him?'

'It gets too complicated but, simply, he got killed when she decided to switch sides, thinking that if Rosamund was abducted and eventually killed, then the Baron might just turn to her again. In my opinion Ingrid Wrangel is completely deranged.'

She looked at Harry and saw that he was looking grim. 'How did she manage to escape justice?'

Bridget shrugged. 'There are those who believe she is a witch and used a broomstick, but I think she managed to escape because of her disguise and also because she wasn't as important as she believed herself to be and was allowed to go free.'

Harry was silent. 'A madness in the light of all you have told me.'

'I would agree,' said Bridget. 'But perhaps after all she is a witch and bewitched those responsible.'

'That is superstitious nonsense,' he said.

'Then she used her womanly wiles,' retorted Bridget pointedly.

Harry was silent, just staring at her.

Bridget moved away from him and gazed out of the window. 'I wonder if we will find the Baron's ship when we get to London. Master Larsson just might be having second thoughts about going to Sweden.'

'It will make no difference to me. He and I fell out,' said Harry.

'You did?' She turned and stared at him.

'He was insubordinate and insulted us both.'

A slow smile lit her face. 'So *you* hit him.'

Harry admitted, 'I lost my temper.'

'I wish I had been there to see it.'

Harry managed a smile. 'The outcome might have been different if I had not taken him by surprise.'

'You do yourself a disfavour, Harry Appleby,' she said firmly. 'What did you tell the master of the other ship about him leaving your service?'

'That Master Larsson was a man of good character and an excellent seaman and that we had disagreed on a matter of principle. I could do no less for it was the truth,' said Harry, fiddling with the quill on the table. 'I told him that I would be glad if he hired him and in return if he could let me have one of his crew who could do his job. I am satisfied with the exchange.'

'No doubt you miss him,' said Bridget.

Harry shrugged. 'I do not regret Christian's departure. He was becoming too judgemental. Now, shall we forget him?'

Bridget nodded, although she knew that she would not forget Master Larsson any time soon.

A few hours later, Harry entered the cabin. 'I have brought you something, Bridget.'

Bridget looked up from her sewing, wondering if this was his way of making amends for not having believed her about Ingrid. 'What is it?'

'The English coast is in sight, so I thought it was the right time to show you a very special gift.' He went back outside and returned carrying a cradle.

Bridget could not believe her eyes. She set aside her sewing and her skirts fluttered about her ankles as she hurried over to where he had placed the cradle on the floor. She fingered a carving of a flower and then that of a bird. 'Did Andrew make this?'

'Who else?' replied Harry, smiling.

'It is a work of beauty. I must thank him.' She glanced up at her husband and caught an expression on his face that moved her. 'It is a lovely gift. Although the baby cannot be due until early next year, it is still best to be prepared.'

'I wanted my son to have the best cradle in the country,' said Harry. 'See how Andrew has made it so that it will swing and rock him to sleep if he ever travels with us by sea.'

'An ordinary carpenter would not have thought of that,' said Bridget, enthralled by the idea. She set the cradle in motion herself. 'See how it will also work on land. How long before we reach London, now that the English coast is in sight?'

'It is the end of May, so there will be light enough for us to sail safely around the coast and anchor in the Thames estuary before nightfall.'

Bridget was delighted and excited by this news. She thanked Harry and the carpenter and looked forward to arriving in London on the morrow.

Bridget gazed through the early-morning haze that hung over the massed roofs of houses, shops and churches towards the towering spire of St Paul's Cathedral.

'Are you ready?' asked Harry from behind her.

She looked into his scarred face and could see how eager he was to go ashore. So much now depended on them finding their friends. Hopefully there might also be news of her father. 'Aye,' she said.

Harry swung down the side of the ship and into the rowing boat below where Joshua waited. He held the boat steady whilst Harry held up a hand to Bridget. She seized hold of his wrist but as she clambered into the boat, she slipped and fell heavily, hitting the side of the boat. The blow knocked all the breath out of her and made her feel sick.

'Are you all right?' asked Harry with concern, putting an arm around her and helping her up.

'Aye, I think so,' she gasped.

Harry settled her on a seat in the stern. He asked her again if she was all right and she nodded, not wanting to make a fuss. The side of her belly was very sore where it had made contact with the wood. She watched as Harry took up the oars and rowed the short distance to the shore. Soon he and Joshua were dragging the boat up the beach.

She found it difficult walking on land again after so much time at sea and staggered about as if drunk. The ground seemed to be moving up and down. Her husband placed his arm about her waist. 'You'll soon get used to it,' he said, helping her up the stone steps that led to the quayside.

She knew he was right, but she still felt sick. After taking several deep breaths she gazed at the scene in front of her. There were warehouses and wooden cranes and goods piled up on the ground. Men stood about talking or hurrying about their business.

Harry had been ashore earlier with his new second-in-command, Hans. They had spoken with the port authorities and discovered that the Baron's vessel carrying Master Larsson had anchored in the river earlier. Harry was now free to give his attention to his wife and his personal affairs. 'I think it best if we visit Lady Elizabeth first. If she is at home she is bound to know of the whereabouts of the Baron and my sister,' he said.

Bridget agreed and the three of them set off in the direction of St Paul's wharf and one of the numerous city churches. Before they reached the cathedral, they turned left to cross a bridge over the River Fleet and then walked along Fleet Street. Eventually they came to the Strand and the gates of her ladyship's mansion.

A guard approached, eyeing Harry's scarred face with suspicion. Joshua called, 'Hoy, Ned, don't yer recognise me, mate?'

The man peered through the bars of the gate. 'Josh, is that you, lad?'

'Of course it's me. Is her ladyship at home?'

'Aye, she's been looking out for yer every day, has been real fretful,' said Ned, unbarring the gate.

Joshua stepped aside, suggesting that Harry and Bridget go ahead of him. 'This is Master and Mistress Appleby, Ned,' he said.

Ned's eyes widened. 'Is that Mistress McDonald who you

went in search of? I thought we'd never see her again. You go and hurry on up to the house, her ladyship will be that pleased to see yer.'

They did not need any encouragement and were soon making their way up the drive to the house barely visible through the trees ahead. As they arrived at its frontage, the door opened and a woman appeared. She was short and stout and was wearing a damson-coloured gown made of a rich satin brocade, trimmed with lace. Her face was pock-marked and on her head was a burnt-orange-coloured wig.

'Lady Elizabeth!' cried Bridget, breaking into a run.

Harry watched his wife fling her arms around the old lady. 'My dear child, you are safe! You can have no notion of how I feared for your well-being,' she wheezed. 'I have prayed morn, noon and night for you. Praise God, that you are here at last.'

Eventually they drew apart and Lady Elizabeth touched the younger woman's cheek with a gentle hand. 'My dear, I fear you have suffered greatly since last we met,' she said in a breathless voice. 'You look pale.'

'All is well now,' said Bridget, wiping her eyes.

Harry stepped forwards. 'May I introduce myself, Lady Elizabeth. I am Harry Appleby.'

The old lady lifted her head and gazed into the scarred face of the man standing before her and her jaw dropped. 'So who have you been fighting, Harry Appleby, to get a face like that?'

Such an honest reaction surprised Harry into a laugh. 'A native brandishing a burning torch in my face.'

'I'll wager it hurt,' she said.

He nodded.

'You might say I have no reason to comment on your appearance when my own is often mocked by the ill mannered,' said her ladyship with a twinkle. 'I used to paint my face to conceal the pock marks, but in the end I gave it up. The paint didn't do my chest any good and eventually one has to accept oneself as one is,' she wheezed, nodding her head so that she almost dislodged her wig. 'Your father was a handsome man, but he was a selfish, thoughtless fool, and you are better off without him,' she continued. 'Your mother, on the other hand, had a lovely nature, and I miss her greatly.' Lady Elizabeth dabbed at her eyes with a scrap of lace.

'You remember her well?' asked Harry hoarsely, deciding to ignore her comments about his father.

The old lady nodded. 'We were girls together. Still, it's water under the bridge now, so what is the point of talking of such times. You must be weary after your journey and have much to tell me.'

Harry wanted to say that he would like to hear all that she remembered about his mother, but decided that perhaps now was not the right moment.

Lady Elizabeth paused for breath before adding, 'You'd best come inside and tell me everything. You will stay here, of course. I will have bedchambers prepared for you both.'

'There is something I need to tell you first,' said Bridget.

'Aye,' said Harry. 'Bridget and I are married, Lady Elizabeth.'

She stared at him and then beckoned Bridget forwards with a beringed hand. 'How did this come about?' she whispered.

'Perhaps we can tell you once we are inside, Lady Elizabeth,' said Harry, who had very good hearing. 'Bridget had a fall earlier and I deem she would be best sitting down.'

Her ladyship nodded and then glanced at Joshua. 'You have my gratitude and will not go unrewarded, but for now you are off duty.'

Joshua winked at Harry, who grabbed his arm and said, 'Return to the ship and bring our baggage. Leave the cradle where it is for now. Tell Hans I will give him his orders in the morning.'

Joshua nodded and hurried away.

Harry turned to face Lady Elizabeth. 'I hope you do not mind, but Joshua wishes to return to Appleby Manor with us.'

'I see you do not intend wasting time, setting your affairs in order. But come, first I would hear everything that has befallen you both, so do not dawdle,' said Lady Elizabeth, leading the way.

Bridget and Harry exchanged smiles and followed her into a parlour. Bridget could tell that her ladyship's honesty about her own disfigurement had had a profound effect on Harry for the better.

'You will not mind dining here?' asked Lady Elizabeth. 'It gets the sunlight at this time of day and is cosier and much easier for the servants.'

'Of course not,' said Harry easily. 'Whatever pleases you, Lady Elizabeth.'

She fixed him with a stare. 'I can see you have not lost the charm you possessed as a boy.'

Harry thanked her. Then he took Bridget's hand and led her to a cushioned settle and sat down beside her.

Lady Elizabeth rang a silver bell and in no time at all a manservant appeared. She gave him orders, including one to have a bedchamber prepared for her guests. Then she sat in a cushioned chair that was like a throne and wheezed, 'Now tell me how you found each other and where you were married? I want to know everything.'

Bridget glanced at her husband. 'I was washed up on the shore in Madeira and Harry found me.'

'I thought she was a mermaid at first because she swims like a fish,' he said. 'She jumped into the sea from a slave-trader's ship. I have never seen such courage.'

Bridget blushed. 'I am not the only one who has courage. You have, too.'

'A slave-trader's ship!' Lady Elizabeth shuddered.

Bridget realised her mistake. 'I should not have mentioned that but, as you see, I survived the ordeal intact.'

Harry gazed at her and realised she was trying to communicate to Lady Elizabeth that she had not been raped.

'I am glad to hear it, my dear,' said her ladyship, looking relieved.

'Perhaps we should leave the telling of our more perilous adventures to another time,' said Harry.

'I agree,' said her ladyship. 'Tell me about your wedding, instead.'

'We were married in Madeira,' said Harry, smiling into Bridget's eyes.

She was transfixed by his smile. Afterwards she wondered if she had been bewitched by it to say what she did. 'Aye, it was very romantic. The ceremony was in a chapel built over the graves of two lovers. One of them was English and the other French. They'd had to flee from the lady's tyrannical father, but instead of landing in Brittany, their ship was blown off course. That is also how the slaver's ship ended up exactly where I wanted it to be. Harry saved my life when he fished me from the sea. He could not have been more caring. I could so easily have died because I caught a disease and was covered in spots.'

'And Harry still chose to marry you. Well!' She beamed at Bridget. 'All's well that ends well. So where is your father?'

The light in Bridget's eyes died. 'We do not know where

my father is. It is possible that he arrived in Scotland after I left England in search of him and that he might have come to London.'

'What is his name? I have quite forgotten,' said Lady Elizabeth.

'Callum McDonald,' said Harry, adding helpfully, 'Red-haired with a weatherbeaten, freckled face.'

'I feel I have heard that name recently.' Her ladyship sighed. 'The Baron would know.'

'Where is the Baron?' asked Harry.

'He is staying here, but has gone out on business. It is possible that he is at your house in Cheap Side,' said Lady Elizabeth.

Harry glanced at Bridget.

'You wish to go and see if he is there for yourself?' she said.

'Aye.'

'Would you mind if I stayed here whilst you go?' asked Bridget.

'Of course not,' said Harry, taking her hand and squeezing it. 'It is probably best you rest after your fall.'

She agreed and did not tell him that her side still ached where it had hit the boat and that she felt a megrim coming on.

'You will excuse me, Lady Elizabeth?' asked Harry. 'But it is important that I see the Baron as soon as possible.'

'Of course, Harry. You go. Bridget and I will be happy here on our own.' She waved him away.

Harry kissed Bridget's cheek and left the room.

Chapter Eleven

As Harry approached the house in Cheap Side, he saw a flaxen-haired, strong-looking man standing in the doorway and immediately recognised the Baron. He was having a low-voiced discussion with another man whom Harry had never seen before. Their exchange came to an end and the Baron went inside before Harry could hail him. He hurried across the street and hammered on the door. There was a short delay before he heard footsteps approaching.

'Who is it?' called a voice.

'It's Harry.' He drew a deep breath. 'Harry Appleby.'

He heard a bolt being drawn and the door opened. His Swedish friend stared at him with a mixture of delight and incredulity in his blue eyes.

'God's Blood, it *is* you, Harry! I had almost given up hope of ever seeing you again. What the hell have you done to your face? That must have been some battle you were in.'

'It was,' said Harry grimly. 'I'll tell you all about it some time.'

'I look forward to hearing about.' Alex placed a hand on his shoulder and squeezed it. 'What were you thinking of, disappearing the way you did? If you knew the trouble you've caused us, you wouldn't have gone hiving off across the ocean.'

'I'm pleased to see you too,' said Harry drily. 'Can I come in, Alex?'

The Baron's lips twitched. 'It's *your* house, actually, although there are a few legal details to be sorted out before the deeds can be handed over to you.' He opened the door wide and his expression was sombre now. 'Do you know aught about Bridget McDonald? She went in search of you and her father.'

'Aye, I know,' said Harry. 'She found me, or should I say that I found her. Then we encountered Joshua in Lisbon.'

'God's Teeth!' Alex's fair eyebrows shot up and disappeared beneath his hair. 'That is wonderful news!'

'I'd say it was almost a miracle,' said Harry, smiling.

Alex seized his arm. 'Come in and you can tell me all about it. I must admit that when I sent Joshua chasing after Bridget, I had my doubts about his ever finding her. I was deeply concerned about her safety.'

'And you had need to be. She was sold into slavery.' Harry closed the door behind him and glanced about the entrance before allowing himself to be drawn further into the house. He said in a marvelling tone, 'It was a while before I could believe I had a name that truly belonged to me, never mind a business, a town house and a manor. This is all mine?'

'Aye, I can imagine how you would find it hard to believe,' said Alex. 'No doubt your feelings would equal Rosamund's when she discovered you were still alive. But if it were not for Bridget we would not have known where you went after you disappeared without a farewell. What about Bridget's father? Did he find Bridget?'

Harry flashed him a startled look. 'What do you mean by that? Callum never set sail for Madeira with me but set off alone across the northern ocean back to Scotland. We feared he was at the bottom of the northern ocean.'

'I know about that! The old reprobate was here in London. You'll never believe what he told me,' said Alex.

'You're telling me that he did survive the crossing!' Harry almost shouted the words.

'Aye! And that's not all he did. But first, come and have a drink,' said Alex, opening a door and showing him into a room. 'You've just missed the man I appointed to run the business in your stead, by the way. He's been lodging here. I thought it best not to leave the house empty.'

'Never mind him right now! Where's Callum?' demanded Harry.

'All in good time,' chuckled Alex. 'I'll get those drinks.'

Harry sat down on a plain wooden chair and drummed his fingers on the table. If Callum had returned to Scotland, he could see that he was going to have to chase after him and bring him back. At least Bridget was going to be happy that her father was alive. So was Harry, if the truth was known, because it meant that his ship was safe and he had an odd fondness for the old reprobate.

Alex entered, carrying two tankards of ale. He placed them on the table and sat opposite Harry and raised his tankard, 'To your good health, Harry, and future prosperity.'

Harry drank half the contents and then put down his tankard. 'How is my sister? Is she well?' he asked.

'Aye, she's carrying our second child, so I left her at Appleby Manor, rather than have her endure the long journey whilst she is suffering from morning sickness.'

Harry decided to keep quiet about Bridget's condition for the moment, but maybe he would have to leave her behind in London whilst he made the journey to Appleby Manor. 'Congratulations. I believe you already have a fine son.'

Alex grinned. 'Wait until you see your nephew. You'll be proud of him.'

'I am impatient to see them both,' said Harry gruffly, 'and I'll have more questions to ask you about them, but first tell me about Callum—and is my ship in one piece?'

Alex looked a little uncomfortable.

'What is wrong?' asked Harry immediately, who knew his friend well.

'Callum took the *Odin's Maiden* with him, Harry. I suppose he thought two ships were better than one.'

Harry scowled. 'What do you mean by that and where has the old pirate gone?'

'In search of Bridget. He sailed into London in his own ship, bringing yours, as well. He left the same way, no doubt believing that if he was going after pirates he would need plenty of men. He had hired a skeleton crew in Ireland and sailed for Scotland, believing he would find Bridget at his brother's castle. Instead he found his nephew who told him that his mother had died and his father had taken Bridget to London. Apparently the nephew is a mariner, too, so Callum put him in command of his ship whilst he remained in command of the *Odin's Maiden* and they both sailed into the Thames.'

Harry was astounded. 'He went to Ireland first?'

'Aye, he only *borrowed* your ship, so he said, having in mind to recover his own vessel and take back as much of his hoard from Patrick O'Malley that he could find.'

Harry downed the rest of the ale in his tankard and wiped his hand across his mouth. 'Why did I not think that he might have that in mind? He went on enough about his hoard and O'Malley.' The question was irrelevant because Harry had believed above all else that Callum's intention was to be reunited with Bridget. 'So Callum managed to get his ship back, but what about his treasure?'

'He enlisted some of Bridget's mother's kin and with their help, Callum took what was his with interest and set fire to O'Malley's ship.'

Harry let out a long low whistle before saying, 'If Callum ever reaches Madeira, he'll be better staying there. He could have the whole O'Malley clan after him.'

'He reckons they would not know it was him because they wouldn't be expecting him. Besides he says it was dark and he was in and out in no time.' Alex shook his head. 'I should have had the river authorities impound your ship until you could reclaim her, but I never expected him to leave so suddenly. His first reaction to the news that Bridget was a prisoner of pirates was to get drunk, but when he sobered up he wanted to know where she'd last been seen. Then he started blaming himself and saying he'd have to go and find you both.'

Harry swore. 'Bridget's here in London with me. I've left her at Lady Elizabeth's mansion. She slipped getting into the boat and hurt herself, so I thought it best to leave her behind.'

'I hope she is all right,' said Alex, looking concerned.

'She's strong, Alex,' Harry said with a hint of pride in his voice. 'She's had to be to survive what she's been through. I admire her courage as well as her beauty. This will come as a shock to you, but Bridget and I are married and we are expecting our first child.'

Alex slammed down his tankard. 'God's Teeth! How did you persuade her? She was mad as an angry bee with you for separating her from her father. It's not that she was—?'

'What? Raped by the slave trader and needed my good name? No, nothing like that, although I reckon there was a danger of it after the slave-trader's woman died of disease. That is when Bridget jumped into the sea and swam for shore despite how stormy it was.' Harry took a mouthful of ale.

'She did what? And what slave trader?'

Harry told him.

'I should have gone with them,' said Alex, frowning.

'Don't you start blaming yourself,' said Harry. 'Your presence very likely wouldn't have affected the outcome.' There was a silence and then he continued, 'Putting all this aside, I confess I received the shock of my life when I was told you were married to my sister. I thought you were mad for Ingrid or I wouldn't have left the way I did.'

'Ingrid is not the woman I believed her to be,' said Alex, his eyes clouding.

'So I have heard. I'd like to know what your experience of her ill doings are some time.'

Alex nodded. 'Your sister is worth ten thousand of her.' A smile tugged at the corners of his mouth. 'Rosamund is another such as Bridget. She has much courage and she is as lovely inside as she is out. We love each other dearly.'

Harry experienced a pang of envy. He wasn't certain what real love was, but had to admit that he would hate Bridget not to be part of his life now that he had found her once more. He cleared his throat. 'I'm glad you and Rosamund found each other and are happy.'

'I, too.' Alex stared at him. 'But tell me more about you and Bridget.'

Harry told him as much of the truth as he wanted Alex to know and then said, 'I can imagine what Bridget is going to say about her father.'

'As long as she doesn't expect you to go chasing after him all the way to Africa and Madeira.'

'No chance of that,' said Harry firmly. 'The next travelling I do will be to Appleby Manor.'

'On horseback or by ship?' asked Alex.

Harry hesitated. 'I haven't considered travelling there by ship, but where is the nearest port?'

'Preston. It is situated inland on the River Ribble that flows into the Irish Sea. You could anchor there and travel by horseback to Appleby Manor. But it would probably take longer than travelling from London on horseback because you would have to sail right round Land's End and up the coast of Wales.'

Harry rubbed his scar. 'How are you travelling?'

'By horse,' replied Alex, 'although one of my ships will be setting sail for Preston in a day or two. It'll be picking up a cargo there and then Rosamund and I will join her and sail to Scotland before returning to our house in Sweden.'

'When?' asked Harry, displeased to hear this news.

Alex sighed. 'I know how you must feel, Harry, about having such a short time with Rosamund before we have to leave, but we have spent little time in my own country since our wedding.'

'I understand that you have been tied up looking after my affairs and I am exceeding grateful,' said Harry. 'It is just that I am concerned about Bridget travelling by horseback in her condition. Perhaps I should leave her with Lady Elizabeth whilst she is still suffering the sickness and travel north with you.'

'You can't do that, Harry!' exclaimed Alex. 'I'll be leaving London tomorrow with Lady Elizabeth. I promised to escort her to Colleweston, the Countess of Richmond's mansion in Northamptonshire, on my way north. You have matters to attend to here and will need at least a few days to sort out the legal paperwork.'

Harry frowned. 'But if you and my sister are to depart for Scotland soon, then I cannot spare more than three days in London if I am to spend any time at all with her.'

'I agree. Besides, the sooner she knows that you and Bridget are both alive the better. It is not good for her to fret in her condition.' Alex rose to his feet and changed the subject. 'So what about *Thor's Hammer* and your seafaring life? I presume you are prepared to give it up?'

'If you'd asked me that two years ago, I'd have said never, but now my circumstances have changed, I must settle down.' Harry's dark brows knit. 'But what am I to do about my ship now I am a landowner? I am reluctant to part with the gift your grandfather gave me.'

'You'll be able to make use of her in your business still. What about Christian Larsson—surely you can promote him to master?'

'He is no longer a member of my crew.'

'What happened? Is he dead?'

'No. He is now working for you, Alex,' said Harry with a wry smile.

'Why?'

'He resented Bridget and was insubordinate. His replacement seems a reliable man. I think I can safely leave the *Hammer*—or the *St Bridget* as I renamed her—in his care,' said Harry. 'As for the *Odin's Maiden*…' he sighed '…I will have to leave her to her fate and pray God that Callum returns with her intact.'

Alex nodded. 'Now shall we return to Lady Elizabeth's? I would like to see Bridget and tell her how glad I am to see her safely back and to congratulate her.'

Harry agreed, thinking that he was not looking forward to telling his wife about what her father had been up to in Ireland.

Alex said, 'I'll take you to meet your father's lawyer and your man of business before this day is out. In the meantime, can you tell me how you came by that scar?' he added, opening the front door.

Harry thought with a sinking heart how his scar could never be ignored, even by his dearest friend, but he set aside such a depressing thought and began to tell Alex about his adventures. They were still deep in conversation when they came to the gates of Lady Elizabeth's mansion.

Bridget had given up watching out for Harry as soon as she spotted Joshua trundling a cart towards the house. She had a niggling pain in her belly, but dismissed it as of no importance and was about to go outside when Lady Elizabeth bumbled into the parlour.

'So I didn't imagine you were here,' she said, beaming at her. 'And Harry Appleby, where has he gone?' She gazed about as if expecting him to suddenly pop out from behind the settle.

'To visit his house in Cheap Side. I was just on my way outside. I have noticed that Joshua has arrived with our baggage. Will you excuse me?'

'Certainly, my dear,' said Lady Elizabeth, settling herself in her chair. 'You'll want to go upstairs and unpack. I'll have one of the maids to show you the way.' She reached for the bell and a maid came running.

In no time at all the cart had been emptied and Bridget and Joshua were following the girl upstairs. She opened the door on to a bedchamber that was luxurious by any standards. Bridget took a deep satisfying breath and went inside, followed by Joshua. She wasted no time unpacking, trying to ignore the fact that the niggling pain in her side had become a positive bellyache. She undressed, washed her face and hands and donned her robe, thinking to have a rest on the bed. But first she went over to the window, hoping to see Harry coming back to her.

Her heart lifted as she set eyes on his familiar, well-built figure walking up the drive. She saw that he was not alone, but accompanied by the Baron. She wondered what he had told his old friend about their marriage and the baby. She was about to go downstairs when she felt suddenly wet underneath. With a sudden sense of doom, she unfastened her robe and saw a trickle of blood running down her leg. Her heart began to bang with fright as she realised what was happening.

Blindly she reached for the door handle, but then draw back her hand. She couldn't go rushing for help, trailing blood all over the place. She remembered the bindings she had purchased in Lisbon and where she had put them. Having recovered them from the chest, along with the belt to tie the ends to, she bound herself up.

The tears were rolling down her cheeks as with shaking hands she removed her bloodied robe and donned a clean shift. Only then did she place a drying cloth on the bed and lay down. She could not stop crying. How big would her baby be? Only a tiny creature. No one could even tell if they looked at her that she had been carrying it. *Had!* Was she really miscarrying, then? She did not want to believe that was happening. She prayed that by lying down the blood would tail off and her child would be saved, but the pains in her belly were growing stronger and she groaned as they intensified.

There was a knock on the door and it opened and Harry stood there. 'How are you feeling?' he asked. She pushed herself into a sitting position and could do no more than stare at him. 'You've been crying,' he said, hurrying over to her.

'What is wrong? You look as if you are in pain. Do you have a megrim?'

'I—I—I deem I am miscarrying the baby!' A sob burst in her throat. 'See the blood on my robe.'

'What! Oh, dear God!' Harry had not expected this and was shocked to the core. Bridget was strong. She had endured so much. How could she be losing their child?

She clutched his sleeve. 'God must have decided that we don't deserve to have a baby.'

'Nonsense,' said Harry, feeling sick inside. 'You must be mistaken.'

'About what?' she cried. 'God's intentions or about my miscarrying the baby?'

'I suppose I mean both. What should I do?' he demanded, running a hand through his hair. 'Should I ask Lady Elizabeth to send for a midwife or a physician?'

'I don't know.' Another sob burst from her.

'Don't cry!' said Harry, unable to bear to see her in tears. If she were to die—! He did not know where the thought came from because it was not as if she had gone full term and was giving birth. He felt a chill run down his spine. 'I'll speak to Lady Elizabeth, she's a woman.'

Bridget tried to pull herself together. 'Aye, and no fool. She has had no children of her own, but she will know what to do.' She gazed up at her husband from tear-drenched eyes. 'Oh, Harry, hold me for a moment!'

Harry hesitated, deeming he should fetch help, but there was such sadness in his wife's face that he could not deny her. He put his arms around her and rocked her, resting his damaged cheek on her hair. 'It will be all right,' he said.

Bridget could only cling to him and cry against his shoulder. He could feel tears in his own eyes and knew he had to be strong and leave this bedchamber and fetch help. 'If I let you go, you'll be all right, won't you?' he said huskily.

She nodded, but a sob caught in her throat as she let him go. He kissed her quickly and almost ran out of the room. He raced downstairs with his heart thudding in his chest. Only for a moment when he gazed down at Lady Elizabeth with her ridiculous wig and pock-marked face did he wonder how he was going to put into words the tragedy that was taking place upstairs.

'Something is wrong, isn't it, Harry? Tell me!' she demanded.

He told her.

She wasted no time in ringing for a servant and sending him to fetch her physician and a woman she knew of good repute. Only then did she ask Harry to help her upstairs as she wished to see Bridget for herself. She told him to make haste and he complied with her wishes.

As soon as her ladyship set eyes on Bridget, she told Harry to leave them alone together. Reluctantly he did so and went in search of Alex with a heavy heart.

'I am so sorry, Harry,' said his friend, putting an arm about his shoulders. 'But perhaps if Bridget rests, the bleeding will stop and the baby will be saved.'

Harry was silent. Bridget's tears had convinced him that the baby could not be saved. What if he was to lose her as well? He felt helpless in the face of what was happening and could only pray that she would not die, too. At the moment that was all he could do for her.

Harry sat at Bridget's bedside, gazing down at her slumbering pale face. He remembered how he had felt when she had been ill in Madeira and he had watched over her. Fortunately she had recovered and he had to believe she would do so now.

Both the physician and the midwife had tried to reassure him by telling him that she should be up and about in a few days' time, but until then she should rest as much as possible.

The midwife had told him that it was not unusual for a woman to miscarry a first child in the early months and that there was no reason why they should not have another child. Her words were of some comfort to Harry because he had begun to worry that not only might Bridget not be able to conceive again, but that he was to blame for the miscarriage. He remembered her slipping and hitting the side of the boat. If he'd had a firmer grip on her that would not have happened. He was convinced that the fall had caused Bridget to lose their baby.

Bridget suddenly opened her eyes and gazed up at Harry. 'You're still here,' she murmured.

'Aye.' He took her hand and squeezed it. 'How do you feel?'

'As if I have been kicked by a horse,' she murmured. 'The physician gave me some poppy juice to help with the pain, so I am still a little sleepy. I am sorry I lost your baby.' Tears filled her eyes.

'It is not your fault,' said Harry hastily, needing her to be the strong Bridget—the one who had jumped into the sea and showed such courage. 'The midwife assures me that there can be other babies,' he continued. 'But for now I will ask Lady Elizabeth for the use of another guest chamber, so as not to disturb you. You need to rest if you are to make a swift recovery.'

She did not want him to leave her, but could see the sense in his words knowing that he wanted to go to Appleby Manor as soon as he could. 'If that is what you wish. I regret that I will not be able to travel for a few days, but if you wish to go to Lancashire without me, then—'

'Shall we wait and see how you fare?' interrupted Harry. 'I have business to do in London that will take a couple of days and I need to purchase horses and what is necessary for the journey. I would prefer not to leave you behind.'

Reassured by his words, Bridget drifted into sleep. Harry remained there a while longer, just gazing down at her, thinking that some time soon he was going to have to tell her about Callum and worried about how she would take the news.

He went downstairs and found Alex and Lady Elizabeth in her parlour, conversing together. They looked up as he entered the room. 'How is dear Bridget now?' asked her ladyship.

'She is sleeping,' said Harry.

'Sit down, dear boy,' bid Lady Elizabeth. 'You look exhausted.'

'Well, that is not for any work I have done,' he said with a wry smile, seating himself on the settle. 'It is oddly tiring just sitting and waiting and worrying.'

'Your priority at the moment is Bridget, so Lady Elizabeth and I have decided to postpone our departure and will leave the day after next. Tomorrow, if Bridget's condition is improved, I will take you to meet your man of business and your father's lawyer.'

Harry thanked him.

'Also, dear boy, you may stay here as long as you consider it necessary,' said Lady Elizabeth. 'Treat my home as you would your own.'

Harry thought about how he and Bridget had never had a proper home of their own. 'Thank you, Lady Elizabeth, your offer is much appreciated. I fear the house in Cheap Side is a gloomy place and in need of renovation.' He grimaced. 'Besides, I would not wish to uproot my man of business. After all, at least for the summer, I do intend to make our home at Appleby Manor.'

'You will find much to keep you occupied there,' said Alex, 'although you will probably need to spend some time in London before autumn.'

Harry agreed, although he was hoping that would be unnecessary and he could leave the bulk of the business in his man's hands. If Alex had chosen him then surely he could be trusted until then. He did not wish to leave Bridget alone in an unfamiliar house when there was much that she had to learn, too. He remembered the moment she had told him that she thought she was with child. He felt so sad that they had lost this baby that had helped bring them together again and set aside their hurt and anger. He had so looked forward to the three of them being a family.

Chapter Twelve

The following day Harry and Bridget were sharing breakfast on a tray in her bedchamber. She was looking more herself, but was still pale and there was a sadness in her face that made his heart ache. He insisted that she stay in bed at least for another day.

'I will do as you say, Harry, but you do not have to stay with me all the time. Go and have some fresh air.'

'I will. I shall go now and walk in the garden and then I will back for a while because I will be going out later with Alex on business.' He smiled down at her. 'Is there aught I can get you before I go?'

'If you could ask if I could have some hot water?'

He nodded and went downstairs and relayed Bridget's request to one of the maids. Then he went out into the garden. The gardener was already up and about and impulsively Harry asked whether there were any roses in bloom.

'Aye, there are some early ones,' replied the gnarled old man, gazing at him intently. 'Is it that yer wanting them for Mistress Bridget?'

Harry nodded and resisted the temptation to cover his scar with his hand. 'Indeed, I do.'

'I'll cut some for her while yer have a stroll round the

garden. I'll have them ready for yer when yer get back here.'

Harry thanked him and continued his promenade, thinking that if Bridget's condition improved even more by the morrow, then he would begin to make arrangements for them to travel to Appleby Manor. He would also have to make time today to visit his ship, and that reminded him that he must tell Bridget about her father. He had very mixed feelings about doing so because he did not want her to get all tearful again.

He collected the roses from the gardener on his return, had one of the maids place them in water in a vase, then he carried them upstairs.

'Good morning again, Bridget,' he said, slightly anxious because she was worrying her lower lip with her teeth.

She lifted her gaze and smiled hesitantly. 'What have you there? Did you enjoy your walk around the garden?'

He placed the bowl of roses on the table by the bedside. 'The gardener allowed me to have these for you.'

She touched one of the velvety dark pink petals and sniffed the flower's heart. 'How—how beautiful they are, and so different from the blossoms you plucked for me when we were in Madeira.' Her eyes were shiny with unshed tears.

'Please, Bridget, don't cry,' he pleaded. 'Or I will never bring you flowers again,' he teased, sitting down on the bed and taking hold of her hand.

A small laugh escaped her. 'You are too kind, Harry. I love you bringing me flowers.'

I wish you could love me. The thought seemed to come out of nowhere and he forgot what he was about to say. Then he collected himself together. 'They're only a few roses from her ladyship's garden,' he said casually. 'Wait until you're gathering armfuls from our own garden.'

'I would like that,' she said softly. 'I have never had a garden of my own and no one has ever given me flowers before but you.'

'No? I admit that I've never given flowers to anyone else but you,' said Harry, toying with her fingers.

She clung to his hand and blurted out, 'Harry, I am worrying that there might not be another child. I was an only child. My father would have liked a son but—what if I cannot conceive again?'

Harry felt a peculiar sinking feeling in the pit of his stomach. 'You conceived the baby we lost quickly enough. I don't see why it shouldn't happen again. Besides, Callum was at sea for long stretches of time. It is possible that is one of the reasons he and your mother didn't have any more children. I am giving up the sea so there will be opportunity enough for us to—' He wanted to say make love but the words wouldn't come.

It seemed it was not necessary for him to say them aloud because her colour was suddenly heightened. 'I am glad you will not have to battle with such storms as we have experienced at sea.'

He agreed.

Then they both fell silent.

Harry knew the moment had come when he had to tell her about Callum. 'Bridget, I have some tidings about your father—and before you think the worst,' he added swiftly, 'he is not dead. At least—'

'Where is he?' asked Bridget.

'He's gone in search of you. Alex told me that he came here with his own ship and *Odin's Maiden*.'

Bridget felt quite light-headed. 'With his *own* ship! I don't understand. How did he get it back?'

'Think, Bridget,' said Harry gently. 'I have lost count of

how many times Callum told me the story of Patrick O'Malley stealing his ship and you both narrowly escaping death. Over and over he spoke of having his revenge. I did not give it serious thought until Alex told me that your father used *Odin's Maiden* to strike at O'Malley and get back his ship. He waited until nightfall and took back all that was his and extra. Then he set fire to O'Malley's ship.'

Bridget was dumbfounded and for several moments she could only stare at Harry. Then she found her voice. 'How *could* he?'

'You mean how did he get away with it or why didn't he go to you first and tell you of his plans? You must have still been in this country when he was busy doing that. If he'd come to find you first, you'd never have left on your voyage to try to find him,' Harry pointed out.

'I know why he didn't come to me first! He knew I'd most likely try to persuade him not to take such a risk. No doubt he bribed your men to crew *Odin's Maiden* for him with promises of a reward if they helped him regain his treasure,' she said waspishly.

'I did always wonder how he persuaded them.'

'I wager he had been drinking when he attacked the ship,' said Bridget.

Harry said, 'Highly unlikely. He'd need a clear head to achieve what he did.'

She was silent for a long time and then, with eyes glinting, said, 'How dare he have me worrying all this time! If he had come straight home to me, I would never have gone in search of him. I would never have been taken by pirates and captured by that filthy slave trader! You would not have asked me to marry you because I was penniless and in need of a protector and I would never have miscarried,' she said bitterly.

'Are you regretting our marriage?' asked Harry bluntly.

'I was thinking of it from your point of view. I really didn't marry you because I knew you were Harry Appleby, you know. I did so because you suggested it and provided me with a way out of my predicament. I just wish I had my father in front of me now. I'd tell him what I thought of him.'

Harry scowled. 'If I had him here right now, then I would shake him like a dog would a rat and make him grovel and beg your forgiveness for the inconvenience and suffering he has put you through. As it is I do not know what you expect me to do about him, but I—'

Bridget looked taken aback. 'I expect you to do *nothing*, Harry! You have your own affairs to tend to and so I can only wait and see if he returns. It could be that he will lose his life in another battle with pirates or in Africa and I will never see him again. As for his treasure, that will be gone for good, unless he has put it somewhere safe this time.'

'Let us try to not be pessimistic, Bridget. He is likely to anchor at Lisbon for fresh water and supplies. It is possible that he will ask for information about both of us and someone will inform him that we left for England.'

'But he mightn't get that information and then he'll sail for Africa and—' She shrugged, feeling angry and helpless in the light of her father's latest venture.

'Let us not waste time worrying about what might or might not happen to him. We have been through all this before where he is concerned.' He reached out and drew her close to him.

She sighed and closed her eyes, wanting nothing more than to rest in his arms, but the moment did not last because after a short while he released her. 'I must leave you and go with Alex,' said Harry, getting to his feet. 'Is there anything you wish me to bring you?'

Bridget shook her head. 'I only need to know when you plan to leave London. If you feel you must go sooner, then I could stay here and follow you on. Perhaps you could leave Joshua and he could accompany me.'

He stared at her, wondering why the sudden change of heart. Yesterday she had not wished him to leave without her. It had to be because of what he had told her about her father. Surely she wouldn't be foolish enough to wait until he was out of the way and then set out in search of her father?

'I need Joshua with me, and what kind of husband would I be if I were to leave you after the trauma you have suffered?' he said firmly, not giving her time to consider answering that question, but leaving her to ponder on what he'd said.

Bridget thought about Harry's parting words for several moments before she pushed back the bedcovers and slid her legs out of the bed. She stood up, only to discover that not only was she all a-tremble, but she felt a rush of menstrual blood. She resigned herself to having to change her bindings and remaining there in the bedchamber for at least another day.

Weak tears filled her eyes. She was foolish to have even considered for a moment staying here in the hope of her father returning in the following week or so. There was much she wanted to say to him, but not in Harry's company. Her husband had been very forbearing when he had told her about the latest episode in her father's adventurous life. He had not even hinted that his own ship could have been blown out of the water by Patrick O'Malley if the raid had gone wrong. She wanted some of her father's hoard to give to Harry as a dowry—he deserved it. If she could do that, she would feel much happier. Harry might have deceived her before marrying her, but she had not lost by it and she wanted them to be on a more equal footing. Perhaps it would not matter so much if she had not miscarried her precious baby. Tears threatened again, but she blinked them back.

Bridget was sitting by the bedchamber window in her night rail, gazing out as the daylight faded. Stars were twinkling on in the sky and the fragrance of roses perfumed the air. A dog barked in the distance, but otherwise all was still and quiet. Then she heard the door open behind her. She turned her head and looked at her husband. 'You've been a long time.'

Harry gazed across the bedchamber to where he could make out Bridget's shapely silhouette by the light of the dying sun and yearned to make love to her. 'Shouldn't you be in bed?'

'I have not been up long and have only sat here, gazing out of the window and thinking of all that has happened since I last saw my father.'

'There are things you would change, of course?'

'Naturally.'

He waited, but she said no more, and he wondered if one of them would be his shaving off his beard before they had taken their marriage vows. Involuntarily he touched his scar and then dropped his hand. 'I have spoken to my man of business and intend to introduce him to Hans on the morrow. If you feel strong enough, do you wish to go into the city and purchase a new robe and aught else you might need?'

'I do not like taking your money,' said Bridget, walking carefully over to the other side of the bed to Harry and sitting down. 'I have been thinking that my father must have gone to Scotland before he came to London as he would have not known I was here. He might have left some of his hoard up there.'

'Perhaps, but let's not talk of your father's money,' said

Harry. 'I just came in to see how you fared and to let you know I have seen the lawyer.'

'No doubt the lawyer was surprised to see you?'

'Aye. Documents are being drawn up even now and will be copied during the night. As Alex will be leaving London in the morning and is unlikely to return for several months, it was decided that the business of signing everything over to me would be dealt with straight away.'

'That is good news,' said Bridget.

'Aye, but now you must get back in bed as the days ahead will be wearisome.'

'You will still sleep in the other bedchamber?' asked Bridget, barely able to distinguish his features.

'If that is what you prefer. I would like to stay in case you need me during the night.'

'Then you must stay,' said Bridget, climbing into bed.

His decision pleased her because, despite her ladyship coming to sit with her for part of the day, she had felt bereft, unable to stop thinking not only of the baby but of Harry being absent for hours. On board ship she had been so accustomed to his being in close proximity, even when they were not speaking and angry with each other.

He climbed into bed clad in a nightshirt. Her leg brushed his and he rolled over, giving her space. Bridget would have appreciated his cuddling her because suddenly she felt low spirited and the ready tears pricked the back of her eyes.

She had no idea how long she lay there before stretching out a hand to touch him. When he did not react, she slid her hand further around his body. A fingernail caught on one of the curls on his chest and she had difficulty freeing it. She drew herself closer to him and slid her other arm around him so she could free her fingernail. It was when she was withdrawing her arms that she felt the scars on his back and remembered his mention of being whipped on the pirate ship. She pressed her lips against his back, believing him to be asleep. Then she closed her eyes and drifted into slumber.

Harry wondered if he had imagined that light caress on his back. But if he had not, what was he to make of his wife's behaviour? A faint smile played about his lips as he closed his eyes.

The bedchamber was filled with light when Bridget woke to find herself alone in the bed. She sat up and realised that physically she was feeling much better. She could smell Harry's roses and sat up and looked for him. Then she saw him, clad only in a drying cloth slung about his hips, gazing out of the window. She could not take her eyes from the way the sun played on his skin, so that it seemed to glow, and thought what a fine body he had.

She cleared her throat. 'Good morning, Harry.'

He turned and his gaze rested a moment on her bare shoulder where her night rail had slipped down. 'Good morning, Bridget. You sound better today.' He reached for his shirt. 'I beg pardon, but I cannot linger. Alex and Lady Elizabeth are leaving today and I want to wish them Godspeed.'

Immediately Bridget said, 'Then I must also do so. If you would be so kind as to wait until I am dressed.'

His brow puckered. 'Are you certain you feel well enough to go downstairs?'

'If I do not try, I will not know. You will wait for me?'

'Of course I will wait for you.' He paused before saying, ' I have decided you must have a personal maid now we have a position to maintain.'

'Could that not wait until we arrived at Appleby Manor?' she asked, startled.

'No. It is best you have a female with you in the circumstances.'

'If that is what you wish.'

She climbed out of bed and for an instant she swayed. Harry was there in a moment to steady her. 'Are you certain that you are well enough to go downstairs?' He frowned.

Bridget was touched by his concern and was glad to rest against his chest for a moment. 'Aye, I am sure I only felt odd for a moment because I stood up so suddenly. If you could fetch me the scarlet gown and cream shift from the armoire, that would be of help.'

Harry removed his arm from about her waist and she placed her hand on the bedpost and watched him carry out her request. What did it matter if her father had disappointed her? She had a husband who was proving himself far more worthy and who was prepared to fetch and carry for her and who had brought her flowers.

'See,' said Harry, placing the garments on the bed, 'you do need a maid. Do you wish me to help you dress?'

'I—I deem I can manage,' she said, remembering she would need to change her bindings. 'If—if you could turn your back?'

Harry turned away and finished dressing himself.

'I would appreciate your arm, Harry,' she said a short while later.

He turned and the breath caught in his throat. 'That is an unusual gown and suits you admirably.'

She blushed and thanked him, holding out a hand to him. He opened the door before sweeping her off her feet and carrying her out of the bedchamber. She would have protested, but from previous experience guessed she would be wasting her time, so, placing her arms around his neck, she allowed him to carry her downstairs. Yet when they reached the bottom, she requested that he set her on her feet. 'I do not want her ladyship thinking that I am not fit for her to leave and delay her journey again.'

'I hope to see you at Appleby in ten days' time if the weather stays fine,' said Alex, embracing his brother-in-law.

Harry returned his hug and then they drew apart. He would have been happier travelling north with the Baron, keeping them company as there was safety in numbers. Yet his worst fears were not that they would be attacked by footpads or be delayed by bad roads, but rather that Bridget might find the journey arduous and fall ill and that his sister would take one look at his scarred face and be repulsed by him.

Alex turned to Bridget and kissed her on the cheek. 'I cannot wait to see Rosamund's face when she sees the two of you together. It will be a blessing to her that she will not be leaving her brother all alone at Appleby when we depart for Scotland.'

'But we will see each other again?' said Bridget anxiously. 'I know that Sweden is far away, but you will visit England often?'

'As often as we are able and you must visit us, too.'

'Come, Baron, we must be on our way,' interrupted Lady Elizabeth, touching his arm. 'I wish that I could accompany all of you to Appleby, but my old bones and this chest of mine cannot cope with such a long journey on the road. You must take care that you do not overtire Bridget, my dear boy,' she said, holding her cheek up for his kiss. 'I look forward to a happier outcome for you both in the future.'

He kissed her and then she and Bridget exchanged kisses before her ladyship accepted the assistance of both men into her carriage. Alex would be riding alongside the vehicle with another four outriders.

Bridget and Harry waved until they were out of sight before going back inside the house. He suggested that she sit inside her ladyship's parlour whilst he went to have a word with her ladyship's housekeeper, Mistress Tyler, about hiring a young, respectable and reliable girl who would be willing to travel with them to Lancashire.

'I will make enquiries for you, Master Appleby,' she replied, 'but I must warn you that there are some, I know, who'd like the position, but who would be alarmed at travelling to northern parts, believing folk up there to be no better than savages.'

'Just do your best, mistress, and I will make it worth your while,' said Harry. 'Tell the one you choose that I will pay her well. If she finds after we arrive there that she is not happy, then we will hire a local lass so she can return to London.'

'Now that is a generous offer, Master Appleby, and should make my task easier,' said the housekeeper, her eyes alight.

'Then waste no time and go to it.' Harry went to tell Bridget what he had done.

She was warmed by his thoughtfulness. 'I was wondering, Harry, if when we reach Appleby it will stir memories of your boyhood?'

'I, too, have thought of that. In the past I often asked myself how is it that I have not forgotten how to put on my shoes or to remember how to string words together that make sense, but could not remember my own name and scarcely anything about my family?'

'At least you now know the truth about yourself and how you came to be on that pirate ship,' said Bridget, hesitating before adding, 'I hope you can forgive me for not telling you sooner about your being Harry Appleby?'

'Let us forget the past,' he said. 'I know now who I am and just wish that the seas could be rid of pirates. They are a scourge.' He thought how there would be no peace whilst so many men believed it was their right to raid ships that traded in their waters. He only hoped that Callum's luck would not run out and that he would return safely. It would do Bridget no good at all if after more days and weeks or even months of worry about her father, he did not return.

Mistress Tyler was as good as her word and later that morning informed Harry that she had found a girl whom she thought might be suitable for his purpose, although she hadn't had much experience, but she was willing to go north. Was it possible for him to see her now? He agreed and, as Bridget was present, suggested that she stay whilst he interviewed the girl in case she should have questions that she would like to ask her.

Shortly after the housekeeper returned with a maiden of perhaps some twelve summers, whom the woman informed them was an orphan. Once the door closed behind the housekeeper, both Harry and Bridget turned their attention to the girl. She was slight of build with a slender face that would have been pretty if her nose had not been broken at some time, as it gave her a belligerent look.

Yet when Harry asked her name, she answered in a voice that belied that impression, for it was soft and hesitant. 'My name is Dorcas Saddler, Master Appleby.'

'Mistress Tyler has explained to you what this position involves?' Harry asked.

'Aye, sir.'

'And you have no qualms about travelling north with us?' asked Harry.

'I wouldn't say that, sir, but it can't be any worse than the life I'll be leaving behind. I'll be glad to get away, to tell you the truth.'

'Your last employer treated you roughly?'

'No, it was me father who did this to me.' She touched her nose. 'But he got killed in a brawl last Monday when the landlord gave us notice to quit. If it hadn't been for ol' Tyler I'd have been living on the streets.'

'Your mother is dead, then?' asked Bridget.

'Aye, she's well gone and deserves to be with the angels for all she suffered from me father.' Her eyes filled with tears and she sniffed and wiped her face with the back of her hand.

'Then this job must appear fortuitous to you,' said Bridget, pitying the girl.

Dorcas stared at her. 'What's that mean, mistress?'

'That this job is just what you need,' said Harry.

The girl's face lit up. 'Aye, it's that all right. I'm all alone in the world now. Me brothers ran away because me father was beating them up and I don't blame them, although I wish they'd taken me with them.'

Bridget was filled with pity for the girl. She might have had little experience of being a lady's maid, but she could train her to do all that she would need of her. Besides, she needed a home and looking after herself. She darted a look at her husband. 'I think Dorcas will suit us, Harry.'

Harry thought he knew what was going on in his wife's head. In the short time she had been with child, her maternal instincts had been roused and taking this girl under her wing could go some way in helping her recover from her loss.

'As you wish, but you must make certain that Dorcas has all that is necessary for the journey. No doubt she will need another set of clothes and a pair of shoes.'

Bridget's eyes brightened. 'I know of a used-clothes dealer, not far from St Paul's Cathedral. We will pay them a visit.'

The girl beamed at her. 'I know the place. Yer talking about

Walther and Maud's place. Yer can have no notion of just how grateful I am to yer both for giving me this position.'

Bridget smiled, remembering how she had been feeling quite desperate when Harry had proposed marriage. 'When we reach Appleby Manor, then we will see about having new clothes made for you. That is, of course, if you do not change your mind about staying in Lancashire.'

'Those barbarians can't be any worse than me father,' said Dorcas stoutly. 'And it's an adventure, isn't it, Mistress Appleby? I've never set foot outside of London in me life, so I'm really looking forward to it.'

'Good,' said Bridget, delighted. 'And we can be thankful, Dorcas, that we are making the journey whilst the days are long, the weather is clement and the countryside looks its best.'

Chapter Thirteen

Not long after, Harry accompanied his wife and Dorcas to the used-clothes dealers. He had used their services in the past when he had needed a disguise for his undercover work with the Baron. They were delighted to see the newly married couple and Harry conversed with Walther for a short while before leaving his wife and Dorcas in their capable hands and going off towards Cheap Side.

Maud produced suitable clothing for Dorcas and Bridget sat on a chair provided and was glad to partake of a cup of Maud's homemade mead and a bun. She found pleasure in watching the expression on the girl's face as she tried on different items. For once she did not worry about spending Harry's money and even bought herself a cloak, a robe, a gown, a hat and gloves of fine quality.

After leaving the shop they made their way to the shoe-makers' row where they were able to buy ready-made shoes for Dorcas. Then Bridget decided there were several other purchases she wished to make for the journey, so they hired a lad to carry all that they had bought back to the house.

By then Bridget was feeling tired, so she lay on her bed and told Dorcas to put away the items they had bought and discussed what she expected of her. Afterwards they had a light meal. Then Bridget decided to sit in the garden and have Dorcas keep her company whilst the girl shortened the hem of the gown Bridget had purchased. She wondered how much longer Harry would be out and hoped he would not be late.

Harry had gone down to the Thames with his man of business, having sent a messenger to arrange with his second-in-command, Hans, to meet them at a local tavern. They had discussed those customers who remembered Sir James and would be willing to do business with his son. They had talked about luxury goods and how his father had had dealings with the wool merchants in Preston and debated whether to rekindle that line of business.

When the meeting was over, the three men parted company. Harry was about to visit his lawyer when a once-familiar voice stopped him in his tracks. 'So you have returned, Harry.'

He whirled round and stared at the woman standing in the shadows. His eyes narrowed. 'What are you doing here, Ingrid? You're taking a risk, aren't you?'

She responded with a tinkle of laughter. 'I am flattered you recognised me so easily despite my disguise. Now I am known as Sister Birgetta,' she said, dancing out of the alley next to the tavern into the light and within a couple of feet of him. Instantly she started back. 'I was told about your disfigurement, but I did not expect it to be so ugly,' she gasped. 'Master Larsson was right. You are not the man you used to be.'

The muscles of Harry's face tightened. 'You should have stayed in the convent, Ingrid. Then you might not have turned out so cruel, murderous and treacherous.'

She fixed him with cold pale blue eyes. 'I see you have

been discussing me with that conniving, crafty Scottish witch you married. No doubt she tricked you into it, but now you know who you are, Harry, you must realise your mistake?'

'Don't refer to my wife so rudely,' said Harry in a dangerously low voice. 'If you think because you are dressed as a religious that I won't treat you as you deserve for that insult, then it is *you* who are mistaken.'

Ingrid laughed. 'Why so angry, Harry? Is it because you know I am speaking the truth? I'm surprised at you for allowing yourself to be fooled into marrying a thieving pirate's daughter. But perhaps it was because Bridget told you that she could lead you to her father's treasure. You can't trust her, Harry.'

'You're the person I cannot trust,' said Harry, seizing Ingrid by the front of her white habit and lifting her off her feet. 'Another remark like that and I'll throw you in the river. What are you doing snooping around here, anyway? You should have more care for your life, Ingrid. You should be punished for your actions, especially your involvement in my sister's abduction.'

'Bridget speaks falsely! I order you to put me down,' screamed Ingrid, clawing at his hand.

'And if I don't? What will you do?' He raised her higher in the air.

Her screams now began to draw attention to them, but Harry ignored those who were watching. She cursed him and Bridget in her own tongue and Harry decided enough was enough. He carried her over to the edge of the quayside. 'Do you really want me to put you down, Ingrid?'

Fear caused her face to twitch. 'You wouldn't, Harry. Remember the good times we had when we were younger. You loved me then.'

'What I felt for you was not love, but the foolish longings of a youth.'

'I don't believe you!' She spat in his face.

He noticed that there were a couple of men tending their nets on the shore not far away, so he opened his hand and released her. She seemed to float in the air for several moments and then she landed in a patch of mud a few feet beneath with a splat. She scrabbled to gain a foothold and her white habit swiftly became smeared with filth. Obscenities streamed from her mouth. Harry saw that the two men had paused in their task and were now watching Ingrid's struggles.

'God's Blood, captain, yer've done it now,' said Joe, appearing at his shoulder. 'She'll be putting a spell on yer next. I heard from a lad I know who works in one of the taverns that she talks to some right unsavoury characters.'

Harry wiped his face on his sleeve and turned round. 'You recognise her, Joe?'

'Aye, Captain. She's Ingrid Wrangel who yer were friendly with once. I saw her talking to Master Larsson early this morning.'

Harry frowned. 'Where is the Baron's ship anchored? I would speak with Christian myself.'

'She's already set sail for Preston, Captain.'

'Do you know if Master Larsson was aboard?'

'I couldn't say. Do yer want me to keep an eye on the so-called nun down there? I wouldn't like her to cause yer trouble. According to Josh, she was hand in glove with one of those hard-up lords whose father was killed at Bosworth. They stole her ladyship's jewellery box from her mansion, yer know. The lord then went and got himself killed in an attack with several ruffians on a party of pilgrims.'

Joe's words gave Harry cause for serious thought. 'Aye, Joe. You do that for me. I must speak with Hans again and tell him that I want him to set sail for Preston as soon as possible. He might even catch up with Alex's ship that's heading that way.'

'So what will you be doing, Captain?'

'I want to get my wife away from London. Who knows what Ingrid might have been plotting? After I have spoken to Hans and seen my lawyer, I will return to Lady Elizabeth's mansion, and Josh and I will make ready the horses. I would like to set out for Appleby Manor early this evening. We will travel only as far as that inn we stayed at in St Albans a few years ago. A horse will be left for you if you are not back by then. Follow us as soon as you are able and meet up with us there.'

'I remember the inn,' said Joe, his eyes bright with excitement.

'Good. Keep your head low and I will see you later.'

'Aye, aye, Captain.' Joe saluted.

Harry clapped him on the shoulder and strode away.

'How are you feeling, Bridget?' asked Harry.

Bridget looked up into her husband's face and instantly rose from the garden seat. 'What has happened?'

'Naught for you to fret about,' he said easily. 'I have decided that I would like to spend a little more time in my sister's company, so we should set out early this evening. That way you will be on horseback only for a short time and I have bought a pillion seat for you. You will be able to rest at the inn in St Albans. Do you feel well enough to agree to that plan, Bridget?'

Bridget hesitated, wondering if he was being completely honest with her about his reason for setting out this evening. She knew him well enough now to know when he was keeping something from her. Still, she decided not to waste time asking him again. Instead, she said, 'It sounds a sensible plan. I shall have Dorcas help me to pack our belongings.'

'Good!' He looked relieved and wasted no time in hurrying to the stables.

Bridget turned to Dorcas, but the girl was already on her feet and it was obvious that she had overheard Harry's words. They wasted no time going inside the house. It took them scarcely any time at all to pack their belongings, but it was only at the last moment that Bridget remembered her husband's shaving gear. She pushed it down the side of the leather bag.

Dorcas carried the larger bag downstairs and dumped it outside the front of the house, and Bridget followed with a smaller bag. Already Joshua had brought round one of the horses and he began the task of tying the baggage on to the beast.

Mistress Tyler came outside to see what was happening. Bridget explained to her about Harry's reason for them leaving that evening. She suggested that although they should be able to have supper at the inn, that they should take some bread, cheese and cold meats, as well as a flagon of ale, just in case they couldn't. 'No doubt the roads will be dusty and you'll get parched.'

Bridget thanked her.

In no time at all Bridget was accepting Harry's help up into the pillion seat. She settled herself into it and when he asked was she comfortable, assured him that a cushion would not go amiss. Instantly he sent Dorcas to fetch one.

It was only as Dorcas was handing up the cushion that she confessed that she had never ridden a horse in her life. She glanced up nervously at the other beast.

'Then you will have to ride with the baggage,' said Bridget, smiling encouragingly. 'Hang on tightly and Josh will ride his horse and attach a leading rein to the baggage horse. You should be safe enough as we will not be doing any galloping.'

Mistress Tyler appeared with food and the flagon of ale, and Harry placed it in one of the saddle bags. The house-keeper wished them Godspeed. Bridget thanked her for her assistance, and soon they were riding down the drive and out of the mansion gates.

They travelled in the direction of Fleet Street, but instead of heading into the city centre, Harry turned up Shoe Lane which led to Fleet Hill and eventually out into the country-side. There they paused to look down on London. Suddenly Bridget realised that Joe was missing and asked why he was not with them.

'He'll follow us on,' said Harry, tossing the words over his shoulder. 'He had a task to do for me, but hopefully it will not delay him for long and he will join us at the inn in St Albans.'

Bridget wondered if this task had aught to do with her father. Suddenly it occurred to her that Harry might have discovered that Patrick O'Malley had found out that her father was to blame for torching his ship and had set out to revenge that act. He could be in London and looking for her. She had hoped that she and Harry could be honest with each other now, but perhaps she was mistaken. Of course, it was possible that he was keeping such a secret from her because he did not want her worrying. Perhaps he realised that she was still fretting over losing the baby and would do so for some time to come. She decided to keep quiet about her suspicions for now.

Bridget was weary and stiff by the time they arrived at the inn in St Albans. Harry helped her to dismount before going inside the inn to make enquiries about a bedchamber. When he returned, Bridget was relieved that he had managed to bespeak one. He suggested that she go upstairs immediately with Dorcas and rest. He had arranged for a supper to be sent up to them.

'But what about you?' she asked.

'I'm going to retrace some of our journey to see if there is any sign of Joe.'

'Could Joshua not do that?'

'He is seeing to the other horses. I will not be long, so do not fret.' The next moment he was gone.

Her husband's attempt to stem any worry she felt only served to make her believe that there could be some truth in what she had thought earlier. She had no doubt that if Patrick O'Malley could not get his hands on her father, then he would like to capture her. Harry obviously considered it his primary duty as her husband to protect her and that is why they'd left London so swiftly and so late in the day. She decided that she had no option but to do as he suggested and retire to the bedchamber and partake of supper when it arrived. She would leave the provisions that Mrs Tyler had provided for the morrow.

Bridget woke from a dream in which she was cradling a baby in her arms and realised that she must have dozed off. She felt that ache of loss inside her chest and sighed. Then she opened her eyes and saw to her amazement that dawn was not far off. There was a scratching at the door and she heard her husband's voice whispering her name. She felt a burst of unexpected joy and scrambled out of bed and went and unlocked the door.

Harry was leaning against the door jamb, looking wind-blown and weary. He smiled down at her. 'I beg your pardon for arriving so late.'

She took hold of his arm and drew him inside. 'You are safe and that is all that matters. Did you find Joe?'

'Aye. His horse had thrown a shoe.'

'As long as that is all it was that kept him.'

'What else could there be?' asked Harry, gazing down at her sleep-flushed cheeks.

She hesitated and then said, 'I thought you might have had tidings about my father.'

'No, I would have told you if I'd had news of him.' Harry glanced in the direction of the bed where Dorcas was curled up fast asleep. Bridget's eyes followed his and she said, 'I am sorry. She kept me company and she was telling me about her mother and of how she had looked after her younger siblings who sadly died young when she suddenly fell asleep.'

Harry frowned. 'You should have discouraged her from telling you such tales. They will only upset you. I suggest you wake her and we make an early start.'

'I know children can die at such an early age. One cannot close one's eyes to the realities of life,' she murmured, reaching out and picking a length of cotton from his doublet. 'But Dorcas and her brothers survived, so I am not downcast.'

'Joe brought me news that the *St Bridget* has set sail for Preston in the wake of the Baron's ship. It could take her two weeks or more to reach there.'

'Is the cradle still aboard?'

Harry nodded and thought he caught the sheen of tears in her eyes. He felt a sudden lump in his throat, wondering if the child had been a boy or a girl as lovely as her mother. He reached out and placed his gloved hand against her face. She rested her cheek there a moment and then drew away from him as there came a sound from the bed. Both glanced in that direction and saw the humped shape of Dorcas moving.

'We'll talk some more later,' he said, and pressed a kiss on his wife's mouth before leaving her alone with Dorcas.

Bridget ran a finger over her tingling lips and would have liked to have had the chance to kiss him back. Then she remembered the need for haste and went over to the bed. 'Up with you, Dorcas. My husband has returned and we must be on our way.'

The maid poked her untidy head out of the bedcovers and blinked at her like a drowsy cat in the dawn light. 'So what kept the master?'

'Joe's horse threw a shoe. You've yet to meet Joe. He is an orphan the same as you. Now we must be out of here before the master returns and hammers on the door, asking us why we are taking so long.'

A few hours later Bridget was feeling reasonably cheerful. The sight of so much greenery and trees in blossom as well as wild flowers growing in meadows and rampantly in the hedgerows was wonderfully uplifting after being at sea for so long.

'Do you think you will ever become accustomed to the countryside as you were to gazing out over the sea, Harry?' she asked, resting a hand on his muscular shoulder and bringing her head close to the back of his.

'I wonder,' he murmured, overwhelmingly aware of her physical presence and enjoying the *frisson* of pleasure caused by her breasts pressing against his back. 'What are *your* feelings about living in the countryside? It is not as if you have done so in the past. I remember Callum telling me that your grandparents' home in Ireland was near the sea.'

'That is true and it is also true that my Scottish grandfather's castle overlooks a sea loch.'

'Appleby Manor is miles from the sea, but I have been told that the Irish Sea can be seen from a tower that is part of the manor house.'

'I suppose Josh told you that or perhaps it was the Baron,' said Bridget.

'They both told me of it,' said Harry, 'and I was reminded of a recurring dream of mine that Josh has now convinced me is no dream, but a memory.'

'Tell me about your memories?' asked Bridget.

So Harry told her and she listened intently and eventually said, 'I agree that these are memories. It is possible, Harry, that you cannot remember everything about when you were a boy because one does forget places and faces and events if they are commonplace and one is not seeing them constantly.'

'That does make sense,' said Harry.

'Perhaps when you have spent a few days at Appleby and ridden about your fields and woods you will have that sense of having been there before.'

'That is what I am hoping,' said Harry. 'But you have not answered my question. What are your feelings about living in the countryside?'

I would be content living anywhere with you, said a little voice in her head. That thought had only come to her recently and she did not yet have the courage to speak it aloud. For it could only mean that she had grown to love him despite that which had threatened to keep them apart.

'I accept now that my place is by your side and I am looking forward, a little apprehensively, I confess, to making our home there.'

He glanced over his shoulder. 'I, too, am apprehensive.

What if those in my employ take a dislike of me and consider me a complete lackwit? They will know that I have been a mariner for most of my life and that I come to the role I am to fill knowing so little.'

'I am certain if you confess that to them, then they will know you are not an arrogant man, but a master prepared to learn and do your best for them,' said Bridget. 'Besides, it is my opinion that they will be glad to welcome you. They must have known for some time that Rosamund will eventually have to leave with the Baron and wondered what would happen to Appleby Manor if you were not found. It could be that they thought the manor might be sold to someone who has no real attachment to the home where you were born.'

Harry nodded. 'I had not thought of that.'

She smiled. 'Then consider it now and do not worry so much.'

'I will do what you advise, but it would have been so much better if—' He stopped, about to say *you had not miscarried our child.*

'If what?' asked Bridget. 'If you had never been abducted and been able to grow up in the place where you belonged?'

'Aye,' said Harry, relieved that she could not read his thoughts.

'Yet, Harry, so much that is good would not have happened if you had remained at home. Most likely you would never have made the acquaintance of the Baron and other folk who I am sure enriched your life.'

He could see the truth of that and fell silent, thinking back over his life and thinking that Bridget had not mentioned the most important person in his life. Herself.

'Did you get to see Master Larsson?' she asked, taking him by surprise.

'No, I did not,' said Harry. 'Why do you ask?'

'It just occurred to me that he might still be serving aboard the Baron's ship. If that is so, then he will be in the north at the same time as we are,' said Bridget. 'Do you think he will want to see you?'

'For what reason?'

'Perhaps he has had time to regret what he said to you and would like to ask your forgiveness and be friends again? I do not like the man, but you knew each other for such a long time.'

'I'd like to believe that,' said Harry, thinking that in the light of what he knew of Christian Larsson's behaviour since reaching London, he was more inclined to believe the opposite.

'But you don't,' said Bridget.

'No,' admitted Harry.

After their exchange about Christian Larsson they were silent for a long time. She thought that he thought she was foolish to have made such a suggestion, while Harry wondered if he should have told Bridget his reason for feeling the way he did, but then he would have to tell her about his meeting with Ingrid, and just thinking of that encounter left a bad taste in his mouth. He would also have to tell her what Joe had told him about the company Ingrid was keeping lately, and he would rather not worry Bridget about that.

Their small party halted only for a short while to take refreshment at an inn, then they were on their way again. Now Bridget rallied and they passed the time talking about what might need doing at the house and the proximity of the nearest market town and port. They discussed furniture, something that neither of them had ever had need to do before. Bridget still found it difficult to believe that she was to be the lady of the manor. She thought about her father and what he might say if he returned and learnt that she was married to Harry Appleby, alias Black Harry. She would have felt pleasure to have been able to tell him that he was to be a grandfather. She wished for the umpteenth time that she had not miscarried their baby.

Soon after Harry insisted on Bridget having a rest and during that time there was a heated exchange between Joe and Dorcas. Changes had been made when they had set out again, which resulted in Dorcas having to sit behind Joe, holding on to his belt, whilst Joshua led the baggage horse and kept a watch out to the rear for sign of any trouble. The problem was that Joe was not pleased about Dorcas sharing his horse.

'She never stops talking,' he told Harry. 'I called her a lackwit and had to tell her to shut up.'

'And what did she say to that?' asked Harry, trying to look severe.

'That she was no fool and stuck her tongue out at me, so I caught hold of it and she didn't half get annoyed.' He grinned at the memory. 'She's got plenty of spirit. If it weren't for her broken nose, she wouldn't be half bad looking.'

Bridget was amused but said, 'Be kind to her, Joe. She had a tough life even before she became an orphan. Her father was cruel to her and she is not to blame for her appearance. It is what comes from our heart and thoughts that matter, not what we look like.'

Her words caused not only Joe to look thoughtful, but Harry, too. Did his wife really mean what she said and was it possible that she accepted the way he looked? Perhaps she now believed that the sad loss of their baby was the foulest thing to happen to them since they exchanged their vows. He could only pray that was so as he watched Joe helping Dorcas on to his horse with a kind word and a smile.

They set out again and Harry thought what a great responsibility it was rearing children, so that they were able to cope with all that life threw at them. Despite Dorcas's father's treatment of her, the girl had not lost her spirit. He wished he could remember those early years of his life when he had known his parents. Joshua had spoken of them at length, but he had not been there with Harry during those times he was alone with his father or mother and his sister. He could only pray that when, if, he and Bridget did have other children, he would be able to make a decent job of being a father. At least the begetting of them would be a pleasure. Just the thought of making love to Bridget roused him, but he decided it would be sensible not to allow his thoughts to wander along such paths whilst on horseback!

Chapter Fourteen

It was early evening on the fifth day that they arrived at an inn in Leicester. The road had been busy because it was that time of year when people were going on pilgrimage and the only spaces available were in a communal sleeping chamber. They spent that night sleeping fitfully on pallets. Harry was concerned about Bridget's comfort and safety.

The following evening the next inn was just as busy, so that Harry felt it necessary that he, Joe and Joshua took turns to keep watch during the night. In such a situation one never knew whether there was a thief or even a cutthroat amongst those lying on the floor.

It was Dorcas who hinted that they could be being followed the following evening. 'Why d'yer think that?' asked Joe, helping her down from the horse. 'There's that many folk on the road yer'd have trouble spotting any one person unless yer'd seen them before.'

'It's just a feeling I have,' said the maid with a sniff. 'Me mother used to have these feelings, too.'

'I think the captain will need more than just yer feelings before being convinced,' said Joe.

Dorcas jutted her chin. 'Yer can say what yer like, but I'm going to keep me peepers open. I don't want to wake up with me throat cut in the night.'

Joe chuckled. 'Yer'd have a job doing that.'

She giggled. 'See what yer mean.' She hurried into the inn in Bridget's wake, leaving him staring after her.

Joe knew that he couldn't just ignore her words and so, with an air of embarrassment, he mentioned what Dorcas had said to Harry. 'I know it sounds daft, Captain, but do yer consider there is a possibility of us being followed?'

'Maybe,' said Harry, stroking his scar. 'You take the horses to the stables and I'll have a word with Dorcas, yourself and Josh later. Now I must see what accommodation is available.'

He knew that Bridget was beginning to flag and that she needed some privacy and a good night's sleep, so he hurried inside the inn and spoke to the innkeeper. He was smiling when he came out of the inn and found Bridget leaning against the wall. 'I have bribed the innkeeper to let us have his own bedchamber,' he said.

Her face lit up. 'Thank you, Harry. I know if I had to lie on a hard pallet on the floor again I must, but I am so glad I do not have to listen to people coughing and shifting about tonight.'

He wondered if she thought that he should have done more for her comfort and felt as if he had proved less than the best of husbands. 'I must speak to the others. You go inside and the innkeeper's wife will show you the room. I will join you as soon as I can and we will have supper together in private.'

Bridget walked wearily into the inn and Harry's eyes followed her. He would be glad when they reached Appleby Manor. He only spoke briefly to Dorcas before suggesting that she go to see if her mistress needed her help. Then he told Josh and Joe that he wanted them to take turns keeping a watch that night and to let him know if they saw anyone they recognised.

When Harry entered the bedchamber not long after, Bridget had already changed out of the clothes she had worn day after day and was wearing her night rail and robe. She had loosened her hair and he could not resist kissing her whilst twisting a strand of her wavy auburn hair between his fingers. 'You are so beautiful,' he said.

She blushed and briefly touched his cheek. He wondered what she was thinking when she touched his scar. Was she remembering the first time she had done so in the darkness of the cabin on the ship? How he had deceived her? Had she forgiven him for doing so? Perhaps she could forgive, but never forget. She had wandered over to the table and now sat down. 'We must be sensible and eat this supper that the innkeeper's good wife has prepared for us,' she said.

He sat down at the small table and soon they were making short work of the stewed rabbit in an herb, onion and barley broth with crusty brown bread. The food was washed down by an excellent ale and they talked little, content to be alone and tired after the day's travelling.

Once the food had been cleared away they went to bed. Bridget was drowsy and appeared to have fallen asleep to Harry, who lay with an arm across her. He wanted her, yet found it comforting just to cuddle up close. Completely relaxed he was not, because he had to keep under control his desire for her and also part of his mind was occupied with thoughts of those who might be following them. He gave serious thought to Ingrid's wish for revenge because of his losing his temper and dropping her in the mud. At least Bridget was safe here in this bedchamber with him.

Bridget felt the aches and pains and tensions of the day drifting away as she relaxed beneath her husband's protective arm. She had a sense of well-being because at last it seemed that all was coming right between them. Harry might not love her, but she believed that he cared for her, and for the moment that was enough. Whether in the days to come that would prove to be so, she was not going to worry about now. Sleepy with fresh air and exhausted with travelling she fell asleep.

When Harry woke it was dark and at first he had no notion of what it was that had woken him. Cautiously he sat up in bed, so as not to disturb Bridget, and could not resist pressing his lips against her bare shoulder where her night rail had slipped down. She did not stir.

Suddenly he became aware of whispering voices outside the window. He strained his ears, hoping to be able to make out what was being said, but when he couldn't, he slid out of bed and carefully parted the curtains.

Harry was just in time to see a robed figure go over to the stables. There was no sign of whoever it was he or she had been conversing with, but Harry's suspicions were aroused. He wondered where Joe or Joshua were and whether they were aware of what was happening outside.

As he turned away from the window, there came a tapping on the door of the bedchamber. He snatched up his hose from the floor and dragged them on before tiptoeing across the floor. 'Is that you, Joe?' he whispered.

'No, Master Appleby, it's Dorcas. I thought I'd best let yer know that neither Joe nor Joshua have come to their pallets.'

'All right, Dorcas. Go downstairs and unlock the back door if need be. I'll join you in a few moments.'

He wondered if Joe had fetched Joshua because he needed his help, both having decided not to disturb him and Bridget. He dressed swiftly and was fastening his doublet when Bridget's sleepy voice said, 'I've been dreaming and a thought has occurred to me.'

'Tell me later,' said Harry.

He crept downstairs and when he reached the bottom, Dorcas came out of the shadows. 'Is them being missing aught to do with what I told yer, Master Appleby?' she whispered.

'Aye, most likely.'

Harry opened the outside door cautiously, looked about him and, seeing no one, went outside. Dorcas followed him as he headed for the stables. The door was open. He paused and listened and thought he heard groaning. He ordered Dorcas to wait and slipped inside. There to his relief he found Joe still alive and trying to sit up. He left him a moment and searched the stables, but found no one hiding there.

Joe had sank back on to a heap of straw. Harry shook his shoulder and the lad tried to sit up again, but had trouble doing so. Worried, Harry hoisted him on to his shoulder and carried him outside and leaned him against the wall. The lad's knees sagged and Harry said, 'Come on, Joe, wake up!'

'Is he gonna be all right?' asked Dorcas.

The lad opened his eyelids, only to close them again. He winced and then peered between his eyelids at Harry and Dorcas. 'God's Blood, Captain, I should have seen her coming. I've a terrible head.'

'I shouldn't have left you to keep watch alone,' said Harry.

'Not your fault, Captain. I shouldn't have allowed myself to be distracted by the sight of the Danish witch.'

'Ingrid!'

'Aye, Dorcas was right and we were being followed by one of the bully boys she recognised as living in her street. He was with Ingrid and there was another man dressed as a monk. I didn't see his face,' said Joe.

He staggered away from the wall and, before Harry could prevent him, doused his head in the horse trough. 'That's better,' said the lad, shaking his dripping head and wiping his hand over his wet face. 'I tell you what, Captain—'

But Harry was not listening; he had already whirled round to make his way back to the inn. He had remembered that he had not locked the bedchamber door and was worried in case Ingrid or either man reached Bridget. He was stopped in his tracks by the sight of his wife hurrying towards him.

'What is happening?' she called in a low voice.

Harry seized her arm. 'You shouldn't have left the bedchamber, but stayed there and locked the door.'

'Too late for that now. Is it Patrick O'Malley?' she asked, gazing up into her husband's shadowy features.

'What has he to do with this? Don't answer that right now,' he said swiftly. 'Explain later. I want you back inside. You shouldn't be outside in your robe and slippers. Dorcas, go with your mistress back to the inn.'

Bridget did not move. 'If Patrick O'Malley is not following us, then who is?' she asked.

Harry hesitated. 'Do as I say, Bridget! This isn't the place for such a conversation.'

For a moment he thought she was going to disobey him but then she turned quickly and walked away with her robe fluttering about her ankles. Dorset followed her.

'So what do we do next?' enquired Joe. 'And where's Josh?'

'We'll think about that after we've seen the women to the bedchamber,' said Harry. 'I wouldn't put it past our enemies to have slipped inside whilst we've been talking.' Without more ado he and Joe followed Bridget and Dorcas across the stable yard towards the inn.

Bridget glanced over her shoulder once and then disappeared inside. Harry wasted no time in following her and Dorcas upstairs, but when they reached the bedchamber, he pushed them aside and went in first. He could see no sign of entry via the window and after a quick search knew there was no one hiding in the room. 'You and Dorcas remain here until I return,' he said to Bridget. 'Lock the door after me.'

Bridget opened her mouth to protest, but he was gone.

Joe looked up at Harry, but he held his finger to his lips and the lad was silent until they were downstairs. Only then did he whisper, 'What do yer think has happened to Josh, Captain?'

'We'll make a search for him. He's either followed them or is unconscious and concealed somewhere.'

'Yer don't think he's dead?' asked Joe, a tremor in his voice.

'Let's not think the worst,' said Harry, looking down at the lad. 'Perhaps you'd best stay here and rest after that knock on the head.'

'I'd rather watch yer back, Captain.'

They went outside and instantly Harry became aware of the sleepy chirruping of birds and realised that dawn was not far off. He made a quick search of the outhouses and the surrounding area and found a man sprawled under a tree. For a moment his heart misgave him, but then he realised that it was not Joshua. He felt for a pulse and discovered the man was dead. Had Joshua killed him, or someone else? He would inform the innkeeper and leave him to deal with the corpse.

'I'm going to check our horses, Joe,' he said quietly, for he had not done so earlier whilst in the stables.

He did so and discovered that Joshua's mount was missing. 'He's followed them,' said Harry, coming outside.

'What do we do?' asked Joe.

Harry's dark brows knit. 'We continue with our journey. Ingrid and her companion must have realised that we're aware of their presence and won't try anything here again.'

'What do yer think was their plan, Captain?' asked Joe.

'Murder, abduction?' Harry's expression was grim.

'What are yer going to tell the missus?'

'If she hasn't already wormed the truth out of Dorcas, then I will tell her the truth,' said Harry, who was not looking forward to doing so.

He rapped his knuckles on the panel of the door and spoke his name in a low voice. A few moments later he heard the door being unlocked and it swung open to reveal Bridget dressed for travelling. She did not look at him, but moved further back into the room that was filling with daylight. There was no sign of Dorcas.

'So—' said Bridget, looking him squarely in the face as he closed the door behind him.

'What has Dorcas told you?'

'Enough for me to realise that you have kept secret from me an encounter with Ingrid.' She struggled to keep her voice steady, not wanting to reveal how hurt she felt.

'Dorcas could not know the whole of it,' said Harry, rubbing his scar.

'I knew *none* of it,' cried Bridget, turning her back on him and going over to the window.

'I did not want you to worry. I dealt with her as I saw fit.'

Bridget whirled round and her eyes glinted with anger. 'Why did you not hand her over to the sheriff? She is a known felon. Is it that you could not bring yourself to do so because you still feel something for her despite what I and others have told you about her?'

'Now you are talking nonsense,' said Harry, his temper rising. 'I would have thought that by now you would know me better. I despise her as much as you do.'

'I cannot believe that is true.'

'Why? Because I once believed myself in love with her?'

Bridget was silent, sensing that this was an argument that neither of them was going to win. She began to gather her belongings together and put them in a canvas bag.

'Anyway, what is this about Patrick O'Malley?' asked Harry. 'Did something happen whilst I was away from the house that causes you to believe he might have been in London and followed us?'

'No! I sensed that you were keeping something from me and mistakenly believed it concerned him,' said Bridget in a low voice. She changed the subject. 'Will we be making an early start? The sooner this journey is over the better.'

'At least we can agree on that,' said Harry. 'Joshua is missing, but there is little point in us waiting for him. He knows our destination and will follow us on if he has not returned before we go.'

'You think he has followed her?'

'Aye. We found the dead body of a man. Hopefully, Dorcas will be able to identify him before we go.'

'But Ingrid is not alone, is she?' said Bridget, her voice rising. 'Dorcas mentioned a monk.'

'That could be a disguise,' said Harry.

'My exact thoughts.'

'So who do you think it might be?' asked Bridget.

'I cannot say for certain. Maybe we will have an answer before this month of June is out.'

Harry gathered his possessions together and unlocked the door. 'Shall we go?' he said.

Bridget nodded and swept out of the bedchamber, recalling the meal they had shared and how she had felt secure and content beneath his arm in bed. Now that contentment was shattered by Harry keeping secrets from her about a woman he'd once had strong feelings for.

Joshua had still not made an appearance by the time they were ready to leave. They could all only hope that he was safe. Harry especially had come to value his loyalty and common sense since they had met in Lisbon and would not like to lose him. He decided he must have faith in the other man's abilities to survive as his own priority was Bridget's safety.

Both Harry and Joe were very much on their guard as they travelled further north, keeping a lookout for anyone who seemed to be taking too much interest in their small party. He and Bridget barely spoke to each other. She wondered if she would ever be able to trust Harry to be honest with her.

They crossed the Cheshire border and it was now that Harry became obsessed by thoughts of his reunion with his sister. Joshua had told him that Rosamund had been broken-hearted when she had been told that he was dead. He longed to see her, yet still feared that he might be a disappointment to her because the boy she remembered no longer existed, and she would be confronted with the scarred face of a man who was a stranger to her.

* * *

Two days later they had crossed the border into the Palatine of Lancashire, and it was now that Harry began to ask the way to Lathom House, one of the homes of the Earl of Derby. It was a well-known landmark, and only a few miles from Appleby Manor. After a couple of hours they began to pass fields of growing wheat and peas and greens. There were orchards on which the blossom was fading and all seemed peaceful. As they drew nearer to the house that now appeared amongst the trees and shrubs, Harry saw that it was built of sandstone and that sunlight reflecting off latticed windows. He noticed a tower jutting up at one side and knew that this was Appleby Manor house. He felt a leap of the heart and turned to look at Bridget to see what she thought of it, but her eyes were looking straight past him.

The front door opened and a woman emerged. Behind her came a man with a child in his arms. Harry's heartbeat quickened and, within moments, he had brought his horse to a halt. He gazed down upon the dark-haired woman standing a yard or so away from him. She was smiling up at him through the tears that shimmered in her violet eyes.

'Harry, it has to be you because you are as Alex described you,' she said, stretching up a hand to him. 'I am your sister Rosamund and I have longed for this moment.'

Harry forced down the lump in his throat and removed his riding glove. His strong fingers curled about those of his sister and still he could not speak for the emotion he felt.

'Well, Harry, it's not like you to be lost for words,' teased Alex.

'I am remembering a dream in which a dark-haired little girl waved frantically to me from a tower,' said Harry in husky tones. 'The mind is truly strange in what it chooses to remember and what to forget.'

'I was that girl,' said Rosamund, tears trickling down her cheeks. 'It was the last time I caught sight of you and you were shouting a warning to me. Welcome home, my dear, dear brother.'

Harry slid down from his horse and he and Rosamund hugged each other, his scarred cheek resting on her dark head.

Bridget bit down hard on her lower lip to control its trembling as she gazed at her husband and his sister. She almost felt envious of their feelings for each other. She looked away and caught Alex's eye. He winked at her and she brushed away a tear and forced a smile.

Alex summoned one of the maids who had suddenly appeared and handed his son to her. Then he helped Bridget down from the pillion seat.

'I am glad to see this day,' he said.

'I, too. It feels as if we have been waiting a long time for it to arrive,' she murmured, telling herself that envy must have no place here.

At the sound of his wife's voice, Harry lifted his head and gazed at Bridget. As they stared at each other something unexpected happened. In the light of their quarrel over Ingrid, it seemed almost magical. They exchanged smiles and Harry felt such a swell of emotion that he knew that he had to make matters right between them. He held out his hand to her. She moved forwards and clasped it and he drew her close, so that he encapsulated both Bridget and Rosamund in his embrace.

'I am so glad to see you both happy,' said Bridget, knowing she must forgive him for keeping his encounter with Ingrid from her.

The two women kissed each other and then both kissed Harry before bursting out laughing with exultation.

'Can I join in?' asked Alex, grinning.

'Of course! Come, dearest,' said Rosamund, drawing him in to the circle. 'Let us savour this moment before all too soon—' She did not finish what she was about to say because a baby began to wail. She pulled a droll face. 'Is that not typical? Do you not find just when you are in the middle of something that needs saying, it is interrupted?'

Bridget watched as Rosamund took her child from the maid and hushed him. 'So this is your son,' murmured Bridget, gazing down at the child with a tender expression on her face and firmly suppressing her own feelings of loss. 'May I hold him?'

'Of course, but I warn you that he is damp,' said Rosamund.

Bridget took the wriggling baby and gazed down into his handsome features. Then she felt Harry's hand on her shoulder. 'He has your eyes, Rosamund,' he said.

'I wish that you both could have been here when he was born,' said his sister. 'We would have liked you to be Douglas's godparents. Harry, he wore the robe that we wore when we were baptised. You will not remember, but it is made of silk and has tiny seed pearls sewn into it. Perhaps when you and Bridget—' She stopped short. 'I beg your pardons. Alex only arrived a few hours ago and told me of your miscarriage, Bridget. I am so sorry. Let us pray that it will not be long before you conceive again,' she added, touching both her brother's and Bridget's arms with a gentle hand.

Bridget thanked her and darted Harry a glance. 'May I hold my nephew?' he asked.

'Of course,' she said instantly.

Their hands brushed as she passed Douglas to him and she gazed into his face as he clutched his nephew to him and saw it through a sheen of tears.

'Greetings, nephew,' said Harry unsteadily. 'It is a pleasure to meet you.'

Douglas stilled a moment and then, seizing a handful of the sleeve of Harry's doublet, dragged himself up so that he was able to perch on his uncle's other arm. He peered into Harry's face and patted his scarred cheek.

'Don't do that, Douglas!' exclaimed Rosamund.

'It is all right, sister,' said Harry, seizing the boy's hand and pretending to nibble his fingers. Douglas chuckled and Harry grinned. Obviously his nephew did not find him repulsive.

'Well, I never,' said Alex. 'Never did I expect to see you so swiftly adept at entertaining my son, Harry.'

'Nor I,' said Bridget, thinking about what Rosamund had said about her and Harry conceiving another child. She wanted that so much but worried that she might do so and have her hopes raised, only to miscarry again.

Rosamund said, 'It is obvious that my brother has an affinity with children, but it cannot be comfortable for him to have a damp *derrière* sitting on his arm. I will give Douglas to his nursemaid and she can change him. Then he will be in a more pleasing condition to entertain his uncle.'

Harry handed his nephew over to his sister. 'I hope to see a lot of you both before you leave for Scotland.'

Rosamund sighed. 'It is a sadness to me that we will have to leave only too soon, but we cannot delay the journey for much longer.'

'I understand that you and Alex have been putting off the moment for my sake,' said Harry. 'I appreciate all you have done here.'

'It was the least we could do for you,' said Rosamund, her voice husky. 'But let us not mar this time with anticipating the moment of parting. This day is one of the happiest of my life. I feel that we are at last a complete family and, wherever we are, there is naught that can change that now.'

'I thought of you often when I was in places where I was unable to receive word of you,' said Bridget.

'Aye, you, too,' said Rosamund softly.

Alex said, 'You have all suffered greatly, but it is over now. Let us forget the difficult times and rejoice in the present.' He paused and said, 'So what do the two of you think of your new home?'

Bridget and Harry gazed up at the house. 'I find it difficult to believe that this interesting edifice belongs to me,' he said, experiencing pride and emotion.

'It needs renovating inside,' said Rosamund. 'Our step-mother used to complain that Father was always reluctant to spend money on the house. Most of it went back into the business and the land.'

'You'll get a better view of your property from the tower,' said Alex.

'Later,' said Rosamund. 'I deem that Bridget is impatient to see what it is like inside. You lead the way, Harry.'

Harry hesitated and then did as his sister told him. Bridget was only a few feet behind him.

Chapter Fifteen

The hall was far grander than Harry had imagined, with a double flight of stairs leading to the first floor at the far end. The walls had obviously had their spring whitewash to rid the place of the grime caused by the winter fires. There were no hangings, so he presumed they had been taken down to be beaten.

'The house dates back to the time of Edward the Second,' said Rosamund.

'A hundred and fifty years ago,' he murmured. 'Hence the need for the tower and thick walls, necessary during those unruly times. The Scots were known to raid this far south.' He exchanged glances with Bridget and smiled.

'Did Josh tell you that?' she asked.

He did not answer, but continued to gaze about the hall, as the memories came flooding back. It felt most peculiar, remembering the fireplace and the chimney being built. 'No, I remember.' He grinned. 'I deem it is time for a toast. If you could summon one of the servants, Rosamund.'

His sister gazed at him with a wondering expression on her face and did as he requested. The man who responded to her call gazed wide-eyed at Harry.

'Master Harry!' he exclaimed.

'You recognise me?' asked Harry.

'Aye, that I do. Yer've changed somewhat, been through the wars by the look of that scar, but yer've got a look of the old master. It's good to see yer back.'

'Is it, Will?' asked Harry, putting a hand to his head.

'Aye, Master Harry.' He beamed at him.

Harry asked him to bring some wine for the ladies and tankards of ale for himself and the Baron. Will hurried away and Harry was aware that he was the focus of four pairs of eyes. 'I know what you're going to say,' he murmured, and sat down suddenly on a chair.

'Your memory really is coming back,' said Bridget, sitting on a chair and gazing at him in delight.

'How much do you remember?' asked Rosamund.

'I don't know. Information about this hall came to me in a flash.'

'How strange,' said Bridget.

'Isn't it,' said Harry, puzzled himself. 'How could I forget so much about myself, family and this place and now remember it?'

'Most likely it is one of those mysteries that we'll never know the answer to,' said Alex. 'I mean your forgetting all that you did and now remembering it is a puzzle.'

Rosamund smiled. 'So you will not need me to act as your guide and to tell you tales of our childhood and parents that Joshua could not tell you.'

Harry returned her smile. 'I would not entirely agree with what you say. I am certain there is much that I have simply forgotten due to the passage of time.'

There was a silence and suddenly Rosamund asked, 'Where is Joshua, by the way? I did not notice him earlier.'

Bridget and Harry looked at each other and before either could decide what to say in way of a reply, Will and one of the maidservants appeared with their drinks. The girl looked askance at Harry, but all his attention was on Bridget as she asked him in a low voice, 'What are we going to tell Rosamund? In her condition I do not wish to upset her by mentioning Ingrid.'

'Then we will not do so,' said Harry. 'I will say that Josh was delayed on a matter of urgent business and hopefully will arrive soon.'

This Harry did and Rosamund accepted his reason for Joshua's absence. Alex was not so easily satisfied. He took Harry aside whilst Rosamund talked to Bridget about house-hold matters. At some point during their conversations, Dorcas and Joe came into the hall with the baggage, and Rosamund suggested that she take Bridget upstairs to show her the bed-chamber that she had prepared for her and Harry.

'I do hope Harry likes this bedchamber. It belonged to our mother and it has a lovely view,' said Rosamund.

'I like it already,' said Bridget, gazing about her with smiling approval.

'Of course, you will most likely wish to choose your own furnishings once you have settled in here. Most of those were here when my mother was alive.'

'In that case, Harry might wish to keep them,' said Bridget.

She joined Rosamund at the window and looked out over the front of the house to overgrown flower beds and a lawn that looked newly scythed. Fields stretched out to woodland in the distance and she thought she caught the gleam of an expanse of water beyond.

'Is that the Irish Sea?' she asked.

'Aye, but it is a good few hours' journey away,' said Rosamund. 'From the tower you get a better view of the landscape. I will take you and Harry up there, so you can see for yourselves. It used to be Harry's bedchamber before our stepmother decided to shut me away up there.'

'I am glad she is dead.'

'You're glad who is dead?' asked Harry, entering the bedchamber,

'Our wicked stepmother,' replied Rosamund, smiling at him. 'Come and see the view.' She held out a hand to him.

Harry joined them at the window, and both women made room for him between them. He leaned out over the sill and his gaze searched the meadows where he could see a few cattle grazing and long grass rippling in the breeze.

'Soon it will be time for haymaking,' said Rosamund. 'You must speak to your steward and the reeve. The land is not used as it should be. Several fields lay fallow because we could not pay the wages of the labourers you need.'

Harry nodded. His intense scrutiny encompassed the woods and the gleam of water in the distance. 'That is the Irish Sea?'

Rosamund nodded. 'Bridget asked that question, too. Is it that you now remember being taken there when you were abducted?'

'No,' said Harry. 'That I still cannot remember.'

'What about this bedchamber?' asked Rosamund.

He turned and surveyed the room. 'I presume there is something special about it. Did our mother sleep here?'

Rosamund nodded. 'Aye, although this bed was not hers. Our stepmother persuaded Father that there was some evil at work in this room and he had the bed burnt. He certainly never came in here afterwards. Maybe his conscience bothered him due to his marrying that woman so soon after Mother's death.'

'I think she killed our mother,' said Harry abruptly.

Both women stared at him.

'The nightmares I have had for years, I sincerely believe now that they were not dreams, but memories I buried deep because I could not bear the pain they caused. If I am right, it was not in here that she died. but on the staircase to my bedchamber in the tower. That woman pushed our mother down the stairs and she caught her head on the stone wall. I went to her, but she never got up again. That hag seized me and made certain I could not speak of it to my father.'

'I was told she had died of a disease, but I always wondered whether she had quickened Mother's end with the potions she gave her,' said Rosamund.

'Perhaps she did both,' said Bridget, 'but she is punished now and maybe it is time you both laid your ghosts to rest.'

'I would like to visit my mother's grave and lay flowers upon it,' said Harry quietly.

Harry and Bridget stood in front of the grave in the church-yard where his mother's body lay at rest, watching as his sister removed the flowers she had placed in a container there only the other day. She beckoned Harry forwards, and he knelt on the ground and replaced the fading flowers with a posy of myrtle, heart's-ease and pink roses that Bridget had gathered for him.

He bent his head and said a silent prayer and remained in that position for several moments. He gave thanks for the woman who had given him life and whom his sister and Lady Elizabeth had spoken of with such affection. He grieved that he had not been able to save her life.

Bridget rested her hand on his shoulder, understanding some of how he felt. She thought of her own mother buried beneath Irish skies. She felt his hand cover hers briefly as if he knew what she was thinking and then he rose to his feet.

None of them spoke as they left the graveside and made their way out of the churchyard. Harry asked Bridget to excuse him and his sister for a short while as there were questions he wanted to ask her.

Bridget would have liked to have listened in on their conversation, but it was obvious that Harry did not want her there. 'I will have some hot water brought up to our chamber. I am feeling filthy,' she said.

'I will see you soon,' called Harry, as she walked away.

Bridget thought that after all the emotions that had been revealed since they had arrived here that she and Harry might have been able to share their feelings more openly. Perhaps she had misread the expression in his eyes earlier. She went inside the house and, after requesting a pitcher of hot water, went upstairs.

She hurried along the dimly lit passage to their bedchamber, only to trip over an uneven flagstone. She managed to prevent herself from falling by putting a hand against the wall. She must tell Harry that more light was needed here. At last she reached the bedchamber and went inside and searched for what she needed in the armoire and chest. Then she walked over to the window and gazed out towards the Irish Sea, thinking about the *St Bridget* and whether she had arrived at Preston yet.

At a knock on the door, she went to open it, hoping it was Harry, but it was only one of the maids with her hot water. She washed, changed into a fresh gown and then sat waiting for her husband to come.

'So do you remember this place at all, Harry?' asked Rosamund, coming out from beneath the trees and on to the river bank. 'Do you think it was from here that you were abducted and taken to sea? Your clothes were found on the banks of the river, after all.'

Harry smiled faintly. 'I wonder how many times people will say that to me now I have returned.' His sister had talked and talked about their childhood, and he had felt the years slipping away in the same fashion they had done when Joshua Wood had reminisced. 'Josh described the river to me, but I can't see how it would eventually flow into the sea or the Ribble from here. I know seagoing vessels anchor at Preston where woollen cloth is exported.'

'Aye, Flemish weavers came over during the last century,' said his sister. 'I can understand your interest, and you're right in thinking that you couldn't get from here by boat to the Irish Sea further south or Preston in the north. The port that is mainly used for ships going to and fro between Ireland is Liverpool. It is only a small place, but it has its own charter.'

'I suppose it is possible I was drugged and taken there. I wager I probably wasn't even near this river when I was abducted. My clothes would have been planted on this bank to give the impression that I'd been swimming.'

Rosamund agreed.

Harry changed the subject to talk now about one that was close to his heart. 'You know Bridget well,' he said. 'Do you deem that she can be happy here with the occasional outing to Preston or Ormskirk?'

'She loves you, so she will be happy wherever you are,' said Rosamund.

Harry froze. 'How can you tell that she loves me? Has she told you so?'

'Any woman would love a man who found her on an alien beach and saved her life. Especially one who was prepared to marry her despite her father having stolen one of his ships,' said Rosamund, her eyes twinkling. 'In my opinion Bridget had strong feelings for you even when she ranted against you as Black Harry.'

She linked her arm through Harry's. 'I only wish that we could spend more time with you and Bridget and watch all your plans for Appleby come to fruition. It will always hold a special place in my heart. I pray that you and Bridget will have many sons and daughters and that you will find great happiness here.' She hugged his arm. 'Shall we return to the house? You must be famished after your journey.'

It had seemed to Bridget that she had been waiting an age for Harry and could feel herself getting tenser every moment that passed. Eventually she decided that she had waited long enough and went downstairs. Alex was there and immediately offered her a glass of wine. She thanked him and wondered what was keeping Harry and Rosamund so long. She was ashamed that she still could feel envious of their newfound close relationship.

She was sipping her wine when they entered the hall. Harry glanced her way and for a moment their eyes caught. He smiled, accepted a glass of wine from a servant and raised it to her. She saluted him with her own. But there was to be no time for them to talk privately because within minutes they were joined by the priest, steward and reeve.

In no time at all they were seated at table and a meal of pork, roasted apples, onions and spring greens was set before them. After the introductions were made the men discussed the husbandry of the land. Harry broached the idea of rearing sheep and selling the wool to the weavers in Preston. 'Although I suppose we could employ our own weavers,' he added as an afterthought.

'You'd need to build cottages for them, Master Appleby,' said the steward.

'Aye, but we have the land, don't we?'

Bridget listened to the conversation with interest, feeling herself drawn in to that which so interested Harry now he was home.

'Certainly, Master Appleby, and it would give work to some of the local villagers,' said the reeve.

'Then that is settled,' said Harry, smiling.

The men grinned and they began to discuss which fields to turn over to sheep and where would be best to build the cottages.

Harry wondered whether to broach the subject of planting sugar beet, but then decided, as it was only at the experimental stage on Madeira and most likely the climate here would not be suitable, that he had best remain silent. Thinking of Madeira made his thoughts turn to the time he had spent there with Bridget. He remembered that even before he had asked her to marry him, he had feared losing her. He guessed that Callum had coped with losing his wife by turning to drink. Where was the old pirate now? Had he arrived at Lisbon or Madeira? Could someone have given him the information that Bridget was Harry's wife and that they had already set out for England? If he arrived safely, there was much Harry had to say to his father-in-law. He glanced in Bridget's direction, caught her eye and wanted to be alone with her on this, their first night in their own home.

The door to the hall suddenly opened and a man appeared in the doorway. His garments were travel stained and for a moment he just stood there; then he begged pardon and turned and went right out again. Instantly Harry pushed back his chair and asked his guests to excuse him. He hurried across the hall and went outside.

'That was Joshua Wood!' exclaimed Rosamund, turning to Bridget.

'Aye, I am glad he has arrived safely. I wonder what news he has for Harry.' Bridget would have liked to have followed after the two men, but knew she would have to wait until the meal was over and the priest and other men had departed. Only then could she rise and go after them.

Bridget hurried outside, but there was no sign of the two men, so she made for the stables, thinking that she might find them there, only to discover the stable void of their presence. She had no notion where else they could be, so decided to return to the house, hoping Harry might have gone there during her absence.

The hall was occupied only by the servants clearing away after the meal, so Bridget went upstairs to their bedchamber, considering it possible that Harry believed that she had retired for the night. To her disappointment he was not there, but someone had lighted several candles and the bed had been turned down. Had one of the maids done that or had it been Dorcas or Harry?

Where was he? For him to be missing this long, Joshua must have had a lot to tell him. She was disturbed by a knock on the door and hurried to open it. To her disappointment it was Rosamund.

'I wondered if my brother was here,' she said.

Bridget shook her head and invited her inside. 'I have searched, but cannot find him,' said Rosamund.

'I, too, have done so,' said Bridget.

Rosamund went over to the window and Bridget followed her. 'Can you see any sign of him?' she asked.

'No,' replied Rosamund. 'I suppose it is possible that they

have gone to Joshua's old home in the woods if they want to talk in private. I wish I knew for certain,' she added.

'You are behaving as if…' Bridget's voice trailed off.

'As if I am anxious about my brother?' Rosamund moved away from the window and sat in a chair. 'He has been abducted before and I have only just been reunited with him.'

'I deem you worry unnecessarily,' said Bridget firmly. 'But if you give me directions to Joshua's house in the woods, then I will go and see if he is there.'

Rosamund shook her head. 'It will soon be dark. You could easily get lost, and Harry would be very vexed with me if that were to happen. No doubt he will return soon. I will speak to Alex, and he will wait up until Harry returns. I will see you in the morning.'

Bridget wished her a goodnight and closed the door behind her. She could not prevent herself from thinking of Ingrid. Perhaps when she had left with her companion they had met others. Maybe Joshua had scarcely managed to escape with his life? Could they have followed him here? She paced the floor, praying for Harry and hoping she was worrying unnecessarily. Then weariness suddenly swept over her and she sank on to the bed, kicked off her shoes and lay down. Despite all her attempts to remain awake, her head nodded and she dozed off.

It was the sound of a door opening and stealthy movements that wakened her. The candles must have burnt down because the room was in darkness. Her heart began to beat heavily and she wished she had a weapon to hand. Then she heard a muffled curse.

'Harry, is that you?'

'Aye. What are you doing awake, Bridget? You should have long been asleep.'

'I was worried about you. What did Joshua have to say? Where have you been all this time?'

'There's no need for you to worry. Go to sleep.'

Bridget was hurt. She had expected this first night at Appleby Manor to be spent not simply sleeping. 'You sound as if you are not coming to bed.'

He did not answer, but the next moment she felt his arms go round her. She sensed a suppressed excitement about him, and then his warm breath was on her mouth and he kissed her long and hard before releasing her. 'Trust me that it is naught for you to worry about. All will be well,' he replied. 'Now go to sleep, and that is an order.'

Bridget heard the sound of the door opening and closing. For several moments she remained where she was, and then she rose from the bed and padded over to the door and went out into the passage. Her eyes had become accustomed to the lack of light in the bedchamber, but it was darker here and she could see no sign of Harry and only the slightest glimmer of a dying flame from a sconce on the wall. Even so she decided to try to follow him.

She had not gone far when she stubbed her toe and lost her balance. Only by the sheerest good fortune did her hand hit the wall, so she was able to steady herself. Even so this second accident along this passage unnerved her, and when she tried to continue, her toe hurt abominably. She had no choice but to return to the bedchamber. It was a relief to arrive at the open door and go inside and find her way over to a chair. She sat down and lifted her foot and discovered that, as she suspected, her big toe was cut and bleeding. She fumbled about in the unfamiliar room in search of what she needed to deal with the injury. By the time she had finished with salve and binding, she was glad to undress and climb into bed, worn out by the exertions of the day.

* * *

Bridget started awake at the sound of knocking on the door. 'Mistress Appleby, wake up! The hour is late and the Baroness has sent me to see if all is well with you.'

Bridget noticed with a sinking heart that there was no sign of Harry in the chamber. She climbed out of bed and went and opened the door. Where was he? Had something happened to him despite his reassurances? 'Forgive me, Dorcas, I did not get to sleep until the early hours.'

'I was starting to think yer'd both been murdered in yer bed,' said the girl, looking about her. 'Where's the master?'

'That I don't know.'

'I wager Joe will know,' said Dorcas, her eyes bright as she placed a pitcher of steaming water on the washstand. 'Shall I help yer with yer *toilette* or shall I go and see if I can find him?'

'The latter,' said Bridget. 'I will get dressed and wait here for you.'

Dorcas wasted no time going in search of Joe. When she returned she did not come empty-handed, but brought some bread and honey and a cup of small ale for her mistress. Bridget accepted them gratefully, for she had regained the appetite she had lost after the miscarriage.

'Did you speak to Joe?' she asked.

'No, I could find only the Baroness. Apparently the master, Joshua and Joe have gone to Liverpool whilst the Baron has gone to Preston,' said Dorcas.

'How odd,' said Bridget. 'Did she explain why?'

Dorcas shook her head. 'She said you're not to worry.'

Easier said than done, thought Bridget, unable to understand why Harry had needed to leave in such haste whilst it was still dark if there was naught for her to worry about.

She forced herself to eat some bread and honey and drink the small ale, wondering how long she would have to wait before Harry returned.

As soon as Bridget went downstairs she went in search of Rosamund and found her in the herb garden, picking mint. She greeted her friend and then asked did she know why Harry had gone to Liverpool, whilst the Baron had travelled up to Preston?

'The two are not related,' said Rosamund, smiling. 'My brother had already left for Liverpool. A messenger came this morning with the news that Alex's ship has anchored at Preston, so that is why he has gone there.'

Bridget frowned. 'I can only think that Harry's ship has encountered a squall or some such difficulty and has been damaged and that is why it has taken shelter in the Mersey. It would be the first port in Lancashire on the journey up from the south, so the ship could be repaired.'

'It sounds like the most likely explanation to me,' said Rosamund. 'Now what would you like to do today? I can show you round the house and introduce you properly to Cook and the rest of the servants.'

'Later, if you do not mind, Rosamund? First I would like to see Harry's tower.'

'As long as you do not expect me to climb up to the top,' said Rosamund, smiling.

Bridget agreed.

Shortly after, she stood at the top of the tower, getting her breath back and gazing out over fields and woods towards the Irish Sea. She wished there was some means of being able to get a closer look at places so far away, but as that was impossible, she decided to come up here as often as she could during the day and watch out for Harry's return. If she was a man and knew the way, then she would have ridden to Liverpool herself. As it was she was going to have to be patient.

So it was that Bridget spent her first full day at Appleby Manor without Harry there to share that precious time. She felt anxious and more than a little annoyed that he had not told her his plans. Evening came and still there was no sign of the three men. She barely slept that night.

Bridget rose early the following morning and within the hour she was climbing the tower once more. But there was no sign of any riders. Her anxiety increased as the hours passed and still they did not return.

The following morning Alex arrived back from Preston and was surprised and disappointed that Harry was not there. Yet he showed no sign of anxiety.

Whether that was because he believed there was no need for concern or because he had complete faith in Harry to get himself out of any fix, she did not know. She found it difficult to believe that all was well with her husband when he had so wanted to spend these days in his sister's company. Obviously something unexpected had happened, but what?

It was early morning on the fourth day that Bridget climbed the tower again. The air was still, with a promise of heat later. She watched as several birds took noisy flight from the trees and then she thought she caught the sound of men's voices. She had no notion of how far away they were, but it was enough to send her hurrying towards the staircase.

She had barely started on her way down when she heard the sound of footsteps coming up towards her. She thought it was Harry and that he might have caught sight of her and had come running to her. She turned the first corner, expecting to see him, only when she saw the figure there, she knew the shape was all wrong.

Her heart began to thud and it was several moments before she found her voice. 'What are you doing here, Ingrid?'

Ingrid threw back her hood and stared up at her with hatred in her eyes. 'So there you are,' she said. 'I've been looking for you.'

'How did you know where to find me?' Bridget wished Harry was here right now.

'Patience, Bridget. I am really very annoyed with you. You are one of those people who will not stay out of other people's affairs. Here was I impatiently waiting for Harry to return. I knew him to be heir to Appleby Manor and thought I could probably bewitch him long enough to persuade him to marry me. Only you reached him first, so my plan was ruined.'

'You must be mad if you think that Harry would have married you after he discovered you were party to his sister's abduction!' exclaimed Bridget. 'He knows you for what you are.'

'That's as may be, but he once loved me, you know.'

'Not any longer he doesn't.'

'I know that now. The ugly fool told me so, but I could have given him a love potion to bewitch his senses. Although, when he dropped me in the mud, I was not very pleased with him.'

Bridget did not know Harry had done such a thing, only that he had encountered Ingrid and kept that meeting from her. But it certainly didn't sound as though any romance had been involved! 'My husband is *not* ugly. Now, if you would get out of my way…' she said haughtily.

Ingrid's eyes narrowed. 'I did not come all this way, Bridget McDonald, to do what *you* say.'

'Why did you come? You were not invited.'

'Master Larsson proved to be a disappointment. We were supposed to be working together and he was to get Harry out of the way when you were staying at the inn, but he didn't have the stomach to go through with the plan.'

'And what was your plan?' asked Bridget, hoping she could keep Ingrid talking until Harry arrived and rescued her.

'To abduct you and hold you to ransom. Then I would have killed you anyway.'

Bridget could believe that of Ingrid—it seemed she'd totally lost her senses. 'Harry is not such a fool as to hand over money to the likes of you without some evidence that I was still alive.'

'You really do have a nasty habit of pointing out the errors in my plans,' said Ingrid crossly. 'You always were quick-witted, but not as much as I am.'

Suddenly she withdraw a cudgel from beneath her habit and came at Bridget, but Bridget seized hold of the other woman's wrist. The two women struggled and then they overbalanced and went tumbling down the stairs. Bridget made a grab for the rope that acted as a rail, but Ingrid continued to tumble and hit a bend in the wall and then disappeared.

Bridget continued to slither down the stone steps with the rope burning her hands. Then unexpectedly the rope came away from the metal rings that held it and she screamed as she felt herself falling. Suddenly there were arms there to catch her and she was being held tightly against Harry's chest. She could do no more than cling to him.

'It is all right, sweeting. You are safe,' he reassured her.

He had called her sweeting and for that and saving her from hitting the ground he deserved not just one kiss, not two, but many kisses, she thought, and proceeded to pepper his face with them.

'Am I to believe from this behaviour that I am forgiven

for my many failings and that you love me?' asked Harry
humbly.

'I deem you can take that for granted,' replied Bridget, 'but
you do have some explaining to do.'

'Agreed,' said Harry.

At that moment there was the sound of voices outside.
Reluctantly, Harry put her down, but he held her hand firmly
and led her down the rest of the stairs. There at their foot lay
Ingrid, and bending over her were Joe and Joshua. 'Is she
dead?' asked Bridget.

'No, but she's unconscious,' said Joshua.

But Bridget scarcely heard his answer because she had
caught sight of the stocky figure of a middle-aged man with
greying red hair. She could only stare at him, stupefied.

'So Harry was right, and there ye are, lass,' said Callum.

'Father!' she whispered, scarcely able to believe it was
really him. He had aged since last she had seen him, and all
the anger and hurt she had felt towards him evaporated. She
felt Harry release her hand and she went forwards and into
her father's arms. She loved him despite his being an old
pirate and reprobate and having put her and Harry through
so much trouble. She was vaguely aware that Joe and Joshua
were lifting Ingrid and carrying her outside, but all that mat-
tered at that moment was that she had the two men that she
loved most dearly here with her.

After she and her father had both shed a few tears, she
drew back from him. 'How could you steal Harry's ship and
consider revenging yourself on Patrick O'Malley more important than reassuring yourself of my safety and letting me
know you were safe?' she demanded in one breath.

'I did it for ye, lass,' he said, his hands splayed on his
thighs. 'I had to get my hoard back to provide you with a
dowry. Never did I think my brother would turn out to be

such a black-hearted villain, and not for one moment did I imagine you would go off in search of me and Black Harry, here. I never thought you'd be captured by pirates and then taken by a slave trader. I'd go down on me bended knee to ye, if I could get down there and beg yer forgiveness. But I'm getting old and ma joints are stiffening up. I can only ask for yer forgiveness.'

'I don't know if I should forgive you, Father, although I deem some good has come out of what you've done,' said Bridget, her face softening.

'Aye,' said Callum, perking up. 'Yer've married a good man. If only I'd known years ago that Harry was heir to a manor and a business I'd have sought him out after he'd escaped the pirate ship and have arranged a betrothal between the two of you.'

'If only I'd known that as well and had Bridget been a little older, then I might have agreed to it,' said Harry, winking at his wife.

'But it is not too late for my father to pay over my dowry to you, Harry,' she said.

Harry was about to say he had no need of it, but recognised that this was important to her. 'You are worth more to me than your father can ever give me,' he whispered, bringing his head close to hers, 'but I'm certain I'll find plenty of ways to use the money. If naught else we can put it in a trust for our children.' Bridget blushed and murmured that she could not think of anything better. 'Then let us go and break the news to Rosamund and Alex that your father has returned and all is well,' said Harry.

It took some time for Callum's tale to be told and it kept all their attention. Bridget smiled when she heard him say that he had met Juanita in Lisbon down at the quayside. Apparently she had foreseen his coming and was waiting for him. Bridget could easily imagine the old woman speaking those words and felt again that mixture of doubt and willingness to believe in the supernatural. She wondered if she would ever see her again. She also heard how Callum had recognised the *St Bridget* in Dover harbour and after speaking to Hans had set sail in *Odin's Maiden* for the Lancashire coast. His nephew he had sent north to Scotland in his own vessel. Fate had led Joshua to Liverpool in Master Larsson's wake after he had parted from Ingrid. There Joshua had spotted *Odin's Maiden* and the *St Bridget* anchored off Liverpool for some essential repairs. He was swift to carry the news to Harry, who had wanted to see for himself that Callum was alive—and if so to bring him to Appleby and surprise Bridget.

'It certainly surprised me,' she said, when at last they were alone together in their bedchamber.

'Aye,' said Harry, frowning, 'but I should have stayed here at your side and kept you safe.'

'You cannot blame yourself for Ingrid's actions,' said Bridget. 'Now can we forget her and everyone else but us right now?'

'I'd like nothing more,' said Harry. 'I am debating whether it is time we began to start building our family again.'

Her eyes twinkled. 'I am in favour of doing so,' she said boldly.

'You don't mind my scar, then?' he asked tentatively, touching it.

She reached up and kissed the puckered skin tenderly. 'Is that a good enough answer?'

He sat with her on the bed and ran his fingers through her glorious hair and brought her face close to his and brushed her lips with his back and forth until she desperately wanted him to kiss her deeply, madly, passionately.

She took hold of his jaw and said, 'Be still,' and kissed him hungrily.

She had no notion of how long that kiss lasted, but her lips parted beneath his and his tongue dallied with hers in a spine-tingling fashion. Then he drew her up so that they both knelt on the bed and he stripped her to the waist and bent his head and captured the tip of a breast between his lips. She gasped as a shaft of pleasure darted through her to form a curl of heat between her legs as he continued to caress her breasts.

Trembling, she wanted to feel his naked skin next to hers and began to unfasten his shirt and explore the chest beneath. She was aware of the amulet on a chain about his neck and brushed it aside. Her heart was beating rapidly and she was aware of the long line of his thigh against hers. He pushed her gently backwards on the bed. She helped him remove her gown by kicking it off when it bunched around her ankles.

He left her only for a moment, but before her skin could cool, he was beside her once more, caressing her all over with fingers and lips until she was aflame with desire. Then they became one and she could feel the pleasure building up inside her. It unfolded inside her like the petals of a flower as he drove deeper inside her. She was breathless with pleasure and all her senses were sending urgent messages coursing through her body. Her pleasure grew and intensified until it finally erupted. As he reached his own climax, a secondary wave of bliss washed over her and she knew that her husband was a man to keep his word and that she would conceive a child that night.

Epilogue

'I believe I will buy your mother such a gown,' said Harry, gazing down at his daughter Aurora Bridget Jane. She was wearing the Appleby baptismal gown decorated with seed pearls.

Aurora gazed up at her father and waved a fist. She had come with the dawn, following on the heels of her twin, after an exhausting night in labour for Bridget. The children had been baptised straight after the birth in the house as was customary in such cases, but as Harry and Bridget had both wanted Alex and Rosamund to be the twins' godparents, a church service had been decided upon, just as soon as they were able to make the journey from Sweden. Now they were downstairs with Douglas and their baby daughter, Margaret Rose.

Bridget smiled into the face of her son, Henry James Callum, and lifted him from the cradle that had been intended for hers and Harry's first child. She rocked him in her arms and glanced up at Harry with a teasing expression in her eyes. 'You do not approve of the gown I am wearing?'

It was of saffron satin and decorated with amber gemstones

that he had asked Alex and Rosamund to purchase for him in Sweden. It was a gift for Bridget on the anniversary of her nineteenth birthday.

'Of course,' said Harry, 'but I would like to see you in a cream satin gown decorated with large lustrous pearls.'

'They would cost a fortune, Harry,' said Bridget, kissing his cheek. 'And you spoil me quite enough.'

'But your neck is bare,' he said, looking around for Dorcas, who was proving to be an excellent nursemaid.

The girl hurried forwards and took Aurora from him and nestled her in the crook of one arm. Bridget stepped forwards and placed Henry in her other arm. Singing softly to the babies, Dorcas left the bedchamber. Bridget remembered how happy the girl had been a year ago when Joe had returned safely from Liverpool, so much so that she had kissed the youth enthusiastically. Joe had blushed to his ears, but he had kissed her right back. As for Joshua, he had visited the lass he had loved as a boy and discovered she was a widow. They had been married forthwith and they were blissfully happy.

Ingrid, on the other hand, was still confused. The bang on the head she'd received when she had fallen down the stairs had scattered her remaining wits and so she had been transported to the nearest convent and placed in the care of the nuns.

Harry closed the door and unfastened the silver amulet from about his neck. He turned Bridget round and then, lifting her lustrous auburn hair, he fastened the clasp before kissing the nape of her neck.

She faced him with a smile. 'Thank you. I deem this is precious to you, so it will also be to me.'

'It betrayed me, though, did it not?'

Bridget remembered that moment of recognition and smiled. Then she closed her eyes and dreamily began to undo a fastening on his doublet. She poked a couple of fingers through the opening and managed to touch his skin. Reluctantly Harry stayed her hand and then raised it to his lips. 'There is naught I would like more than to toss you on the bed and make love to you, but we have our children's baptism to attend.'

'Our children,' she whispered and her eyes were suddenly bright with tears. 'But we will never forget the one we lost, will we, Harry?'

'Never,' he said.

'I will always be grateful that you found me on that beach in Madeira, my dearest Harry.'

'No more than I, sweetheart,' he said, gathering her into his arms for one last kiss before joining their children and the family that was so dear to them.

* * * * *

HISTORICAL

Novels coming in May 2011

GLORY AND THE RAKE
Deborah Simmons

As if the continual vandalism of the spa she's renovating weren't enough for Glory Sutton, she also has to deal with the enigmatic Duke of Westfield! As they get drawn into the mystery, they must reveal their own secrets in order to uncover the truth…

LADY DRUSILLA'S ROAD TO RUIN
Christine Merrill

When her flighty sister elopes, Lady Drusilla Rudney knows she has to stop her! She employs the help of ex-army captain John Hendricks. Drusilla's unconventional ways make him want to forget his gentlemanly conduct…and create a scandal of their own!

TO MARRY A MATCHMAKER
Michelle Styles

Lady Henrietta Thorndike hides her lonely heart behind playing Cupid—but Robert Montemorcy knows it has to stop! He bets Henri that she won't be able to resist meddling…only to lose his own heart into the bargain!

THE MERCENARY'S BRIDE
Terri Brisbin

Awarded the title and lands of Thaxted, Brice Fitzwilliam waits to claim his promised bride, but Gillian of Thaxted will *not* submit to the conquering knight! Will Brice risk exposing the chink in his armour by succumbing to the charms of his new wife?

MILLS
BOON

HISTORICAL

**Another exciting novel available
this month:**

SECRET LIFE OF A SCANDALOUS DEBUTANTE

Bronwyn Scott

Just another dull debutante?

From boxing at Jackson's to dancing starry-eyed society belles around London's ballrooms, Beldon Stratten is the perfect English gentleman. And he's looking for a perfectly bland, respectable wife.

Appearances can be deceiving...

Exotic Lilya Stefanov is anything but bland. Beldon is intrigued to see the ragamuffin girl he once knew has matured into an elegant lady, poised and polite!

But beneath the mysterious beauty's evening gowns and polished etiquette lies a dangerous secret—and a scandalous sensuality…

MILLS & BOON